"What was the nature of Uncle Horatio's accident? I understand it had something to do with a boat."

Silence fell over the table. Mimi looked scared. Mr. Prinney's face looked like she had asked something indecent and Mrs. Prinney stabbed at a potato that rolled off her plate, across the tablecloth, and plopped onto the floor. She looked down at it for a long time in preference to meeting anyone else's gaze.

Lily was embarrassed, yet didn't know why she should be. Then, realizing that Uncle Horatio was a virtual stranger to her and Robert, but a friend to the others, she started apologizing.

Mr. Prinney said nothing, but looked as if he were thinking furiously.

JILL CHURCHILL

ANYTHING GOES

A GRACE AND FAVOR MYSTERY

AVON
TWILIGHT

This is a work of fiction. Names, characters, places, and incidents either are products of the author's imagination or are used fictitiously. Any resemblance to actual events, locales, organizations, or persons, living or dead, is entirely coincidental and beyond the intent of either the author or the publisher.

AVON BOOKS, INC.
1350 Avenue of the Americas
New York, New York 10019

Copyright © 1999 by The Janice Young Brooks Trust
Excerpt from *Anything Goes* copyright © 1999 by The Janice Young Brooks Trust
Excerpt from *Easier to Kill* copyright © 1998 by Valerie Wilson Wesley
Excerpt from *Yankee Doodle Dead* copyright © 1998 by Carolyn G. Hart
Excerpt from *In Big Trouble* copyright © 1999 by Laura Lippman
Excerpt from *The Merchant of Menace* copyright © 1998 by The Janice Young Brooks Trust
Excerpt from *The Body In the Bookcase* copyright © 1998 by Katherine Hall Page
Published by arrangement with the author
Library of Congress Catalog Card Number: 98-91018
ISBN: 0-380-80244-9
www.avonbooks.com/twilight
Jill Churchill can be emailed at **COZYBOOKS@AOL.COM**

First Avon Twilight Printing: June 1999

AVON TWILIGHT TRADEMARK REG. U.S. PAT. OFF. AND IN OTHER COUNTRIES, MARCA REGISTRADA, HECHO EN U.S.A.

Printed in the U.S.A.

WCD   10   9   8   7   6   5   4   3   2

To Scott Herrington and Mike Autenrieth
with thanks for their very generous help

Chapter 1

August, 1931

Lily was hot and cranky.

She shoved her damp, limp hair back under her wilted summer straw hat and closed her eyes for a moment. She was wearing her last pair of undarned silk stockings, which on such a blistering day had been an awful mistake. The taxicab, which was really just an old black Ford with TAXI inexpertly stenciled on the driver's door, kept lurching along the steep, tree-encroached tunnel of a road, tossing her around annoyingly. And if her brother Robert didn't soon stop that tuneless whistling, she'd have to consider throwing herself out the door and ending it all.

Or perhaps she'd just shove Robert out into the shrubbery.

They'd arrived by train from New York City in Voorburg-on-Hudson at noon on a steamy Saturday, and had taken a quick look around the attractive little pre-Revolutionary town. They'd waited for a taxicab quite a while before finding out that the town had only the one and the stationmaster had to locate the driver for them.

1

"He's usually here to meet the noon train," the stationmaster had said, "but he might still be at Mabel's Cafe."

Robert had laughed heartily at this. "In hard times, it's good to know there really is a Mabel's Cafe somewhere."

"Tired, darlin' Lil?" Robert asked later, as the taxi driver took a sharp turn, flinging them about in the backseat like dice in a cup.

"Tired and hot."

"But it's much nicer here than in the city today," Robert said.

She opened her eyes and glared at him. He looked as cool as an iced drink in a crystal glass. Sometimes she hated her brother. Especially when he was right. It was August and New York City was so hot that sometimes she feared her lungs would scald if she took another breath, and her feet would fry from the searing pavements. For the last week all she'd wanted in life was to be alone and stand dripping wet and naked in front of the squeaky electric fan she and Robert had in their tiny two-room apartment in the tenement in the Lower East Side.

But instead, she'd dragged herself off every weekday morning at eight and walked the twelve blocks to her dreary, menial job at the Chase National Bank where she sat on a high backless stool at a big table all day with seven other women and sorted checks into tidy piles. A comfortable chair and interesting conversation would have made the job more tolerable, but Lily had so little in common with the other women that they might as well have been speaking different languages. In fact, English wasn't the native language of several of them.

By the time she reached home at six, Robert had usually fixed her a light supper and was dressing for his evening of earning his living, such as it was. The jobs changed—sometimes he was a bartender in the more socially acceptable speakeasies, sometimes he hired himself out as a dancing partner and escort to elderly ladies who fawned over him and introduced him to their friends as their favorite nephew.

His 'dear old biddies,' he called them privately.

Occasionally he substituted for the maitre d' at the Cafe Savarin, Fraunces Tavern, Luchow's or the Algonquin—restaurants that catered to those who had, against all odds, held onto their wealth. Lily often thought it must be humiliating for him to come down to being an employee rather than a customer, but he had never complained.

The only things Robert's jobs all had in common was that he had to look spectacularly handsome, speak well and own a tux.

This was good, because playing a fair game of polo, looking and acting top-drawer, and being relentlessly cheerful were Robert's only skills, highly developed as they were.

"We didn't have to come all the way up here, you know. It was all your idea," Robert said amiably. Robert was almost always amiable.

Lily wondered if she could reach the door handle on his side of the taxi before he could become aware of her intentions.

"And miss something that might help us crawl out of dire poverty?" she asked. "Attorneys don't put ads in the papers asking specific people to contact them for news to their advantage for no reason."

"I still think it's a con," Robert said cheerfully. "Some rumrunner is going to meet us at this cottage and tell us we can make a fortune with just a few illegal trips across the Canadian border. Still, it's a lark and gets us out of town for a day. Dear God,

Lily, everything's so damned *rural* here, just a couple hours' train ride out of the city. Who'd have thought . . ." He gazed out the window as though it were as foreign as a desert or an arctic landscape. "I'm just the tiniest bit afraid of trees, you know. You can never tell what they're going to do."

That made her laugh, as she knew he intended. "Trees don't *do* anything, Robert."

He grinned. "They get hit by lightning and splinter. I've read about that. And they drop leaves and bark that somebody has to pick up and discard. And sometimes peacocks nest in them overnight and mess up your car. That happened to me once at the Breakers."

In another life . . . Lily thought. *Our* other life.

"Here you are, folks," the taxicab driver said, taking a sharp turn between two stone pillars that were nearly covered with ivy. "Honeysuckle Cottage."

Lily gawked at the structure, wondering how anyone could have misnamed it so badly. It wasn't a cottage. It was a great hulking monster of a mansion. And if there was honeysuckle growing anywhere, it was having to put up a good fight with the weeds, coarser vines and acres of ivy that almost entirely obscured the facade of the house and most of the windows. Aside from the few random turrets sticking up bravely through the greenery, it looked more like a burial mound with extremely luxuriant foliage than a house.

Lily counted out the driver's tab and added a frugal, but not downright stingy tip. "You'll come back for us in an hour?"

The taxi driver was counting the pile of change she'd given him. "Uh-huh," he said reluctantly, grinding the gears and chugging off.

Lily and Robert stared at the house for a long moment and Robert was the first to spot what might be a front door. He pushed aside an especially aggressive vine and knocked firmly. They heard footsteps, a crash that sounded like a small table falling over and a muffled curse, before the door opened.

The man standing in the semidarkness was small, elderly and had badly dyed black hair and a matching pencil-thin moustache. "You must be Miss Lillian Brewster and Mr. Robert Brewster. Come in, please. We'll talk in the library."

They followed him gingerly down the dark central hall, alongside a massive staircase and into a room at the back of the house. Robert amused himself by pretending to be blind and having to feel his way. Lily gasped as the stranger ushered them into the library. This room was magnificent. It was flooded with light from a pair of French doors and ranks of large windows in the back wall. Lily walked forward and realized the room presented a breathtaking panorama of a long green lawn and a superb view of the Hudson River, curving gently below them. None of the voracious vines were allowed to obscure the view from this room. The other walls were covered with bookshelves with elaborately etched glass doors protecting them from dust.

"I'm Mr. Elgin Prinney, Esquire," the elderly man said as he fastidiously swatted a large handkerchief at the seats of three chairs grouped at the end of a long, gracefully proportioned library table. "Please sit down."

Lily had to make a real effort to tear her gaze away from the river. She sat down in the chair facing the windows.

Pretending to fuss with the lock on his document case, Elgin Prinney secretly studied the young pair. A very good-looking young man who seemed frivolous but pleasant. And a girl with obvious good breeding who was far too thin and tired-looking for her own good. At least she loved the view. He hoped they really were the young people that he'd been searching for.

"I believe you've brought the documents I requested when you telephoned me?" Mr. Prinney said.

Lily opened the small case she'd been clutching for hours. She removed two baby books, hers and Robert's, which had family trees filled in on the front pages. Each book also had a formal invitation to their respective christenings, giving their parents' names and the dates of Lily's and Robert's births. She'd also managed to acquire copies of birth records from city hall, an obituary noting their mother's death and a more recent death certificate for their father.

October, 1929. Cause of death: suicide by defenestration.

She handed these items to Mr. Elgin Prinney, Esquire, and took a long envelope from her handbag. This contained her father's will, a picture of him from a newspaper clipping, another picture of him with Lily and Robert on the long porch of their summer home in Nantucket shortly before his death.

Mr. Prinney studied all the documents slowly and thoroughly, even looking at the backs of the newspaper clippings. Robert caught Lily's eye, grinned and winked at her.

"This seems to be quite convincing."

"Convincing of what?" Robert inquired.

"That you are the children of Caroline and George Brewster."

"Of course we are. Why would anybody be benighted enough to pretend to be us? Look here, old chap, what's this all about?"

Mr. Prinney sighed, leaned back in his chair and tented his short fingers. "Were you aware that your father had an uncle named Horatio Brewster?"

Robert looked at Lily. "Were we?"

"Yes, he visited us one winter at the Gramercy Park apartment when we were about six and eight. You must remember. He gave us lemon drops and we ate so many we were both sick all night. He's listed here on the family tree."

"And you had no further contact with him?" Mr. Prinney asked.

Lily shook her head. "My mother used to write everybody in the family a chatty Christmas letter and send pictures with it. And when she died, I used her address book to send cards. But I never received anything back from him so I stopped sending them."

"Do you remember what his address was?"

"Somewhere in Connecticut. I didn't think to bring Mother's address book. Uncle Horatio's address was in a town that started with an 'S' as I remember."

Mr. Prinney nodded approvingly. "Very well. I think this adds up to adequate proof of your identity. I'm sorry to have to inform you that Mr. Horatio Brewster died two months ago in a boating accident on the river. This had been his home for the last five years. He has left it to the two of you—in a manner of speaking."

Lily and Robert exchanged a quick glance.

"In a manner of speaking, you say?" Robert asked. "Would you mind explaining what you mean by that?"

"It's somewhat like a grace and favor benefice, with your Great-uncle Horatio's own alterations."

"Grace and favor?" Robert asked. "That sounds terribly upper-crusty. What does it mean?"

Lily interrupted. "Robert, don't you remember Great-aunt Winifred in Coventry? We visited her when we were teenagers. She lived in a grace and favor house. King Edward gave it to her and Uncle for use during their lifetimes, as an honor to Uncle's outstanding civil service career."

"So, we inherit this . . . uh . . . house," Robert said, casting a wary glance back at the gloomy hallway, "but it doesn't really belong to us? We can't sell it, for instance?"

"That is roughly correct," Mr. Prinney said. "The will stipulates that you must both live in the house for ten years without being away for more than two months apiece in any given calendar year. But unlike a true grace and favor, it would then be entirely yours, to do with as you wish. If you fulfill this requirement, the house becomes yours."

Robert laughed heartily. "Live here for ten years? Mr. Prune . . ."

"Prinney!"

". . . Prinney, we couldn't afford to buy the wood to heat one room in the winter."

Mr. Prinney actually said the words "Tut-tut," which delighted Robert. Then he went on, "You need not concern yourself with that. Mr. Horatio Brewster also left a substantial amount of cash and assets in trust, the management of which is in my hands as trustee and executor. It allows for the maintenance of the house, the furnishings and the grounds, which I must admit have been sadly neglected. At the end of the ten years, the balance of the trust will also revert to the two of you, if you have fulfilled the conditions therein."

"A substantial amount of cash?" Lily murmured. "How substantial . . . exactly?"

Mr. Prinney removed a folded sheet of ledger paper from his suit pocket and carefully opened it up. "As you know, the real estate holdings are worth only what someone is willing to pay for them, so they're difficult to assess accurately. And I admit I failed to stop at the bank today and check on the current amount of interest and today's gold prices, but as of last Monday the funds in the trust amounted to one million, eight hundred and twenty-three thousand, four hundred and nineteen dollars and seventeen cents."

Chapter 2

Lily was the first to get her breath back. She whispered, "How much?"

Mr. Prinney repeated the figure.

"And this amount and the house will be ours if we stay ten years?"

Mr. Prinney nodded. "In addition to the real estate holdings. There will be debits from the total, of course, and who can guess what will happen to the value of gold over the years? Or the value of all the other properties he left," Mr. Prinney said.

"Other properties . . ." Robert murmured, as if it were part of a song lyric.

"Your great-uncle held title to diverse properties. Some were his alone, but the majority were co-owned with other business associates of his," Mr. Prinney said. "He owned land in Florida, Michigan, several ranches and a mountain in Colorado, orange groves in California, some of which he sold to moving picture studios, others which are still in the estate."

"And these would be ours?" Robert asked.

"In ten years, if you agree to fulfill the requirements," Mr. Prinney said. "In that case, I would be in charge of financial decisions during that period, but would explain my reasons to you and instruct you in the process."

"You'd be better off instructing my sister," Robert said. "She's the one with a head for figures."

"The house and grounds need a great deal of work to be considered livable," Mr. Prinney continued. "As trustee, I'm inclined to be liberal in that regard. It's not economically sound to let a potentially valuable property go to wrack and ruin. And then there will be upkeep. That will come out of the capital as well. But once the original expenditures are made, the interest on the capital should pay for the upkeep without diminishing the total."

Lily's mind was reeling. Almost a million dollars each and half the house at the end of ten years. Plus these 'other properties.' She'd be thirty-four years old by then. Not so young, but not terribly old, either.

Mr. Prinney, in the face of their stunned silence, was inspired to chattiness. "Your Uncle Horatio was an astute man. And was good enough to share his financial advice with me. He had invested heavily in stocks through the years, but never on margin, as so many did. And he saw the end looming. He sold his stocks at their peak, bought gold and land, and urged me to do the same with my pitiful few investments."

Nearly a million dollars, Robert was thinking. *But we have to live here. Here! Dear God.*

"Mrs. Prinney and I would be in dire straits indeed if Mr. Horatio Brewster had not warned me," the lawyer was going on. "I suppose you'd like to have a tour of the house now."

"Will there be any sort of allowance for us? For food and clothes and such?" Robert asked.

Lily was surprised at Robert asking such a practical question.

Mr. Prinney shook his head with regret. "No, I'm afraid not."

"Then how would we eat?" Lily asked.

Mr. Prinney shrugged. "I suppose you'll have to get jobs."

"Mr. Prinney, we *have* jobs," Lily responded sharply. "Dreadful jobs. We are no longer ranked among the idle rich."

"I'm so sorry, Miss Brewster. I meant no criticism. Let me explain. Your great-uncle's stipulation of your remaining here for ten years was very specific. You are to take up full-time residence in Voorburg-on-Hudson at Honeysuckle Cottage. Keeping your jobs in the City would require a two-hour train trip each way and I was assuming that the train fare alone would make living here and working in the city impossible. Besides . . ."

"Besides what?" Lily asked suspiciously.

"Should anyone dispute your claim when the ten years have passed, they might have grounds to argue that your daily presence in the City counted against your time here."

"Who would dispute our claim?" Robert asked.

"You have other living relatives," Mr. Prinney said. "I'm not suggesting that any of them would cause trouble, but it's a possibility you must consider."

Robert's eyes narrowed. "Cousin Claude!" he exclaimed.

"But surely . . ." Lily started to object.

Mr. Prinney put up a hand. "Your uncle's will is quite unusual. It follows no standard for which there is precedent that I know of. That leaves it more open to legal challenge than I like."

Lily glanced at Robert. His normal level of cheer-fulness had dropped several notches. In fact, he looked downright serious, a very rare sight.

"I may, however, have a partial solution for you," Mr. Prinney said. "Mrs. Prinney and I have quite a large house in Voorburg. It was her mother's home and now that our daughters are grown and married, it has become onerous to maintain. Since I, as trus-tee, must be able at the end of the ten years to doc-ument and testify to your residence here, I would make so bold as to suggest that Mrs. Prinney and I could become boarders at Honeysuckle Cottage. It would be far more convenient to me, it would please Mrs. Prinney and relieve her of many responsibilities and such an arrangement would give you a modest income."

"How modest?" Robert asked.

"That can be negotiated," Mr. Prinney said with a sniff. "In good time."

Lily was doing furious and largely inaccurate mathematics in her head, trying to tote up Robert's irregular income, her extremely meager pay at the bank and the cost of train fare and figure out how much would be left. The figures she came up with didn't make her happy. And there was greedy, stuffy Cousin Claude to consider.

Mr. Prinney rose. "I believe you should see the rest of the house."

While the interior of the house hadn't been as se-verely neglected as the grounds, it was certainly not an aesthetic pleasure to view. It wasn't even *easy* to view properly. Electricity had been installed, but most of the light bulbs had burned out. The vines that covered almost all the windows gave everything a dark, underwater look, although they also kept it a good ten degrees cooler inside.

All the furniture except for that in the room with the Hudson River view had been dust-sheeted and lurked greenly in the shadows. Lily lifted a few of the sheets as they toured and found that there were decent, if a bit oversized, sofas, chairs, tables and beds hiding beneath. Nearly every room had rugs that had been carefully rolled and covered. A few quick examinations revealed that at least they weren't frayed at the edges.

Moreover, the house was huge. Besides the library, entry hall and grand staircase, there was a parlor, a reception room, a huge dining room, a morning room, a little office, a ballroom and several other unidentifiable rooms on the ground floor alone. On the second floor, bedrooms and bathrooms stretched down the long upper hall in both directions from the staircase. Mr. Prinney explained that there were even more, but smaller, rooms on the third floor for servants and guests' servants. "And there are attics, of course," he added.

But neither Lily nor Robert were really ready to take in the details. Such a windfall, Lily thought. A fortune. But ten years in this house? With Mr. Prinney? And what if Mrs. Prinney was a terror? Mild, prissy little old men often had tyrants as wives. On the other hand, there was that magnificent view of the river that would be a positive balm to the soul. She wouldn't have to bang elbows with Robert in their tiny apartment, or walk the hot pavements or go nearly mad at the thought of years at the bank stretching before her.

The kitchen was awful enough to bring her out of her reverie. The lock on the kitchen door had been broken and hobos had apparently taken up residence at some point. There were empty bottles and tin cans and newspapers all over the room. It stank of desperation, sweat and despair. Still, the hobos hadn't invaded the rest of the house, which Lily found remarkable. Even cleaned up, the kitchen would be horribly old-fashioned, dark and grim.

"Perhaps I should have warned you," Mr. Prinney said as Lily swayed. "The cooking facilities would have to be updated considerably."

"Isn't that . . ." Lily could hardly bring herself to say it. ". . . a wood-burning stove and pump-handle water supply?"

He nodded sadly. "But Mrs. Prinney would be very happy to help you fix things up. She's an excellent cook and knows precisely what a kitchen needs to function efficiently."

"That's good to know," Lily said. Before the stock market crash the family had a number of homes. Lily had never even seen the kitchen in two of them. And her only experience with cooking since then had been opening tins into saucepans and warming them on the hot plate in the apartment. She didn't imagine that would qualify as the 'board' part of 'room and board.'

"You don't suppose," Lily said sweetly, "that your wife would consider cooking for all of us? I'm really not a cook and I'm afraid both of you would starve otherwise."

Mr. Prinney beamed. "How fortuitous a thought. Mrs. Prinney's sole regret about leaving our own home has been the thought of having to eat what others prepare for us. She's really quite particular about good food. And there's nothing she loves better than cooking for a lot of people. I josh her that she must have been a cook for an army in some previous lifetime."

Robert had, for the duration of the tour, been whistling a rather frantic tune that resembled a fractured version of "The Flight of the Bumble Bee." He now stopped abruptly and cleared his throat.

"Lil, old girl, hadn't we better talk this over a bit before we commit to details?"

Mr. Prinney answered for her. "By all means. No financial decision should be made in haste, no matter how advantageous it might look."

"And are we to understand that this arrangement must include both of us?" Robert asked.

"Oh, yes. Mr. Horatio Brewster was very clear on that point. I believe that unpleasant noise outside must be your taxicab returning." He hustled them out of the kitchen, through a dining room with the most awful wallpaper Lily had ever seen and into the nearly pitch dark front hall. Opening the door, he said, "You young people go back to your home and let me know your decision within the week, if you would."

"I don't think it will take that lo—"

Robert interrupted Lily's remark. "What will happen to this place if we decline to accept it?"

"Robert! Are you mad?"

Both men ignored her outburst. "Your cousin, Claude Cooke, will inherit but could not sell the property. Should he turn it down, the house and grounds will become an animal orphanage. Mr. Horatio Brewster was fond of cats and dogs, but, alas, he was highly allergic," Mr. Prinney explained. "Funds will be set aside to maintain it and the rest of the holdings will go to various charities."

"And not a penny for us," Robert said.

"I'm afraid not."

The taxicab driver honked his horn again.

As Lily and Robert climbed into the vehicle, Mr. Prinney said, "I look forward to your telegram telling me when to expect you."

* * *

Brother and sister hardly exchanged a word all the way home.

Robert whistled recent show tunes. Many of his 'dear old biddies' were enamored of the musicals and he had a good ear for a tune he'd heard only once.

Lily stared out the train window at the river as it moved along, ancient and untroubled, beside the railroad tracks. She knew Robert didn't like this idea. She also knew they had to move to Honeysuckle Cottage. How was she going to resolve this without making him unhappy? Robert was a thoroughly cheerful person and that was too rare a trait, especially in these difficult days, to risk spoiling. Countless times she'd fallen into utter despair and Robert had pulled her out with a willing hand, a bad joke and a sincere smile.

She owed him a lot. She owed him his continued happiness.

When they got to the city, Robert donned his tux, examining his appearance critically in the pier glass Lily had insisted on bringing along from the family's Park Avenue apartment. It was the one item of furniture she knew her mother would have risen from her grave, shrieking, to save from the hands of strangers.

"It's getting a little shiny at the elbows, isn't it?" he asked. "Good thing I'm not."

"Let me sponge it a bit to bring up the nap. You have a job tonight? You didn't say."

"Not really, but one of the waiters at Sardi's might like to take the night off. It's hectic but fun on Saturday night."

When he'd gone, Lily sat down by the window

and turned the squeaky electric fan on and got out a small ledger book in which she recorded their income and expenses. There was really no good reason to keep track of the dismal figures, but it had become something of an obsession.

She flipped to the first page. Eight hundred dollars. That was all that had been left of her father's enormous fortune. He'd mortgaged all their homes to the hilt and borrowed besides to invest heavily in the stock market on margin. When the market collapsed and he committed suicide, the homes had all been sold for much less than they were worth because there were relatively few people left who could afford them. The probate judge had let Lily and Robert have their own clothes, family pictures and personal items and, at Lily's tearful insistence, the pier mirror. The judge had ordered the estate's attorney to sell everything else. The furniture, the pianos, even the kitchen pots and pans and the as yet unused cemetery plots the family owned were sold. When it was all done, the debts all paid, there were exactly eight hundred dollars left.

Lily and Robert had hung onto the money like grim death for almost two years now, moving three times into successively more dreadful apartments. With Lily's pitiful but regular wages and Robert's erratic income on the credit side and the expenses for their horrible tiny apartment and food on the debit side, they now had eight hundred ninety dollars and forty-two cents. Lily consulted a calendar. She'd been keeping track for two months short of two years. She subtracted the original eight hundred dollars, and divided the remainder by twenty-two months.

They were 'getting ahead' at the rate of four dollars and eleven cents a month. Robert desperately needed a new tux and his shoes had been resoled as many times as possible. Lily's everyday clothes, too, were threadbare and ink-stained. She had trunks of party dresses, of course, but she'd look like a fool wearing them to work at the bank unless she could get on the night shift, which was entirely women who, she'd heard, took off their dresses and worked all night in their slips to save wear and tear on their shabby outer clothing.

She put her head down on the table and cried. She wasn't sure if it was out of happiness for herself or despair for Robert. Dear Robert, who was 'afraid of trees.'

Chapter 3

Even Robert agreed there was no choice when he came home a bit tipsy around three in the morning and was forced to look at Lily's computations.

"So, at the rate we're going," he said, "we *might* have another five hundred dollars in ten years if we keep on the same way. And nearly a million each if we stick out the ten in ghastly great house in the jungle."

"Not a jungle, Robert. Woods. It won't be so gothic when we get it cleaned up and it won't cost us a cent. I promise you we'll make sure it's a place you'll like."

"I don't think that's possible, but anything's better than this," he said, making a sweeping gesture that caused him to almost graze his fingers on the door. "But how on earth are we to even feed ourselves? I'm sure if Mrs. Prune does the cooking, the food and service will cost as much as they're paying us. We really can't live on absolutely nothing at all. You know how hard it was to get a job in the city. How will we get one in the wilderness? I, for one, have no wilderness skills, as you may have noticed. And

I don't think the tips at Mabel's Cafe would be much to write home about."

Lily fussed about, tidying the rickety, ugly table where she'd been going over her paperwork and said offhandedly, "I've thought about that, too. And I have an idea. Even if we come out even with the Prun . . . Prinneys, we could take in another boarder. Just one, mind. Somebody we can like. Someone young. And even though that will make the food cost a little more, we ought to at least clear five or six dollars a month, which is better than what we're doing now. And it won't be as hard on us. Surely Mr. Prinney's idea of a household budget will run to at least one maid to do the cleaning."

Robert sat down on the lumpy sofa. Grinning, he said, "And what else have you been thinking about?"

"Me? Don't be silly, Robert. Nothing, really."

"Lil, old dear, you know you can't fib to me. I *taught* you fibbing."

She sat down next to him. "Well, I thought if one boarder extra worked out well, we might eventually take in more. Not soon, Robert. And only if you agree."

"I might, at that. But only if they're amusing and interesting."

Lily's idea of the Good Life didn't include a houseful of 'amusing and interesting' paying strangers, but if that was the price of keeping Robert happy, so be it. She'd get out of this dismal apartment, away from the dreadful bank and off the scalding pavements and Robert would have his very own circle of entertaining friends. A fair enough trade.

Robert was deep in thought. "It's a bit of a vacation spot, isn't it? Hunting, fishing, yachting and all that? We could make it a classy spot to spend the summer or fall. Not for boarders, for vacationers. Dressing for dinner and such. You could wear your good frocks again, Lily. We might even get me a new tux if we got a bit ahead. When we get the house fixed up, I could invite Bunny and Dodo and Tank up here and show them the place. They'd tell everybody else what a great joint it is."

Lily smiled and bade him good night. As she was dropping off to sleep, she could hear him bashing around, punching his pillows into the hollows in the sofa in the other room and muttering things like, "Boomer Feldman! How could I have forgotten him! He's rolling in dough and he loves to fish!"

On Sunday Lily and Robert treated themselves to a heavy breakfast at the greasy spoon on the ground floor of their apartment building and made lists of things to be done. Early Monday morning, Lily went to the bank for the last time to give her notice and withdraw their money. Her supervisor, who had given her the job because he had once known her father, couldn't disguise his relief.

"I had orders this morning to either fire one of the women in your group or put you all on four-day weeks with only four days of pay. I hate it that you're the one leaving, Lily, but you've saved the others a pay cut."

Lily didn't say goodbye to the women she had worked with. She hoped never to see or even think of them again. They were all older than she—or at least looked older. Several had husbands out of work and starving children to feed. They either worked through their lunch break in order to get home a half an hour earlier, or they brought food from home that was even more disgusting and meager than the sandwiches Lily took to work. They never joked or smiled. It wasn't their fault, but Lily was enormously relieved to be free of them.

While Lily was quitting her bank job, Robert sent a telegram to Mr. Elgin Prinney, Esquire, letting him know they would arrive to take up residence on Tuesday. He also rounded up a couple furniture movers to carefully crate up the pier glass. By the time it was padded with old quilts and had a wooden frame built around it, it took up nearly the entire room. None of the rest of the terribly shabby furniture belonged to them, so it wasn't a concern.

When Lily got back to the apartment, bedraggled and hot, but with a light step, she took the moving men to the basement of the building to show them the four large trunks stored there that contained everything else they owned and struck a hard bargain on the price of having the trunks and mirror shipped up to Voorburg-on-Hudson.

Meanwhile, Robert informed the landlord of their plans to leave and didn't manage such a good bargain. There was a long waiting list of tenants who, like Lily and Robert, had come way down in the world and couldn't afford their previous comfortable accommodations. The tiny apartment would be reoccupied practically before they could close the door, but the landlord refused to give them back the half month's rent they'd paid ahead.

Brother and sister went across the street to sit on the bench at the trolley stop. It was the only place to get out of the way while the pier glass was wrestled out of the apartment and onto a truck. Robert whistled quietly for a while and Lily hurriedly read the last of a library book, a mystery story, that had to be returned before they left the city.

Robert stopped in the middle of a fairly awful

whistled rendition of "Ain't Misbehavin'." He didn't quite have the range for it. "This is good," he said.

"What is?" Lily closed her book.

"Doing something different."

Lily put her arm through his and her head on his shoulder. "I'm so glad you feel that way. I do, too. It can't be worse than living here and it might be better."

Robert patted her hand, but didn't look at her. "Sometimes—not often, but sometimes lately—I've had this dream that I'm suddenly fifty years old. Still wearing the same tux. Working where we had breakfast instead of Sardi's. Being too old to interest the old ladies who want a dashing pseudo-nephew. Fading away. Becoming passé and dreary."

"Not you, darling," Lily said. "Never dreary. When you're fifty, you're going to be a dashing old roué with beautiful young girls hanging on your every word. But I know what you mean. One day last week, when I got to the block the bank is on, I had to stop and have a little cry. Not because I had to go there that day, but because I suddenly had a shivering horror of having to go there every day for years and years and years. That I'd start looking like the women I worked with. That, God forbid, I'd start *thinking* like them!"

"This is one good thing that's come out of this last couple years," Robert said.

Lily looked up at him, confused. He was remarkably good-natured, but it defied reason that even *he* could think there was anything good in their lives since late 1929.

"I mean that we've gotten to know each other, Lil. We spent all those years passing each other in big rooms in big houses and at big parties. If we were still rich, you'd be married by now to some wealthy, handsome banker who probably kept a showgirl mistress on the side. And I'd be playing polo superbly well on some green field in England with no idea of what I'd do next and only a vague recollection of having a sister."

"Oh, Robert, stop! You're making me cry again."

"Look! Here comes the mirror."

They watched as the two burly men squashed themselves and the crated treasure out the door of the apartment building and expertly hoisted it onto the truck.

Once the mirror and trunks were gone, the telegram dispatched to Mr. Prinney, their last night spent in the ghastly apartment, the keys turned over to the landlord and the decision rendered irrevocable, Lily was eager to get on with the next stage of her life. She'd have happily gone straight to the Grand Central station first thing in the morning in the hope of getting an earlier train. But Robert still had some courtesy calls to make on friends. He'd hand-lettered a small blank calling card with their names and new address to show to Lily the night before.

"Honeysuckle Cottage," Lily said doubtfully. "Do you hate that name as much as I do?"

"I do. What shall we rename it?"

"What would you think about Grace and Favor Cottage, since that's what it is—in a way."

He printed a new card in his finest hand and showed it to her:

Miss Lillian Bodley Brewster
Mr. Robert Vanderkell Brewster
Grace and Favor Cottage
Voorburg-on-Hudson
New York State

"Robert! It looks so grand!" she'd said. "We *are* doing the right thing, aren't we?"

"If not, we can come back here. I'm sure there's an apartment with an even more grotesque view than the side of another building five feet away. Something overlooking the trash alley, perhaps."

They spent their last three hours in the city delivering the cards to homes with elegant addresses on Fifth Avenue, Central Park South and Park Avenue before boarding the train for the second greatest change in their lives.

Chapter 4

When they disembarked in Voorburg-on-Hudson for the second time, Robert inquired about the mirror and trunks.

"Yes, sir, Mr. Brewster, they came on the early freight," the stationmaster, Mr. Buchanan, said. "Mr. Prinney says you folks are moving into Honeysuckle Cottage."

"We are. But we're calling it Grace and Favor Cottage from now on," Robert replied. "Now, how do we get everything up the hill?"

The stationmaster said he had a couple of men in town who shared a truck and moved big pieces for fifty cents each and would take care of it.

"Please tell them to take special care of the big crate," Lily said. "It's our mother's mirror." As she spoke, she became aware of someone standing behind them and turned.

"You're Miss Lily Brewster?" the young man asked. "And Mr. Robert Brewster? I'm Jack Summer. Reporter for The *Voorburg-on-Hudson Times*. Mr. Prinney said you were moving here today. Our readers will be interested in the new folks at Honeysuckle Cottage. Have you got time for an interview?"

Lily said, "Not right now, if you don't mind. We're anxious to get settled in."

"Tomorrow, then? In the morning?"

"That would be fine," Lily said.

"Nice-looking chap," Robert said as Jack Summer departed with a tip of his hat. "All that curly blond hair."

"Oh, really? I didn't notice," Lily said.

"Fibber."

The taxicab driver entered the station a moment later. "Sorry I'm late. Mr. Prinney sent me for you, but I had to take Mrs. Welling to her doctor's appointment first. Goiter, you know."

Robert barely repressed a snort of laughter.

As they followed the driver out, Lily whispered, "Do you suppose Mr. Prinney's put up a public notice of our arrival in the town square? Everybody seems to know about us."

It was a little cooler today and the ride wasn't so harrowing. This time Lily paid more attention to the route, thinking that it wasn't really quite as far from town as it had seemed only a few days earlier. And this time she noticed, too, that there were several rather grand homes along the way. They were in wooded settings and weren't very easily visible unless one looked for them. She wondered what sort of neighbors they would have.

As they turned into the drive between the pillars, Robert exclaimed, "Holy Toledo!"

Mr. Prinney had thrown himself into fixing up the grounds with astonishing gusto. There must have been half a dozen men already hard at work. One old man who looked like a cartoon of Father Time was scything the tall grass. Two younger men with ladders were tearing down the vines around the front door. Another pair, whose dark hair and stocky shapes made them look as if they were probably father and son, were cutting out the dead limbs of a big tree. Yet another man was sawing up the limbs and stacking them as firewood.

Most amazing of all, Mr. Prinney was striding about in jodhpurs, a sporty cloth cap and Wellington boots, directing the activities.

"A sight to be savored," Robert said.

As Lily was counting out the taxicab driver's fare, Mr. Prinney spotted them. "Welcome! Welcome!" he said. "You can see we're making good progress."

"You are indeed," Robert said. "I wonder if I might have a private word or two with you."

Had Robert read her mind? Lily wondered. While the two of them strolled off, she went into the house, meaning to pick out the room she wanted before Mr. Prinney could assign her one. The front hall had been lighted and dusted, and the marble tiles gleamed, which was a huge improvement. Even the dreadful wallpaper in the huge dining room didn't look nearly as bad as it had in the watery gloom.

Lily went up the wide stairway and heard sounds of someone working in a room halfway down the hall. As Lily approached the room, a woman came out with an armload of dust sheets.

She was slim, platinum blonde and quite glamorous, even in a faded, sleeveless housedress. Her hair, figure and carefully made-up face gave her the appearance of someone in her early twenties, but her neck, upper arms and hands suggested mid-thirties.

"Oh!" the woman exclaimed. "You did give me a fright! You must be Miss Brewster."

"Yes. Are you Mrs. Prinney?"

The woman laughed shrilly. "Goodness, no! I'm

Mrs. Mimi Smith. Mr. Prinney's hired me to tidy things up for you. I started with this bedroom because I think it's the nicest and you'd like it. And it has its own bathroom. Come and see what you think."

Mrs. Mimi Smith had made a good choice. Lily couldn't imagine how she could have failed to remember this room on her previous tour. It had a cabbage-rose-patterned wallpaper, a large floral rug that picked up the same pinks and deep greens and a single bed with a dark cherry headboard and footboard and was topped by a lovely cream lace canopy. There was a matching cherry desk and chair in front of the window and a rather empty area on the inside wall that would be a perfect place for the pier glass.

Best of all, it had a river view. Or would, when the vines were removed. As it was, Lily could only catch glimpses of the long, sloping lawn and the river beyond.

The bathroom was tiny, with a dainty claw-footed tub that was hardly larger than a hip bath. Mimi Smith had even found some fairly fresh-looking pink towels to hang on the porcelain towel bars.

"I couldn't have made a better choice myself," Lily said. "And to even find such pretty towels!"

Mrs. Smith preened. "I'm glad you like it, Miss Brewster. But I'm the one who put the towels away when the house was closed up, so it's no surprise I could find them."

"You've worked here before then?"

"Oh, yes. And my mother, too. She was nurse to old Miss Flora."

"Miss Flora?"

"Right you are. Mr. Horatio's maiden aunt what raised him."

Lily frowned. "I'm confused. I thought Mr. Prinney said Great-uncle Horatio had only lived here for a couple years."

"Well, that's so and it isn't. He grew up here, then he left when he was grown, and came back when Miss Flora died and left him the place," Mrs. Smith said, straightening a hand towel that wasn't precisely squared up. "Haven't you got no bags?"

"I left my suitcase outside. My brother will bring it up. And some trunks will be delivered later."

"Then let me show you the room I've fixed up for Mr. Brewster. It was Mr. Horatio's room. I don't much like it myself, but it's a manly room."

By 'manly' Mrs. Smith seemed to mean huge and dreary. It was a big, dark room with green-shaded lampshades, dark paneling and enormous somber pieces of furniture. Tearing away the vines that entirely covered the windows here would help. But not much. The thing Robert would like was the bathtub, which was approximately the size of Vermont.

"I don't like it either," Lily admitted, "but maybe Robert will. Is Mrs. Prinney here now? I need to introduce myself to her."

Robert and Mr. Prinney were inspecting the work that was going on outside. "My sister and I are awfully grateful that you've arranged for all this to be done," Robert said.

"Just doing my duty as executor and trustee, Mr. Brewster. It's good to see the old place coming back so nicely. It's a fine house."

Robert looked at the house. There was some very good ornamental brickwork emerging. "There's just one thing I'd like to ask, old chap, and I mean no offense," Robert said with his usual friendly smile. "My sister and I understand that you have the final word on the money that's spent on the house, but where do we stand?"

"I'm not sure I take your meaning," Mr. Prinney said, looking wary. Maybe this young man wasn't as frivolous and friendly as he'd originally thought, he mused.

"Well, decisions about what's to be done and whatnot. Suppose you want to pay someone to take out a big tree and we like the big tree, for example? Or we all agree that a bedroom needs new paint— who decides on the color?"

"You're not pleased with the work I've hired out?" Mr. Prinney looked wounded.

"Pleased? Why, we're thrilled to death, but don't quite understand the rules and—" He added with all the false sincerity he could muster, "We don't want to break them or cause you distress."

"Yes, yes. I can see this might make problems," Mr. Prinney said, no longer offended. "The will, of course, doesn't specify this sort of detail. I feel it's a great mistake to try to cover every possible contingency in a legal document and told your great-uncle so. As soon as you list fifty things that *might* happen, the fifty-first *will* happen. Common sense and decency are the key."

"Of course they are!" Robert agreed enthusiastically, hoping they could get it thrashed out quickly and not have to have any more serious discussions. It was so difficult maintaining a sober, businesslike demeanor around a little elderly man in jodhpurs who sported a funny moustache. Robert could hardly keep himself from flinging himself on the newly shorn lawn and laughing hysterically.

Mr. Prinney, hands behind his back, deep in lawyerly thought, took a few steps to the left, a few to the right and finally said, "Let me think about this for a bit."

Rats! Robert thought.

"Would you like to be shown around?"

Robert sensed this was an order, disguised as an offer. Ticks, gnats, little furry things, big furry things with fangs, thorny things and spiders were in the forefront of his mind as he smiled charmingly and said, "I'd love to."

Mrs. Prinney wasn't much taller than her husband, but was much bigger. Her tightly corseted bosom was an awesome structure and her upper arms were like hams. In contrast, she had lovely hands, great kind baby-blue eyes and a porcelain-doll complexion, which was quite pink and dewy from her exertions.

"Mrs. Prinney? I'm Lily Brewster."

Mrs. Prinney had removed all traces of the hobos' residency and now laid down a strange implement with which she had been cleaning a big oak table. Wiping her elegant hands on her apron first, she shook Lily's hand in a firm, forthright manner. "Glad to see you, Miss Brewster. Right awful kitchen, eh?"

"Terrible," Lily said. "And you must call me Lily."

"Miss Flora and Mr. Horatio had no cause to ever come in here, but if this is going to be my home and I'm going to do the cooking, it's going to have a lot done to it. I thought about having that outside wall knocked farther out and a nice big window put in so it's a more sociable place."

Lily was suddenly angry and knew it was entirely unjustified. Mrs. Prinney was right to feel that way. The Prinneys had moved in. It *was* her home now, too. And since Mrs. Prinney was willing and prepared to do the cooking, Lily had no right whatsoever to determine what was done to the kitchen. She should be grateful. Instead, she was as suddenly, irrationally furious as a child who'd missed her nap. She'd been looking forward to a more independent life and suddenly everybody else was making decisions for her as if she were a simpleton.

As well-schooled as Lily was in keeping her emotions under control, her face must have reflected the tenor of her thoughts.

"Oh, dear. Now I've gone and stepped in it again," Mrs. Prinney said. "Mr. Prinney is always telling me to think more before I speak. I'm sorry, dearie, if I scared you with my brash talk."

Lily's anger sputtered out. "No, no. You're right about the kitchen. It's too small and dark. A nice big window would help keep it cool in the summer and bright in the winter. Perhaps a pantry could be built out to the side, too. I'm being far too touchy lately," she said with a weak smile.

"Being uprooted so sudden does that to folks," Mrs. Prinney sympathized. "You need to rest from your journey. I went to New York City once, and I swear I was as limp as a wet rag for a week afterward."

Lily grinned. The woman could scrub the whole top layer of a table off with something that looked vaguely like a potato masher, but a short train ride defeated her.

Lily ran into Robert in the front hall.

"We have a car! A gorgeous Duesie!"

"A what?"

Robert was dancing in place. "A Duesenberg Model J. The Derham Tourster. Almost brand-new.

A big monster of a car that will hog the whole road! It goes with the house," he exclaimed. "It's been neglected. Battery's dead. Out of gas. But picture us swanning around Voorburg in it when I get it running!"

"Thank God! No more taxicabs," Lily said.

"We had a yacht, too. Or we would have if it hadn't sunk. It's odd, though," Robert said, trailing Lily up the stairs. "I asked Mr. Prinney if that was the boating accident he mentioned as the cause of Uncle Horatio's death and he suddenly clammed up. He'd been chattering away like a squirrel on cocaine until then. He just drew himself up, twitched his silly moustache and said, 'That's something we don't need to discuss,' very curtly, and changed the subject."

"They were probably friends and it's an unpleasant memory for him."

"Or it wasn't an accident," Robert said.

Lily stared at him for a moment and involuntarily shuddered. "Oh, Robert, don't be melodramatic. Maybe Mr. Prinney just hates boats."

"Well, it was odd," he said. "I wonder—"

"Take a look at your bedroom," Lily said. "It's that big door at the end of the hall."

She watched as Robert walked away jauntily and strolled through the door. He came back out a few seconds later, looking wild-eyed. "I'll turn into Edgar Allan Poe if I have to sleep in that room!" he declared.

Chapter 5

Lily ran water into her tiny bathtub to soak off the dirt and smell of the train trip. Although the tub was very short and narrow, it was tall and by scrunching down a bit and leaving her knees high and dry, she could submerge to her chin in the cool water. If she let her legs hang over the front, she discovered that she could even wash her hair, though rinsing it out was going to be problematic. This was the first time since they'd left the Gramercy Park apartment almost two years earlier that she'd taken a full, all-at-one-time bath. The hideous apartment in the city had only a showerhead and a drain in the cramped bathroom. There hadn't even been a curtain around it until Robert rigged one up. And half the time the canvas curtain ended up falling on her like a moldy tarp. The water supply had been fitful, sometimes flooding the room, more often dribbling out in a cold, gray, gritty stream.

How simple and spoiled she'd been most of her life, assuming that baths were commonplace. They were, she had learned, a fabulous luxury when you're poor. And a pretty bar of scented soap was an intoxicating addition.

She lathered herself with the bubbling lilac fragrance, which made her dizzy with delight. She still had no money. There would be no more scented soaps when she'd used this one up unless Mr. Prinney could be persuaded that they were a household necessity. She'd have to go on wearing the darned stockings, the shoes that were getting so thin-soled she could feel the ground through them, the everyday dresses that had seams that often gave out.

But she could be clean. She could take a bath in privacy without hearing the toilet in the next apartment flush. She could smell nice. She'd taken all that for granted for twenty-two of her twenty-four years. The last two years had taught her otherwise.

Robert would appreciate a return to these formerly ordinary amenities, too, but not as much as she did. Robert was a social butterfly who would desperately miss the bright, brittle cafe and polo crowd. While Lily had thoroughly enjoyed the parties, the fine champagne in fragile crystal glasses, the elegant dances and trips to Europe in the best shipboard suites, it had been simple enjoyment of what she thought life was like for pretty nearly everyone. How could she have been so stupid and blind to the realities?

Robert, in contrast, thrived on that life. Those witty companions, the late nights of drinking and dancing and then sleeping well into the next afternoon were what sustained him. Even when he had to become the waiter instead of the diner, he'd chosen to pretend to himself that he was still part of that world. He'd chatter about the latest society gossip he'd picked up as if he'd been sitting at the table, instead of hovering around it with the wine bottle.

For all his silliness and good cheer, Robert wasn't stupid. He knew as well as Lily did that Uncle Hor-

atio's will had saved them from despair and star-
vation. He'd stick out the ten years, but would
regard it as an imprisonment with a reward at the
end that would let him go back to his previous life.
But what would those ten years do to him? Would
he lose his wit and charm, or were they so deeply
ingrained that he'd come out of the required decade
still himself?

Lily's thoughts were interrupted by a tap on the
bathroom door. Mrs. Smith called out, "Miss Brewster, there's a truck here and the men are asking
where you want things put."

Lily said, "Ask them to wait just a minute. I'll
hurry." She frantically rinsed herself, threw on her
clothes and rushed downstairs with a towel around
her dripping hair. She identified and assigned Robert's trunks and hers to the proper bedrooms, and
followed the men up the stairs as they grunted and
groaned under the weight of her mother's mirror.
As it was being uncrated, she dithered and fretted
and drove the workmen nearly mad with her im-
patience to see if it had come through the move in-
tact.

"Thank God," she said, when it was finally free
of the quilted pads.

Mrs. Smith had been watching the process from
the doorway. "That's so beautiful," she said. "Like
something you see in them fancy museums. What's
in these trunks?"

"We'll open them in a minute," Lily said, tipping
the workmen generously to make up for her annoy-
ing behavior, then fished around in her handbag for
the keys to the trunks.

She thought for a second that Mrs. Smith was going to faint when the first trunk was opened and an
apricot silk ball gown was revealed. Mimi slapped

both hands over her mouth and tried to muffle a scream of appreciation. After a few gasps, she said, "Oh, Miss Brewster, Miss Brewster! That's purely the most beautiful frock I ever did see. I'd be afraid to even touch something so pretty."

Lily lifted the dress out, put it on the bed and hunted down the tissue-wrapped slippers, long gloves and evening bag that had been specially made to match it. "The last time I wore this," she said, "was the night Dickie VanBuren proposed to me and acted like he was going to cry when I turned him down. I wonder what's become of him."

"I'm surprised every man in the room didn't propose to you," Mrs. Smith said. "You musta been beautiful in this dress."

Lily smiled. "I think I was, Mrs. Smith. Now it would hang on me as if it were on a coat hanger. I've lost so much weight."

The older woman frowned. "If you wouldn't mind, Miss Brewster, I'd rather you just called me Mimi, like everybody else does. I don't much like being called Mrs. Smith."

"Oh . . . I see. All right, Mimi."

"It's just that Mr. Smith—Billy Smith, that is— isn't really my husband. Well, he is, far as the law's concerned, but we don't get along. Not since—well, never mind that. Now, how are we going to take care of this dress until Mrs. Prinney fattens you up?"

Lily was stymied. "I have no idea. It's a bit wrinkled, but I don't think it can be ironed since it's silk. Steamed, maybe?"

Mimi studied the ball gown, frowning. "Might not be good for it. I'll ask Mrs. Prinney."

Suddenly Lily realized how ironic their conversation was. Mimi had never seen a silk ball gown and Lily herself had never wondered how the servants took care of one. They were both approaching the problem with utter ignorance. Somehow, she found this oddly comforting.

They unpacked the rest of the clothing and hung it all in a cedar closet down the hall—a closet that was larger than the entire New York apartment she and Robert had shared. Two of the day dresses had been a bit large on Lily to begin with and would probably never fit her again. She gave them to Mimi, who was about Lily's height, and a bit heavier. Thrilled, Mimi went off to show Mrs. Prinney her new navy and white suit dress and full-skirted floral cotton shirtwaist.

Lily unpacked her smaller trunk, which contained more personal items. Several expensive, uncomfortable corselettes, a selection of satin slips, silk camisoles and nightgowns with hundreds of tiny tucks. Her childhood diaries were in this trunk, as well as school papers, party invitations, graduation certificates, a few love letters she'd received from smitten adolescent admirers and family pictures. Lily took out the clothing, put it away in drawers and left the rest of her past in the trunk, which she stuck way back in the closet where she wouldn't run across it very often.

Dinner was lovely. Lily wore a slinky red skirt and a red and white silk polka-dot blouse she'd always loved. Robert wore his summer whites and lacked only a boater hat and tennis racket to look thoroughly sporty. Mrs. Prinney had cooked a wonderful meal of Yankee pot roast with potatoes and carrots and tiny pearl onions that nearly melted on the tongue. There were fresh, yeasty rolls, and a salad of tender greens that Lily didn't recognize. Mimi, wearing one of the dresses that Lily had given

her, served the meal, then sat down in the remaining
vacant chair.

Lily was puzzled. Did Mimi live here, too? It
wasn't a question she wanted to ask at the table. She
supposed it made sense. But she was the maid. An
employee. She was serving the dinner and eating it
with them, too. And so were Mr. and Mrs. Prinney
employees in a sense. But they were also guests and
tenants and their hosts and jailors as well. Lily was
going to have to readjust a lot of her ideas of social
precedence.

"What are you grinning about, Lil?" Robert asked.

"About our new 'family' around the table here,"
Lily said.

Everybody beamed. Mr. Prinney loosened up
enough to actually smile.

Talk was general and pleasant. The weather, the
progress on the grounds, Mimi's extravagant appreciation of her new frocks, what should be done to
the car to make it usable. Mrs. Prinney asked about
Lily and Robert's food preferences.

"We'll eat anything that doesn't bite us first,"
Robert said.

While Mrs. Prinney was still laughing uproari-
ously at this, Lily asked Mr. Prinney, "What was the
nature of Uncle Horace's accident? I understand it
had something to do with a boat?"

Silence fell over the table. Mimi looked scared. Mr.
Prinney's face looked like she had asked something
indecent and Mrs. Prinney stabbed at a potato which
then rolled off her plate, across the tablecloth and
plopped onto the floor. She stared down at it for a
long moment in preference to meeting anyone else's
gaze.

Lily was embarrassed yet didn't know why she
should be. Then, realizing that Uncle Horatio was a

virtual stranger to her and Robert, but a friend of the others, she started apologizing.

Mr. Prinney said nothing, but looked as if he was thinking furiously.

Mrs. Prinney abandoned her study of the escaped potato and cut Lily off. "If everybody's nearly done, I'll just pop the pie in the oven for a minute to toast the meringue." Robert and Mr. Prinney stood up politely as she rose and departed. Mimi followed her. Robert winked at Lily and resumed his discussion of the car battery with the elderly lawyer.

After having second helpings of a remarkably good lemon meringue pie, everybody retired to their various pursuits. Mrs. Prinney, floating on a sea of compliments, went back to the kitchen with Mimi. Mr. Prinney said he had some bookkeeping to do and disappeared. Robert went to change his clothes and take another look at the car.

Lily went to the library and opened the French doors to stand and gaze at the river below. In spite of the heat of August, the trees were still a lush green. There was a breeze off the water that smelled of river, fish, honeysuckle and pines. A person could almost get drunk on a fragrance like that, she thought.

The door behind her opened and Mrs. Prinney said, "Oh, sorry, dear. I didn't mean to disturb you."

"You aren't disturbing me. Please come in."

Mrs. Prinney, still perspiring from her kitchen work and redolent of onions and lemons, came to stand beside Lily at the doors. "Lovely sight, isn't it? When we lived in town, we were too close. Rivers are better from a little distance."

"I'm really sorry I asked that tactless question at dinner," Lily said.

"You had no way to know," Mrs. Prinney said.

"It's just that Mr. Prinney was on the boat when the accident happened and it's a bit upsetting to him."

"He was on the boat? Oh, if I'd known—"

"But you didn't and there's no reason to fret." Her tone was polite and pleasant, but final. It was the end of the discussion.

"Does Mimi live here?" Lily asked.

"I told her she could stay until we had the house all opened up. But it's up to you, dear, whether she stays on."

"Has she a home of her own?"

"Not to speak of. She grew up in this house as daughter to Miss Flora's housekeeper, but since Miss Flora died, Mimi's been pillar to post. She lived some of the time with her husband Billy until a couple months ago mostly. Every time he got drunk and they had a fight, she moved in with two aunts of hers. But the aunts are old terrors and it's a strain on everybody."

"Then she should stay here," Lily said.

Mrs. Prinney beamed approval. "That's good of you, Miss Brewster."

"Not so good, really. I just know what it's like not to have a home," Lily said.

"I'll go tell her now. She'll be so pleased," Mrs. Prinney said.

Lily stepped out on the little parapet beyond the doors and leaned on the railing, watching a small barge being towed upriver. It seemed to move remarkably fast. The tide must have been coming in. Could there still be a tide so far up the river? She'd have to ask someone. The sun was setting and the opposite high bank was casting deep shadows on the river. Lily found herself wondering why, after a lifetime of seeing the Hudson from various points, it seemed so much more beautiful here. More than beautiful—somehow essential to her well-being.

A few moments later, she heard Robert calling for her. "In the library," she answered.

He was in his rattiest clothes and had a smudge of oil on his cheek. "That's some car, toots. Badly neglected, but she'll clean up swell if we can get her running." He joined her at the rail. "You really stepped in it at dinner, didn't you. I told you the boat wreck was a touchy subject."

"I had no idea how touchy," Lily said. "It was stupid of me anyway. Death isn't a suitable dinner subject. I've forgotten my manners."

"That's not a bad thing. You used to be awfully prissy."

"I was not!"

"People far and wide referred to you as Miss Lily Priss."

Lily gouged him in the ribs. "They did not! Mrs. Prinney was here a minute ago. She told me that Mr. Prinney was on the boat when it sank."

"Did it sink?" Robert asked.

"I thought you told me it did."

"No, Mr. Prinney just said there was an accident and it was damaged beyond repair. Admit it, Lily. You're as curious as I am. I want to know what happened. If nobody here will tell us, how will we find out?"

"There must be a local newspaper. Newspaper! Oh! I forgot that reporter is coming tomorrow. What are we going to tell him about ourselves?"

"More important, what can we ask him about the boat accident?" Robert said, rubbing his hands together.

Chapter 6

Jack Summer leaned on the windowsill of the out-side ticket counter of the Voorburg-on-Hudson train station. "Mr. Buchanan, you got anybody going up the hill today I could hitch a ride with?"

"Nope. Not until the five o'clock train, unless there's a passenger I don't know about. No hauling. Why?" the stationmaster asked.

"I was hoping to catch a lift up to Honeysuckle Cottage."

"They call it Grace and Favor Cottage now, they told me," Mr. Buchanan said.

"Silly name. What's it supposed to mean?"

Mr. Buchanan, who knew a lot about a lot of people in town, didn't always give out the information. He knew, for example, that the Widow Baker took a train to Tarrytown every other Tuesday late at night and came back early in the morning. And that a good-looking, if somewhat porky gentleman came to Voorburg on the Tuesdays between on the same schedule. He knew, too, that another widow, who claimed her husband had been dead for a year, made irregular visits to Sing Sing to visit him. But he kept this sort of information to himself.

And in this case he couldn't answer because he didn't know. Yet. He just shrugged.

"Sounds hoity-toity to me," Jack grumbled. "Betcha that girl decided on a new name. She looks the type."

"The type to change the names of things?" Mr. Buchanan asked.

"No, the type to be hoity-toity."

"You appeared to admire her yesterday."

"Admire? Okay. I admit she's a looker, even if she is on the skinny side. But that doesn't mean she has brains to go with it. Those rich girls are usually as stupid as a red brick."

Mr. Buchanan pretended to be examining some paperwork so Jack couldn't see his smile. "You know a lot of them, huh? Rich girls?"

"Just because I live in a hick town doesn't mean I'm a hick," Jack said. "I've been to New York City."

"Yep, that day you went to look for a job with a big-city newspaper. I remember. You looked real spiffy."

Jack strutted to the edge of the tracks, as if looking for a train coming. He didn't like to be reminded of that day. He hadn't known he needed appointments to see real New York newspaper editors and in spite of his neatly slicked back hair, the new suit he'd borrowed from a cousin and the spit and polish shoes he'd spent the last of his meager money on, he never got past the front desk of any paper until the late afternoon.

It was a crummy paper. And he only got through to an underling. "You're trying to see the boss for a job?" the editor's male secretary said. "Got experience?"

"Not much in newspapers, but I've written a lot of short stories and I've got a good education," Jack said. "Two years of college. I'd make a good reporter."

The secretary looked a bit like an amused fox, pointy-faced and hungry, when he replied, "Listen, boy, you go back to whatever burg you're from and you work for their paper. For nothing, if you have to, just to get some bylines. Keep clips of every story you've done for three years. Then, if you're really, really good, you might get a job at a sleazy outfit like this. I know you don't like hearing it, but it's a tough business to get into. Nobody starts as a reporter, even here, let alone at the good papers. You get your clips together, you might get to be a janitor for a year or two, then move up to apprentice typesetting before you get to write a word."

Jack resented being talked down to this way and was about to tell the secretary where to put his advice, when he suddenly had an insight. "You . . . ?"

The secretary nodded. "College degree and two years in the boondocks and here I sit."

Still pretending he hadn't heard the stationmaster, Mr. Buchanan refer to that humiliating day, Jack went back to the window. "Guess I'll have to take my bike up the hill then. Sure you don't know anyone going up?"

"Nope. Why you going if you don't like the new folks?"

"Assignment," Jack said. "Mr. Kessler told me to write up a new-neighbor piece. Hell, I wish something would really happen in this town. A good story I could get my teeth into."

"Things happen," Buchanan said. "Like that boat wreck a couple months back."

"Right, but Mr. Kessler did the story himself. I need something of my own to investigate. Something he doesn't even know about."

"Good luck, boy," Buchanan said. He was going to add some witticism about moving up from new-neighbor stories to the inside gossip of the Bake Sale Club, but decided Jack wouldn't find it funny.

"He looks like James Cagney," Robert said.

"Who's that?" Lily asked.

"Oh, you remember. He was in that moving picture I made you go to last year. *Sinners' Vacation?* No, *Sinners' Holiday.*"

They were standing in the front yard, watching the workmen cut down a grotesque juniper tree, and had noticed Jack Summer toiling up the hill.

Lily studied Jack for a moment. "Yes. He does, I guess. He's got that same sort of rooster strut, hasn't he? Robert, we're not going to talk about why we're here, are we? I mean, not admit we were practically starving before this windfall."

"I don't see how that's anybody's business. Especially a reporter's. I figure anybody who pays attention will quickly realize how utterly incompetent we are, without being told."

Jack, unaware that he was being observed, stopped and wiped the sweat off his forehead, tried to tidy his springy blond hair with his hands and took a deep breath. The chain on the bicycle was making a strange noise and he decided to walk it the rest of the way. Honeysuckle Cottage, now that he had the leisure to notice, was abuzz with activity. Ladders, workers, piles of brush and—standing in the middle of it all, like the idle rich they were—the Brewsters. Of course, you didn't have to be rich to be idle. Look at all the time his boss, Mr. Kessler, spent sitting around the office carving dumb little animals out of bits of wood instead of going out and looking for news.

"Good morning, Mr. Summer," Lily called out as he approached them.

He hated that they looked clean and cool while he was hot, sweaty and disheveled from his long uphill ride. "Good morning," he said, trying not to sound cranky. The one thing he'd learned about interviewing people was to get on their good side. It made them more talkative.

Lily offered him some of the lemonade Mrs. Prinney had made and they went in to the library to talk. Robert dutifully pointed out the view of the river and Jack dutifully acknowledged that it was impressive. But he seemed more impressed by the lemonade. "How'd you get the lemons?"

"Mrs. Prinney's ways are mysterious," Robert said.

"They're awfully expensive, aren't they?" Jack said.

Lily took offense. "Are they really?" she asked coldly. "Is that what you came clear up here to ask?"

Jack's fair face flushed. This wasn't a good start.

"No, my editor assigned me to ask you about yourselves. A way of introducing you to the folks who read the paper."

Robert, who despised conflict and knew from the set of Lily's jaw that there might be open war any moment, flung himself into a chair and said amiably, "Then ask away. Our lives are an open book. Well, except for the epilog."

Jack took out a small notebook and nub of a pencil from his back pocket and sat down across from Robert. "First, I guess, is how did you come to buy this place?" He wasn't willing to refer to it by name.

"We didn't buy it," Robert said before Lily could speak. "We inherited it from our Uncle Horatio."

"Great-uncle," Lily said.

"Great-uncle," Robert said with a smile that he hoped she'd take to mean *Don't antagonize the press, however rural.*

Jack asked the requisite boring questions his editor demanded. How did they like the house? How long had they been here? What (he didn't append 'if any,' though he was tempted) were their professions?

Robert got in before Lily again. He'd once been brutally honest with a reporter about the poor sportsmanship of a fellow polo player and had lived to regret it when his personal views were printed in a society gossip column.

"Right now," he said suavely, "we've put our work aside to give our whole attention to Grace and Favor. There's a great deal that needs to be done, as you can see."

"But what did you do before you moved here?" Jack persisted.

"Oh, any number of things," Robert said, but didn't bother to enumerate them. "More lemonade?"

Mr. Brewster didn't care to comment on his previous employment, Jack planned to say in the article. That would show what an idle, idiotic butterfly the newcomer was without being actionable.

"Do you plan to live here full-time?" Jack asked.

"Oh, yes," Robert said, grinning at Lily, who smiled back at the private joke.

Jack suddenly realized that Miss Brewster was really quite stunning when she smiled.

When he'd completed his questions, Lily said, "Now we'd like to ask you a few things if you have the time. You see, we don't know very much about the nature of our Great-uncle Horatio's passing. I wonder if you could explain what happened."

"It was a boat accident," he said. "Mr. Brewster

took a group of his friends on his yacht up to Bannerman's Castle."

"Where's that?" Robert asked.

"About twenty miles downriver. It's not a real castle and it's officially named Pollepel Island on the maps." Jack was well-informed about the island because he'd done a newspaper piece on it the previous spring. "It belongs to a Scottish family called Bannerman. They buy up war materiel when the wars are over. They started up after the Civil War and when the Spanish-American War was over, they acquired so many cannons and guns and ammunition that they didn't have room to store them in their New York City warehouse. So one of the family built a mock Scottish castle on an uninhabited island for storage of the ammunition. There are living quarters for the family in the upper stories. Imagine trying to sleep when you're a few feet over a huge arsenal."

"Why did they all go there?" Lily asked. "Uncle Horatio and his friends, I mean."

"Just a jaunt, I hear. The island and the arsenal are heavily guarded and your uncle must have asked permission to bring friends to see it. For all I know, he knew one of the Bannerman family."

"So, what happened there?" Robert asked.

"Nobody knows exactly," Jack said. "It's very rocky and the tides can be vicious. Most likely the yacht just ran aground. They raised the thing later and there was a big gash alongside the keel."

"Uncle Horatio wasn't much of a sailor then?" Robert asked.

"I don't know. I wasn't invited along." That sounded petulant and childish even to his own ears.

"Who was?" Lily asked.

"I don't remember all their names. Local bigwigs. Your next-door neighbor, for one."

"Who *is* our next-door neighbor?" Robert asked.

Jack was surprised. Jonathan Winslow was not only the richest man hereabouts, but he, his wife and his daughter were among the most socially prominent. They'd actually had foreign royalty visit any number of times in the past. He mentioned the name.

"Do they have a daughter they call Sissy?" Lily asked.

"I believe so."

"I went to dancing classes with Sissy Winslow," Lily said, more to herself than to him. "And we were in the Mayflower Girls in grade school."

"Mayflower Girls?" Robert asked.

"We all had names of Mayflower people. Brewster, Bradford, Winslow, Billingslea. It was a joke. I don't think any of us were actually descendants."

Jack was still hoping to get something interesting out of the Brewsters and answering their questions and listening to girlish recollections wasn't accomplishing anything.

"You mentioned Mrs. Prinney having made the lemonade. I understand Mr. and Mrs. Prinney have put their house up for sale. Are they living here?"

"To our enormous pleasure, they are," Robert said.

"Why is that?"

"Because they wished to—and this house is much too big for the two of us," Robert replied cheerfully. He wasn't about to mention that Mr. Prinney controlled the money and served as official watchdog on their movements.

"How could we find out more about our uncle's death?" Lily came back to the subject that most interested her.

"What's to find out?" Jack asked. "The boat sank. He drowned."

"Did anyone else drown in the accident?" Robert asked.

"Nope. But my editor wrote it up pretty thoroughly. You could come to Voorburg someday and take a look at the newspaper morgue."

"I think we'll do that," Robert said.

Jack gave him a long, appraising look. "Why are you so interested?"

"Well, he was our great-uncle," Lily said. "And nobody seems to want to tell us what happened."

"You think there was something suspicious about the accident?" Jack asked, his inquisitive mind making a leap.

"Oh, no. Certainly not," Robert said, too heartily. "We're just curious people."

Jack didn't know whether to believe them or not. Surely Mr. Prinney had explained it all to them. But maybe not. Prinney had a reputation for complete discretion.

Jack waited a minute, debating with himself, then said hesitantly, "I shouldn't be the one to tell you, but I've heard he was murdered."

Chapter 7

"Murdered!" Lily exclaimed. "By whom?"

Jack had to admire her grammar—and her delivery. She sounded genuinely shocked.

"I don't know. Nobody knows. My editor handled the story himself and I never heard the details." That was a hard admission to make since it made him look like a mere flunky.

"I don't understand why Mr. Prinney didn't tell us this," Robert said. "Somebody actually killed our uncle? On purpose?"

"I couldn't swear to the truth of it," Jack admitted. "But that's what folks in town say."

"Who killed him?" Lily asked.

"Nobody knows. There are only rumors."

The way he was waffling made Robert suspicious. "I think you have everything you need for your interview, don't you?" he said pleasantly.

Jack took the hint, stuffed his notebook and pencil in his pocket, thanked them for their time and departed.

"Why didn't Mr. Prinney tell us this?" Lily asked Robert when Jack Summer had left. They were standing on the porch watching him set off.

"I don't know. Maybe it's just a silly rumor. Mr. Prune doesn't seem the type to go in for idle gossip," Robert said. "Maybe that's why he clammed up at dinner last night when you asked him about the accident."

"I only asked Mr. Prinney what happened in a general way. He was on board the yacht, and people don't like talking about horrible experiences."

"Lily, don't be daft. Most people *love* talking about horrible experiences. It constitutes the majority of after-dinner talk. Especially among men. And I've overheard women talk about childbirth in terms that make me want to curl up in a ball and whimper. Jack Summer didn't seem to want to talk about it either. He's a reporter. He should have known a lot about it."

"Robert, what are you getting at exactly?"

"Just that I want to know more. And I want to know why nobody will really discuss it with us. You know, Lily, when a man of enormous wealth dies in something called an accident, warning flags should go up everywhere."

"What do you mean?"

"Motives, my dear child."

Lily looked at him patronizingly. "Motives?"

"Since we inherited from him, we have the greatest motive," Robert said. "But we didn't even remember him. At least, I didn't."

"What!"

Robert waved his hands frantically. "No, no. I didn't mean you had a motive and I didn't. But, as far as anyone else knows, in theory we did have a compelling motive. We were about as far down on our luck as a snake on skates and a great-uncle dies in an accident and leaves us his house and fortune.

At least, that's what it must look like to people who don't know us."

"But if, as it sounds, he was murdered on the boat, we're obviously in the clear. We weren't there. And we couldn't have afforded to be there if we'd been invited."

"Lily, I'd bet the only person in Voorburg who knows we haven't two beans to rub together is Mr. Prinney. The people of the town don't know that and neither does Jack Sprat."

"Jack Summer," she said, preoccupied. "Do you think Mr. Prinney suspected us? Or maybe still does?"

"Dear God, I hope not! Why would he let us move in here—unless he had in mind a little detecting of his own."

"Robert, lower your voice. The house and yard are full of people who might be eavesdropping on this bizarre conversation. Let's take a walk."

They strolled, with rather ostentatious casualness, out in the road in front and pretended to be pointing out plants and wildlife to each other as they spoke in low voices.

"There are other kinds of motives for causing an—accident," Lily said.

"You mean murder."

Lily shuddered. "I don't mean murder, precisely. A rejected lover might have wished to simply alarm someone and went too far. Or a cheated business acquaintance or partner. We don't really know anything about Uncle Horatio. We've been thinking about him as a kindly old gentleman because he gave us this house."

"You might think that indicates kindliness. I'm not sure I do," Robert said with a grin. "Uncle Horatio might have been a real horror. And keep in mind, Lily, that he didn't 'give' us this house. He set it up so we have to be incarcerated here for a whole decade to ever really own it. That doesn't precisely smell of milk and honey. Men who arrange things for other people beyond their own deaths certainly aren't fading violets in life. Lily, the fact is, we have no idea what sort of person Uncle Horatio was. He might have given us those lemon drops, or whatever they were, in a deliberate attempt to make us sick."

"Do you really think anybody could seriously consider us as suspects, or are you just entertaining yourself?" Lily asked, plucking a red flower off a vine by the side of the road and putting it in her hair.

"A little of both," Robert admitted. "One does what one can to keep one's wits sharp when one is lost in the wilderness."

Jack had been very angry when Mr. Kessler took over the reporting of the incident. Jack had done a piece on Bannerman Island only a short time earlier and secretly wondered if it had played a role in inspiring old Horatio and his pals to go explore it. And then when the trip became suddenly newsworthy, old Kessler put away his whittling knife, pulled rank and took over the story. Jack had—stupidly, he now admitted to himself—kept a distance from the story out of pure pique and a good journalist would never do that. He'd failed himself.

The bicycle chain was still making a strange clanging noise, but only when he pedaled, so he kept to a slow coast all the way down the hill, allowing his mind to wander freely. When he'd said the word 'murdered,' he'd expected the Brewsters to laugh it off. But they'd taken it very seriously. Jack himself had really considered it merely gossip to fill lonely evenings for the people of Voorburg. But could Robert Brewster, the silly ass, be right? He immediately rejected the idea just because he was resentful of the rich, but his mind kept coming back to it.

Kessler had done his reports in the paper, gone back to whittling and it was all just part of the past to him, Jack thought. The editor had no more interest in the matter. But what if Jack could find out something that Kessler didn't know and wouldn't have had the nerve to ask? Kessler was a bit mealymouthed around the gentry and particularly about Horatio Brewster, whom Kessler seemed to admire beyond good sense.

This, Jack thought, might just be The Story that could get him to New York.

He coasted down the rest of the hill, inventing fantasies of big New York newspaper editors sending drooling telegrams to him, begging him to come to the City and assume his rightful place on their papers as an ace reporter. He couldn't wait to get back to the office and look over those articles.

Mr. Kessler's idea of newspaper writing wasn't in synch with the times. He claimed that when he himself read a newspaper, he wanted the facts, not some damned reporter's opinions. He and Jack were often at odds about this, and since Kessler was the editor, his will always prevailed.

The lead news article in the *Voorburg-on-Hudson Times* was notably sparse and stuck strictly to the facts.

LOCAL MAN DIES IN BOATING ACCIDENT
Mr. Horatio Brewster of Honeysuckle Cottage, Voorburg-on-Hudson, New York, died last Sunday in a boating accident on the Hudson. Mr. Brewster had

invited friends to accompany him aboard his yacht, *Happy Times*, to Bannerman's Arsenal, 15 miles below Voorburg on the Hudson on Pollepel Island. Though the weather was fair at the onset of the journey, an unusually strong storm sprang up as the party approached the island, which is known to be a dangerous landing site.

The yacht, tossed about in the wind and rain, as well as the erratic tides that always surround the island, apparently struck a rock or some other underwater obstruction of substance and sustained major damage. The yacht began to list severely from the inflow of water. Mr. Brewster's guests, with the help of two guards of the island and Castle, all managed to either swim or take the small dinghy to the island.

It was not discovered until the yacht had sunk from view that Mr. Horatio Brewster was not among those who had escaped the sinking vessel and found safety on land. A search was instituted, but was hampered by the storm. As of this date, Mr. Horatio Brewster's body has not been found, though he is assumed to be deceased, according to the authorities.

The other guests on board, Mr. Elgin Prinney, Esq., of Voorburg; Major Jonathan Winslow, businessman of Voorburg; Mr. Fred Eggers, businessman of Poughkeepsie, Mr. Charles Winningham, banker of New York City; Mr. Claude Cooke of New York City, and Mr. David Kessler, the editor of the *Voorburg-on-Hudson Times*, were all unharmed except for the most minor injuries.

Jack read the article several times and then copied it out by hand, telling himself it was for his own reference, but thinking he might later share it with the Brewsters. Then he looked through the rest of that issue. Squeezed in here and there between advertisements, club meeting announcements and pictures of an eyesore of a house in town being torn down by a wrecking ball, Jack found a short interview with some of the others who had been aboard the *Happy Times*. Mr. Elgin Prinney expressed his sorrow at having lost an old and valued client, but said nothing of the accident himself except to say that it would be inappropriate to comment before the proper authorities had conducted a thorough investigation into the unfortunate circumstances.

"Ever the lawyer," Jack snorted. He liked Prinney well enough, but knew the old boy was as close-mouthed as a clam.

Major Jonathan Winslow had been a little bit more forthcoming. After a proper remark of grief about losing a long-time friend, next-door neighbor and occasional business partner, he said that he'd been surprised to learn that Mr. Brewster had not been aboard the small boat that had been hastily lowered into the river. He had observed Brewster releasing the boat and helping guests aboard and assumed he had gone with them. Major Winslow, an excellent swimmer, had preferred, as had Mr. Eggers, to take his chances in the water rather than in another watercraft.

Mr. Fred Eggers said he was too upset about the incident to make any comment at this time and Mr. Charles Winningham of New York City had returned to the City and couldn't be reached. Neither could Mr. Claude Cooke.

No hint of foul play. But then, Kessler had was a cousin by marriage to the chief of police, who was a bumbler, a boozer and a bully. Maybe Kessler had been asked to keep quiet about the nature of the death. That would be in keeping with his stodgy outlook.

Sitting on a great story and not saying, or hinting, anything without permission.

Jack read on. Mr. Kessler, as participant and writer of the article, limited himself to saying merely that it was a very sad tragedy.

Jack grinned as he ran a pencil through the words 'very sad' and wrote in the margin '*tautology*.' He hadn't taken all those grammar classes for nothing. Sooner or later, he'd get a chance to mention that to Kessler.

"I think the Duesenberg might be able to work if I get gas for it," Robert was saying to Lily. "One of the workmen with a truck agreed to drive me to town to get some."

"Who's paying for it?" Lily asked.

Robert looked surprised. "Why, Mr. Prune, out of the trust, I assume."

"Don't assume. Take along a dollar," Lily said. "And please stop calling him Mr. Prune."

Robert got a hangdog look and muttered, "I don't have a dollar."

Lily dug around in her handbag and came up with eighty cents. "That'll have to do." She saw no reason to mention the ten-dollar bill she also had in her bag. She'd hidden the rest of their pitiful savings in the little silk packet where she kept her hosiery.

"If you can actually get it running, I think we should go back to town and have a talk with Mr. Prinney. And I'll have a chat with Mrs. Prinney about dinner while you're gone."

As Lily approached the kitchen door, she could hear voices raised. One, a man's, coarse and belligerent, and the other Mimi's, soft and whiny. She couldn't distinguish the words. Opening the door, she found herself nearly eyeball to eyeball with a revolting individual.

Mimi, looking upset, said, "This is Billy Smith, Miss Brewster."

"Mimi's husband, I am," Billy said. He was short and wiry, and sallow of complexion as if he were seldom out in daylight. His dark hair was too long, too greasy. He was missing several teeth and the remainder of them looked pointy and ominous and disgustingly gray. He had a heavy-lidded look that was probably meant to be sexually attractive and merely made him look stupid.

"What are you doing here, Mr. Smith?" Lily said coldly, bringing many generations of haughty elegance into her voice.

"Just having a word with my wife, lady."

"I'm Miss Brewster, not 'lady,' " Lily said. She couldn't remember ever having taken such an instant and bone-deep dislike to anyone.

"And you ain't my husband," Mimi put in. "Except by law."

"The law's all it takes, honey," Billy sneered.

"It doesn't appear that Mimi wants to have a word with you," Lily said. "It would be best if you leave here. Now."

"Throwing me out of *your* house, huh?"

Lily went cold. What did he mean by that? Had Mimi told him that Grace and Favor Cottage wouldn't be theirs unless they stayed there ten years? No, Mimi couldn't know that. She and Robert certainly hadn't mentioned it around her. And Mr. Prinney seemed to be very closemouthed about his clients' affairs.

The only other person who might know was Mrs. Prinney and Mr. Prinney must have made clear to her long since that anything she knew about clients was confidential. At least, Lily devoutly hoped so.

"No, I'm not throwing you out, but I'll telephone the police and have them do it if you're not gone in ten seconds," Lily said.

He literally snarled. Lily suspected he'd had lots of unpleasant contacts with the police and didn't want another one.

Billy spat on the kitchen floor and slammed out of the house.

"Oh, Miss Brewster, I'm so sorry." Mimi was crying. "If I'd known he was around town, I'd have kept the doors locked."

"No, we can't turn the house into our own jail, Mimi," Lily said. "But I warn you, if I ever find him in the house again, I will call the police. Try to get that message across to him. And please get that floor cleaned."

Lily hated to be hard on Mimi, but since Mimi herself was the attraction, it would have to be Mimi who kept him away.

Or the police.

Chapter 8

Jack Summer turned up at the door to Grace and Favor Cottage quite early the next morning. He asked to see Robert. Mimi showed him to the library and fetched Lily because she couldn't find Robert.

"You're an early bird, Mr. Summer," Lily said.

"I managed to hitch a ride up the hill. And please call me Jack. Mr. Summer is my father," he said with a smile. The first one she'd seen on him. It wasn't a bad smile. Sort of goofy and crooked with a hint of a dimple.

She wasn't quite ready to be on first-name terms with a reporter she hardly knew and didn't quite trust, so instead she answered, "You'll have a nice ride down the hill, too. My brother got the Duesenberg running. Have you had breakfast? No? I haven't either. I'll ask Mimi to bring it in here for us."

"Thanks. Your brother isn't here?"

"He's polishing the car. He was asking me where rags are kept at five this morning. As if I'd know," she said with a laugh.

Lily went to the kitchen to ask for breakfast in the library and when she returned, said to Jack, "What

brings you here? Have you learned anything about
our uncle's death?" After her run-in with Billy Smith
the afternoon before, Jack Summer was downright
welcome company.

"I looked up the articles about your uncle in the
paper and copied them out since you seemed to
want to know more about it."

Robert suddenly appeared at the door, disheveled
and chirpy. "She's a beauty, Lily. Want to take her
for a spin? Oh, Summer, old boy. Didn't know we
had company."

"Mr. Summer came to show us the newspaper articles about Uncle Horatio. We're having breakfast
in here. Tell Mimi if you want some and tidy up a
bit."

Breakfast appeared at the same time Robert returned. As Mimi seemed to have the inclination to
linger, they chatted about the automobile while they
ate, though Lily was itching to get her hands on the
newspaper articles. Robert was the one who insti-
gated the investigation, but he was now obsessed
with the Duesenberg just as Lily was getting really
interested in Uncle Horatio.

She barely remembered her uncle. He was a big
man, but she'd been a child the one time she met
him—everybody had looked big to her then.
"Portly" was more the word. He had a large walrus
moustache and big square yellow teeth like the keys
on an old piano. That much she did recall. He'd
given Robert and her sweets, probably over her
mother's polite objections. Was he the ogre Robert
suggested and had goaded someone to a frenzy or
was he just a nice old man who died tragically in an
accident?

When they were finished eating and Mimi had finally gone off with their plates, there was another
interruption. Mr. Prinney came into the room, look-

ing harried. "You haven't seen my notary seal anywhere, have you?"

"A notary seal?" Lily asked. "I don't think so."

Mrs. Prinney came in from the kitchen as Lily
spoke. "Did you enjoy—oh, Elgin, what are you doing here? I thought you were at your office."

"I brought my notary seal home last night and
can't find it now."

"That's the little thing you stick in the wax? You
dropped it in the bedroom. I have it in the kitchen."

Mr. Prinney headed for the kitchen and Mrs. Prinney hung back, shaking her head fondly. "He's only
done that twice in his life and both times this year.
Last time it went missing, he found it just where it
was supposed to be and he'd looked there three
times already. Men!"

"Breakfast was wonderful," Lily said, hoping to
draw the interruption to a close.

But Mrs. Prinney went into quite a song and dance
about how she made the oatmeal, just as her granny
had taught her when she was a mere slip of a girl.
" 'Emmaline, my girl, if you can make up a big pot
of oatmeal without scorching it and do a hem without the stitches showing, you'll never lack for an oc-
cupation in bad times,' my granny used to say."

Lily feared Robert might go into gales of laughter
over the image of Mrs. Prinney ever being a mere
slip of a girl and gave him a gentle kick and a warning look.

Robert's incipient laugh turned to a yelp.

"Oh, I'm so sorry. Did I kick you?" Lily said innocently.

When Mrs. Prinney finally departed, Lily wasted
no time. "Do you have the articles with you?"

Jack handed over his handwritten transcripts to
her because Robert had bent down and disappeared

under the table to examine his injured leg.

Lily read through the lead story. Then read through it again more slowly. "Claude Cooke was on the boat? Claude Cooke!"

There was a thump as Robert banged his head trying to get out from under the table. "Cousin Claude!"

Lily didn't want to discuss Claude in front of Jack Summer and gave Robert a quick, fierce look warning him. "Do you know any of these people?" she asked Jack. "Besides Mr. Prinney and your editor?"

"Only Major Winslow, your next-door neighbor, by sight. Is this Cooke person a relation of yours?"

"Cousin," Lily said. "And I don't know if it's the same person. Cooke is such a common name. I know about Major Winslow. I must go over and call on Sissy. What do you know about him? Her father?"

Jack shrugged. Did she think he moved in circles that included the Winslows?

"Not much," he said. "I've seen him in town, taking the train to New York. I hear they used to socialize a lot. Not with folks around here, though. With the high-society crowd. Had some prince or princess up for a big to-do a couple years ago, I heard. The whole town turned out to meet the train and gawk."

Robert had taken the first pages from Lily and asked, "What about this Fred Eggers?"

"Never heard of him before," Jack admitted. "Nor the fella from New York. Winningham, was it?"

"And these were the only people on the boat?" Robert asked.

"Yeah, plus Billy Smith and—"

"Billy Smith!" Lily yelped.

Robert looked at her. "Have you gone mad? Who

is this Billy Smith that you screech his name that way?"

"The nasty little man who was in the kitchen; I told you about him. He's Mimi's husband—in a way."

"Billy is a nasty item," Jack said. "A real river rat. But he knows about everything there is to know about getting around on the water. Folks around here call him 'Waterbug'—that is, when they're not calling him something a lot worse. I'll bet he could take a steamboat against the incoming tide with bottles of hootch all over the deck and never lose a drop."

"Was that what he was doing on board? Working?" Lily asked.

Robert rolled his eyes. "You don't suppose Uncle Horatio had invited him along as a guest, do you? What do you mean about the hootch, Jack? Is he a rumrunner?"

"Oh, sure. Everybody knows it. But he's so slick about it that he's never been caught. Last spring a bunch of G-men were up here keeping an eye on him and they couldn't even keep track of him. Of course, everybody knew what they were. Pretending to be traveling salesmen staying at the hotel and bulging with guns."

"So if he's so good with boats, how come the yacht sank?" Lily asked.

"It was a whale of a storm, Miss Brewster. A real freak. And, too, Billy was working for your uncle. If Brewster told him to pull closer to the island, Billy'd of done what he was told. Horatio Brewster was about the only person he seemed to listen to. Talked awful about him, but was afraid to cross him in person."

Lily and Robert were looking at him doubtfully.

"Really," he protested. "Mr. Kessler told me the rain was coming at them horizontally and so heavily you couldn't see more than a few feet. And the boat was rocking and bucking. Even Billy Smith couldn't do anything about that. And he certainly wasn't responsible for the weather turning that way."

"But couldn't he have taken advantage of it?" Robert asked.

Jack stared at Robert for a long moment and said, "Yeah, he could have."

"There doesn't seem to be any mention of murder in this article," Robert said. "Where did they find Uncle Horatio's body? How does anybody know he's really dead? Maybe he got washed downriver and is even now in some poor widow's hovel with amnesia. I can see it," Robert said, waxing romantic. "Poor Uncle Horatio, sitting at a battered oaken table, making paper sailboats and moaning, 'Who am I?' while the widow, a mere slip of a girl, makes oatmeal for him and hems things."

"Robert, stop being so silly," Lily said. "Mrs. Prinney might hear you."

Robert looked slightly contrite.

Jack handed Lily the transcript of another article from a later paper. The piece said that the yacht had been raised out of the water by the Coast Guard, for fear it would drift into the main channel and cause a hazard, and the body of Horatio Brewster, late of Voorburg-on-Hudson, had been found in the galley section of the cabin. He had died, not of drowning, but of a severe blow to the top of his head. Several heavy objects remained in the galley, but the submersion of the yacht had obliterated any evidence of what object he had struck his head against.

Lily passed the paper to Robert, who read it and said, "Or what object had been struck against his head. There's a world of difference. And there's still no direct mention of murder."

"My editor's awfully upright about news being only the bare facts," Jack said.

They fell silent for a moment, then Lily said, "Mr. Summer, what was our Uncle Horatio like?"

"You don't know?"

"We only met him once, when we were children," Lily said.

"And he left you his house and fortune?" Jack exclaimed.

"In a manner of speaking," Robert said. "We must have been his closest living relatives besides Claude Cooke, and nobody in their right mind would leave him anything. What sort of chap was Uncle Horatio?"

Jack thought for a minute. "I didn't know him, really. Just to see around town and hear about. Nobody liked him much, but I don't know that anyone especially disliked him. He was very formal and polite, but he wasn't friendly. But everybody who had dealings with him said he was a fair man. Never cheated anyone. Never *got* cheated, either. He irritated a couple local folks who thought he might pay more for food and gas and such, just because he had the money. He set them straight."

Jack paused to rummage around in his memory. "I don't know where else he lived, but he wasn't here all the time. Mostly when he was in town, he had people staying with him up here in the house."

"Lots of parties, then?" Robert asked.

Jack shook his head. "Not parties that I ever heard of. Business people, I think. Old guys with paperwork under their arms. I guess that's why he didn't bother keeping up the grounds. He wasn't trying to impress society types and figured if a businessman like him didn't care what the outside looked like, none of his cronies would either."

"So that's probably the sort of guests who were on the boat when it sank," Lily said. "No women involved."

"Nobody but Mimi Smith," Jack said.

Lily was shocked. "Our Mimi Smith? She was on board? She wasn't mentioned in the newspaper article."

"She'd been hired to serve drinks and food," Jack said. "Servants don't count with Mr. Kessler, I guess. Billy wasn't mentioned either." He paused. "Wait. I remember something about that. Horatio Brewster had his man hire a pilot and waitress . . ."

"His 'man'?" Robert asked.

"Yes, a sort of butler, valet, houseman. And I heard there was some kind of wrangling about it when they were setting out."

"What kind of wrangle?" Lily asked.

"I'm not sure," Jack said. "I heard it thirdhand and didn't pay much attention. Apparently Mr. Brewster didn't approve of the houseman's choice of Billy and Mimi, but it was too late to hire anybody else. He moored his boat in town, you see. So there were the usual Nosey Parkers hanging around, watching them set out."

"So he didn't want either of them?" Robert asked. "I can understand not wanting Billy around. From what you and Lily say, he's a real blot on the landscape. But what was wrong with Mimi being the waitress?"

Jack shrugged. "No idea."

"Did the houseman go along?"

"I don't think so," Jack said. "He wasn't mentioned in the newspaper articles."

"But neither were Billy and Mimi mentioned,"

Robert said. "Only the toffs. Is the houseman still around?"

"No, he put out a big spread for the funeral, then vanished," Jack said.

"How about the three of us trying to find out more about this trip?" Robert said.

Jack was certainly eager to know more, now that he thought there might be a story in it, but he hadn't intended for his investigation to be a group effort.

Still, the Brewsters lived in the victim's house, as did two of the other people who had been aboard the boat.

"Let's do that," Jack agreed.

Chapter 9

Lily and Robert had decided that they'd go to Voor-burg and beard Mr. Prinney in his den. Questioning him about Uncle Horatio seemed likely to be more effective in an office setting than at home.

But in the meantime, Lily intended to find out what more she could on her own. Two of the men on the boat were unknown; one lived in New York and one in Poughkeepsie. She could do nothing about them. She could write to Cousin Claude, but would be unlikely to get a reply unless she took him on in person. At least she knew where to find him. He still lived with his mother—Lily and Robert's Aunt Hilary.

Major Winslow had been on the boat as well and was close by, but she'd never met him except years ago at a school play she and Sissy had been in. She'd wait on him.

She hadn't met Mr. Kessler, the newspaper editor who was another guest on the boat, and as close-mouthed as he'd been in the reports in the paper, he was unlikely to spill the beans to her.

Billy Smith was impossible. She couldn't bear the thought of speaking to him.

So that left Mimi. She felt Mimi would talk about the accident, but only with some chummy buttering up first.

"Mimi, come sit down for a minute, would you?" Lily said.

Mimi had been cleaning the runner in the upstairs hall with a carpet sweeper when Lily ran across her and looked alarmed when Lily made her request.

"I ain't done nothing wrong, did I?" Mimi asked, gingerly taking a seat on one of the Chippendale chairs that flanked a tiny table in the hall.

"No, of course not," Lily said, also sitting down carefully. She suspected the chairs were probably fragile. "I just wanted to chat with you. I'm curious about something Mrs. Prinney said about you growing up in this house."

Mimi relaxed a little. "Well, my ma, she was Barbara by name, she came to work as a girl for Miss Flora, who was a spinster. Ma started in the kitchens when she was about fourteen, and was a good hard worker and by and by she came to Miss Flora's attention and Miss Flora took her upstairs to be her maid. Miss Flora wasn't old then, but she enjoyed poor health even then. She'd had that infant disease . . ."

"Infantile paralysis? Like Governor Roosevelt had?"

"That's it. She could walk and all when she got well, but had trouble getting in and out of bed and lacing up her shoes and such. So Ma helped her. Then when the housekeeper up and died right there in the front hall, Miss Flora made Ma the housekeeper."

"And when did you come along?"

"Just a year or two later, I think. My ma married, but he ran off with some floozy from town before I was even born. And Miss Flora, who liked my ma a lot, let us stay on here and Ma kept on being house-keeper."

"What about my Uncle Horatio? Did you like him?"

"Oh, no, miss."

"He wasn't nice?" Lily asked.

"It's not that. He wasn't here. He left before I was born. I never met him until this summer."

"Why did he leave? Didn't he get along with his aunt?"

Lily's animated expression suddenly faded. "Yes, miss. They got along well enough, my ma told me. But they had some sort of fight and he went off on his own. Never came back except for when Miss Flora died."

Mimi made a vague gesture toward her aban-doned carpet sweeper. Lily sensed that she had hit a nerve, or maybe Mimi just wasn't interested in talking about Uncle Horatio since she'd never known him.

"What about your mother?" Lily asked. "Does she still live nearby?"

"No, miss. She took the flu something awful in twenty-three and died. Miss Flora died three years later, even though I took real good care of her. I'd have stayed on here, but Mr. Horatio came back and he had his own people to run the house. Mr. Prinney hired me to put everything under covers after Mr. Horatio died and his people went away to other jobs."

"Oh, Mimi. I'm sorry to hear that your mother is gone. Do you have other family?"

"I got two aunts in town—Ma's sisters. I lived with them mostly from the time Miss Flora died un-til you and Mr. Brewster came here. They fight like cats and dogs, my aunts do. Every now and then, I'd get to feeling so bad in that house that I'd go live with Billy for a while, but that was worse.''

"You're married to Billy?"

"Official-like, but not really. Not in my heart, miss.''

"Why haven't you divorced him?''

"Mainly 'cause he won't go along with it. It's hard enough when both want a divorce, but when only the wife does, she's got to have a lawyer and all. That's expensive, you know. Besides, there's nobody else I want to marry, so it don't really matter.''

Mimi paused, and then went on in a rush, "I'm awful grateful to you and Mr. Brewster for taking me in here. I like this big old house. Know every nook and cranny of it. Makes me remember Ma and Miss Flora. And long as you stay and I do my work good, I won't ever have to live with Billy or my aunts again. They liked Billy and was always inviting him over to dinner, hoping, I guess, that I'd go away with him for good.''

"Why did you marry him?'' Lily asked. It was an automatic question. In her own mind she was dealing with the fact of Mimi's gratitude and Lily's responsibility for her, which she hadn't realized until now.

"I dunno. He was real good-looking when we were young. So was I, I figure. Miss Flora had died and Mr. Prinney said Mr. Horatio was coming back here with his own people to take care of the house and all. I didn't know how to do anything except take care of old ladies and most of the old ladies in town who needed help weren't near as nice as Miss Flora. Couple of them were really mean old things. So, it was stay with my aunts or marry Billy.''

Lily was appalled. "But did you love him? Ever?''

"I guess I thought I did at first. I wanted to be in love. All girls do, I guess. He was handsome and had a lot of get-up-and-go then. Always working real hard. I didn't know at first that he was working hard at bad things till he started getting arrested fairly regular. He'd always beat me up when he got out of jail, like it was my fault he went to jail. So I moved in with my aunts. Then he'd be real sorry and come fetch me back and be real good to me for a while and before long it would happen all over again."

"Mimi, I'm so sorry to hear all this. What a hard life you've had."

Mimi smiled and took hold of the carpet sweeper handle. "Ain't your fault, miss. And everything's co-pacetic now."

"One more thing, Mimi ... About the boat accident—"

Mimi seemed to cave in on herself. "No, miss. I don't like to think about it much. It was so awful. I've never been so scared in my life."

"All right, but I hope you'll change your mind someday. You see, it was my great-uncle who died in the accident and I'd like to know more about it. That boat accident is why I'm here and why you're here, too. It seems important to me to know how it happened."

"All right, Miss Lily. I'll try to remember and tell you later." She stood up abruptly and said rather shrilly, "These floors are a mess, what with all the workmen coming and going and dragging leaves and twigs in. I don't like to see the house dirty. Ma and Miss Flora would be rolling in their graves."

That was all she was going to get out of Mimi for now. Lily stood and said, "Thanks, Mimi, for telling me about yourself."

"Weren't very interesting, miss."

Lily laid a hand on Mimi's arm. "Everybody's interesting, Mimi. You included."

"Yes, Miss Lily," Mimi said. "If you say so."

Robert was determined to take Lily to town to speak to Mr. Prinney.

"Why don't we make a courtesy call on the Winslows first?" Lily suggested. "Just to see if the automobile really does work. I'd rather get stranded next door than in town. And I haven't seen Sissy in ages."

"And you're hoping she's improved?" Robert asked.

"Improved? I don't see how she could. She was beautiful when we were in school together."

"That's true, but she was a dumb cluck."

"You prefer brains to beauty, Robert?"

"I demand both."

"I seem to remember that she had quite the crush on you."

"And I gave her the icy mitt," Robert said. "I hope she remembers that and doesn't make a beeline for me again. Get your baggage."

"I just hope Major Winslow isn't around," Lily said. "You're not going to like him. At least, Dad didn't."

"Why not?" Robert asked.

"Because he was both the richest and stingiest man Dad said he'd ever known. Don't you remember Dad raving about the time that Major Winslow gave the ball at their Fifth Avenue mansion for his wife's birthday and had a cash bar? And the buffet food was meager and ran out half an hour after the party started. Dad was appalled and so was everyone else. I remember Sissy saying she had to keep an inventory of her clothing and if she wanted something new to wear, she had to prove to him that some other dress was worn out and beyond repair."

"Sounds like a charmer," Robert said. "I guess borrowing money from him is out of the question?"

"Utterly," Lily said with a laugh. "Give me five minutes to spruce up."

Lily took the time to dress up a little, added a scarf to her ensemble and put everything from her handbag into a slightly nicer, smaller one. By the time she was ready, Robert had the Duesenberg at the front door.

"Isn't this some crate?" Robert said, beaming.

Lily was dumbfounded. It was a great, handsome beast of a car. The paint was a rich yellowish-cream color and there was a huge amount of chrome that Robert had meticulously polished. The grille alone was a work of art. It was not only luxurious, but gigantic and she wondered what would happen if they met up with another car on the narrow road. Fortunately the drive to the Winslow house wasn't long enough to create the problem.

"I should have telephoned first," Lily said, suddenly remembering the proprieties she'd grown up with and which had become rusty in the last two years.

"We'll just say we were taking a spin in the Duesie and dropped in. Which is true," Robert said. "Nice little pile they've got here," he added as they turned into the Winslows' drive.

The house sat a little lower and farther back from the Hudson than Grace and Favor and probably didn't share the same magnificent view of the river. But it was massive and probably much older than many of the great homes in the area. Robert pulled the car around an elaborate circle drive and they walked up the four steps to the portico. He used the great lion's head door knocker enthusiastically.

They waited.

"The butler must be taking a nap," Robert said, knocking again.

Finally the door opened, but it wasn't a stiff-bosomed butler before them, but a beautiful red-haired girl. "Why, it's Lily and Robert Brewster!" Sissy Winslow said with pleased surprise. "Whatever are you doing here? Come in."

"We're your next-door neighbors," Lily said as the girls embraced. Sissy attempted to hug Robert, too, but he gracelessly eluded her with a sudden desire to tie his shoe.

"Neighbors?" Sissy said. "Oh, are you two the new people at Honeysuckle Cottage?"

Lily explained that they did indeed live there and had changed the name to Grace and Favor Cottage.

"What does that mean? Grace and Favor?" Sissy asked.

"Just a pretty phrase we picked up," Lily said.

"I never would have made the connection between Mr. Brewster and you two, in spite of the name," Sissy said. She indicated a table where Lily could leave her things (although Robert wouldn't part with his precious car keys or the violently checkered golfing cap he'd suddenly developed a fondness for), and led them along a marble-tiled hallway to a vast formal front parlor.

"Butler's day off?" Robert asked.

"Oh, we don't have a butler anymore," Sissy said. "Daddy says that with so terribly many people out of work, it's unattractive to live ostentatiously. It's sort of fun, actually, to have practically no staff at all. More private, you know. Not having a maid laying out her choice for your clothes and such. And

I'm learning to cook. Cook! Can you just imagine *me* cooking?"

Lily had forgotten what a high-pitched giggle Sissy had and was insulted that Sissy thought cutting back the staff was 'roughing it' when she and Robert had lived the last two years like rats in a tiny cage. She mentally chided herself. If their father hadn't lost everything, she would be no better informed than Sissy. It wasn't fair to blame her for her stupidity.

"So Horatio Brewster was a relative of yours and left you the house?" Sissy went on.

"Our great-uncle," Lily said.

"Daddy thought the world of Mr. Brewster, you know," Sissy said. "They were great friends. And business associates as well."

"What business?" Robert asked.

"I'm not sure, exactly. But they were always talking about bits of property they owned together. Someplace they were going to build a resort in the mountains out west. But that probably won't happen now, what with your uncle dying."

"Your father was on the boat, too, wasn't he?" Robert said.

Sissy made a Sad Face, which wasn't nearly as flattering as she apparently imagined. "Yes, and it was too, too horrible. It's a good thing Mummy and I didn't even hear about it until Daddy was home safe and sound and told us about it."

"What did he say happened?" Robert persisted.

"Your uncle had invited some friends to go look at that awful island. I can't imagine why. It's so terribly spooky, you know. And dangerous. And this perfectly dreadful storm suddenly came up and the boat was being tossed around horribly and it started sinking right out there in the middle of the river."

Sissy was getting all the drama she could out of telling the story.

"What did your father do?" Lily asked.

"He and your uncle got this little boat—a dinghy, I think it's called—unhooked from the back and started helping people into it. But Daddy slipped on something when the boat rocked violently and hit his head and fell down. He said he must have passed out for a few minutes. When he got his wits back, the dinghy was gone and there was only one other man on the boat that he could see. The other man said he was a pretty strong swimmer and was going to take his chances in the water instead of waiting to see if the dinghy made it to the island and came back. The rain was coming down so hard they couldn't even see where it had gone. Daddy's a good swimmer, too, so they dived in."

"They didn't know Uncle Horatio was still on board?" Robert asked.

"No! Daddy assumed he'd gone with the dinghy. And he was appalled when he finally got to the island and realized everybody was there except Mr. Brewster. Daddy tried to take the dinghy back out to fetch him, but the guards on the island, who had thrown out a rope when they heard the cries for help, wouldn't let him."

"Why not?"

"Because the dinghy had a hole in it by then, too. They said it wasn't safe to take out again. One of them even drew a gun on him. It was an outrage, of course. Daddy says they all staggered around on the rocks clear around the island looking for your uncle. They thought he'd decided to swim to safety, too, and had ended up somewhere else on the island."

"But he hadn't," Lily said. "Poor Uncle Horatio."

Chapter 10

Sissy's father showed up a moment later. He was a tall, stiff, sandy-colored, military-looking man who walked with a cane. He didn't seem to have a limp, and the cane was quite grand, ebony wood with a gold handle in the shape of a flying goose, so Lily assumed it must be an affectation. Or perhaps he sustained some minor injury in the Great War and had once used it out of necessity and now merely kept it out of habit.

"You have company?" Major Jonathan Winslow said in a tone that implied that he didn't quite approve.

Sissy leaped to her feet to make introductions. "Daddy, you've met Lily and Robert Brewster before. But it's been ages and ages. Back when Lily and I were in boarding school."

"Nice to see you again," Major Winslow said, apparently approving the credentials. "Taking a look at the countryside, are you?"

"Yes and no," Lily said. "We live next door to you now. We inherited Honeysuckle Cottage from our Uncle Horatio."

"Imagine that," Winslow said. "I never heard

Horatio talk about his family. I asked Mr. Prinney about the distribution of his assets, of course, thinking I might buy the place and fix it up, but I suppose you know what he's like. Won't give away any information. Just told me it had been left to relatives and it would be up to them. You're not interested in selling it, are you?"

That's blunt enough, Lily thought. "No, not in the least. We're gaga about the place."

"Probably really belongs to your parents anyway," Major Winslow said. "I'll drop by one of these days and ask them about it."

"Our parents are dead, Major Winslow," Robert said.

"Oh, I'm sorry to hear that. Didn't know. Well, I wish you the best with it. And I hope you don't mind a bit of advice . . ."

Robert was smiling his best fake smile. He wasn't any more taken with Major Winslow than Lily was. "What might that be, sir?" Robert asked with exaggerated respect.

"Take it easy with the money. Don't make too many improvements too fast. Don't hire more staff than you need. These are bad times and the wealthy are resented by the locals. If you mean to spend much time here, it'll be better for you to get along well with the local merchants and working people and not let them think you're lording it over them. I imagine Sissy's told you, we've cut back. Everybody who can manage to, should do so. This worldwide financial situation could lead to revolution and anarchy. I've actually heard that there's a club of Reds right here in Voorburg."

Robert smiled and asked, with apparent innocence, "But don't you wonder, sir, if the staff you laid off might be among the revolutionaries?"

Jonathan Winslow got red in the face and started to sputter.

"It's been nice to see you again, Sissy," Lily said, standing up before Major Winslow could say anything coherent. "But we really must be getting along." If she could get Robert out of here fast enough, he might not become so ultra-polite that it would be obvious how offended he was at being talked down to this way. She plucked at his sleeve.

"Robert, come along." She hurried him out of the room, tossing goodbyes over her shoulder, grabbed her purse from the table in the hall and had opened the door before Winslow father and daughter could even catch up with them. Lily hopped into the Duesenberg and gaily waved goodbye to Sissy as Robert put the car in gear and sped away.

"What a patronizing bastard," he said when he'd turned onto the main road.

"Slow down, Robert."

He let up on the gas. "Lily, times are hard. People are out of work. So Major Winslow fires his staff so he'll look good to the locals? Bet the staff wasn't much impressed with being flung out on their ears. They were probably locals, too. No wonder Sissy's so stupid, being raised by a person like that."

"I warned you that he was naturally stingy. He's using this excuse to save money," Lily said. "Let's go to town and talk to Mr. Prinney. Forget about Major Winslow."

"What? Swan around in a great buttercup-yellow battleship of a car in full view of the locals and incite anarchy?" Robert said.

"We could hide it somewhere close to town and then walk," Lily said.

Robert roared with laughter. "That would be like

attempting to tuck Blenheim Castle in a quiet little nook. But we'll give it a try."

They stashed the car a half a mile from town behind a barn and set out on foot to explore Voorburg-on-Hudson. But they only got as far as the village green where there was a statue of a Revolutionary War hero, which the seagulls had seriously abused and needed a good hosing down. The statue stood in front of a bandstand where Lily came to a sudden stop. Robert, who was strolling along slightly behind her, trod on her heel.

"Robert! Look over there. In front of the gasoline station. Isn't that—"

"Cousin Claude!" Robert exclaimed. "What's he doing here?"

Claude Cooke was the oldest son of Lily's and Robert's father's sister Hilary, who was considered to have made an 'unfortunate' marriage to a minister, who was not only *not* Episcopalian, but worse yet, some sort of offbeat semi-Baptist sect of his own devising. Hilary had met him when a school friend, as a lark, took her to a revival meeting. Poor Hilary, only eighteen and never acquainted with anyone like the flamboyant preacher with the bedroom eyes, soaring tenor voice and outright swaggering manner, fell instantly in love.

Hilary Brewster promptly ditched the friend who had taken her to the revival, went backstage to introduce herself to Reverend Cooke and ran off with him to Kentucky the next morning. She claimed a marriage had actually taken place and none of the Brewster clan openly questioned it when she returned to the bosom of the family a year later, wearing mourning garb and carrying a three-month-old Claude in her arms. She told a rambling and hysterically confused story of a train wreck, or train robbers. Nobody was ever quite sure which.

Hilary was silently absorbed back into the family, where she took up an extremely quiet life devoted largely to religious needlework for the Episcopal Church and raised her son in the comfort of a modest family trust from her grandfather. Reverend Cooke's name was never uttered again within her hearing.

But Claude grew up resenting his bizarrely mixed social heritage and was determined to out-snob a rather snobby family. With the help of a New York State Supreme Court judge who had fruitlessly courted Hilary for many years (and received, each Christmas, a petit point pillow with his initials in whatever colors of wool Hilary had left over that year), Claude got a scholarship to Columbia Law School and subsequently a very good job in a prestigious firm of tax attorneys.

Claude was older than Lily and Robert and was a big, rather coarse-featured, crinkly-haired, barrel-chested redhead with a stiff, patronizing manner that made them dislike him almost from the days of their births. When they were complaining bitterly about him correcting their manners one day when they were both teenagers, their father told them the story of Aunt Hilary and the preacher and urged them to try to work up some sympathy for poor Claude.

Neither of them had ever been able to do so.

"Let's find out what he's doing here," Lily said as Claude paced in front of the gas station, smoking a cigarette in a silver holder that probably cost more than the average person's monthly pay. Not that the average person had monthly pay these days.

"Let's avoid him," Robert said.

But the decision was taken from them when

Claude shaded his eyes for a moment, looked across the street and spotted them.

"Too late," Lily murmured. "Besides, I want to know what he was doing on that boat when Uncle Horatio died."

"Trying to get something out of Uncle, you can bet," Robert replied. "I never met a greedier man in my life. Remember how he used to fine us when he disapproved of our manners? Took my whole week's allowance once because I used a bad word and he threatened to tell Dad."

"What was the word?" Lily asked.

"Poop," Robert said. "Not exactly blasphemy."

"We can't pretend we didn't see him. Come along. Five minutes' chitchat and we're done. And don't use the word 'poop,' if you don't mind, unless you're asking him about parts of the boat."

Lily took Robert's arm and nearly dragged him across the street. "Why, Claude, it *is* you," she said brightly. "What are you doing clear up here so far from the City?"

He gazed sternly at the two of them and nodded formally. "Just visiting some friends and business associates. But my car has a flat."

"Could we give you a lift somewhere in Uncle's Duesie?" Robert asked with a wicked grin. "It's just up the road."

Claude's perpetually ruddy face grew redder. "Yes, I did hear something about you two inheriting his estate. But I don't need a ride, thank you. The garage man says he'll have the tire repaired in a few moments."

"I understand you were on the boat when Uncle Horatio died," Robert said.

Claude made a surprised noise which, in a less refined individual, would have been called a snort.

"Where did you hear that?" he asked, apparently hoping he could deny it.

"There was an account of it in the local paper," Robert replied.

"It must have been a horrible experience for you, Claude," Lily said, hoping she sounded encouraging and sympathetic.

"Of course it was. Such a tragedy. I've tried to put it out of my mind." Claude cast a hurried glance back over his shoulder to see if the car was ready.

"Oh, you shouldn't do that," Lily said. "All the brain doctors these days say you should thrash about with your feelings in order to come to terms with them."

"I'm not familiar with any brain doctors," Claude huffed.

"Perhaps you should—" Robert began.

Lily gave him a sharp nudge.

"Claude," she went on, "you weren't injured when the boat wrecked, were you?"

The ploy worked. "Yes, I was, as a matter of fact. A minor injury, fortunately. I got my finger caught in some sort of hook on the dinghy and broke it. It was extremely painful."

Robert said something under his breath that neither of them quite caught.

"So you were on the dinghy," Lily went on. "Why was that? Why didn't you swim like several others did?"

Claude regarded her suspiciously, wondering how she knew this much. "I'm not a swimmer." The tone was that of an upright citizen declaring he was not an arsonist.

"And the dinghy was supposed to go back for the others?"

"Yes, but it sustained too much damage to go

back. I must say, the Bannermans' guards on the island took onto themselves far too many important decisions. One of them actually waved a gun around in a threatening manner."

"Where was Uncle Horatio when the dinghy set out for the island?"

"I have no idea," he said.

"You didn't look back at the boat as you left?"

Claude was finally irritated enough to snap, "Of course not. We were all looking for a shoreline. I don't think you realize what filthy weather it was. A person could hardly see the others in the dinghy, much less the larger craft. My car ought to be ready in a moment. It was . . . interesting to run into you." He tipped his hat and disappeared into the gasoline station.

"Hmm," Robert said, as they walked away. "He's another exception to my rule that people love to talk about catastrophes. Wonder what he's trying to keep from us."

Lily took off her straw hat and fanned her face. It was turning into another hot day. "Do you really think he's trying to conceal something or is he being his usual priggish self? What a damp rag he is! I wish I'd asked him why he happened to be on the boat. I don't ever remember him so much as mentioning Uncle Horatio. Suddenly he's chummy enough to be invited on this jaunt with Uncle Horatio's other business associates. I'll bet he's been secretly buttering him up for years."

"Thank God it didn't work," Robert said. "Or we'd still be in the tenement."

"Maybe it would have worked if Uncle had lived longer."

"Which would mean he had a compelling reason

to keep Uncle alive," Robert said. "Rats. I'd rather have him be a suspect."

Lily rolled her eyes. "Robert, there might not be *any* suspects. But if you want some, you can keep Claude on your list."

"How so?"

"Well, suppose Uncle Horatio got sick of being annoyed by Claude and told him he was the heir— just to get Claude out of his hair. Then Claude might not have minded too much hurrying him along on his way to the afterlife."

"Hmm. It's kind of a thin theory, much as I like it. The mental picture of Claude finding out we were the heirs warms the heart."

They fell into a companionable silence while they strolled around the village green, looking for Mr. Prinney's office. Voorburg was such a Dutch name that Lily had expected Dutch architecture—not that she really knew what Dutch architecture looked like. But Voorburg was a mix of New England styles— lovely little Cape Cods, a miniature saltbox or two and quite a few small-scale Georgian and Tudor homes. There was also a handful of houses and shops that had no identifiable style except as a reflection of some home builder's personal taste—or lack of it.

The village green had shops along the east side, which was slightly elevated. Besides the gas station, there was a greengrocer, a butcher with rabbits and chickens hanging in the front window, and a milliner with a window display of unfashionable and rather dusty hats. Next door was a clothing shop that appeared to deal primarily in fairly good hand-me-downs. Mabel's Cafe was there, too, and had the faintest air of suggesting that illegal booze just *might* be purchased by the trusted locals. A small door between the cafe and the milliner's opened to a stairway. A sign on the door said, MISS PHOEBE TWINKLE, SEWING AND ALTERATIONS.

Lily could hardly wait to meet Miss Phoebe Twinkle.

Homes and offices converted from homes were along the two sides of the green. A post office and jail shared a small, dignified house. A hardware store occupied the first floor of another building with a notice in the window that a cobbler was available on the premises Mondays and Thursdays. There were a number of carefully refurbished rakes, brooms and shovels displayed in front of the shop.

They finally found Mr. Prinney's office, which occupied half of the first floor of a large brick home. A secretary sat in the tiny entryway. She was an elderly lady who looked as if she had her hair in pin curls without the pins. It was either a wig or highly lacquered. Lily introduced herself and Robert, only to be told that Mr. Prinney was out calling on a client and was expected to return within the hour.

Lily and Robert debated going home, but decided to wait and roam around the town a bit more.

The fourth side of the green, the river side, had only two buildings. One was devoted to boats, oars, nets and various fishing tools. Attached behind it was a tall sail loft and to the side was a fish market. The other building, which was minuscule, was a boat rental and boat ticket booth. A sidewalk between the two ran to a steeply staired walking bridge that crossed the railroad tracks next to the river, presumably leading down to docks that weren't visible from the green.

Lily turned slowly, savoring the warm, slightly salty, fishy smell of the river mixed with a divine fragrance of fresh bread from a bakery she'd failed to notice earlier. The people of Voorburg were probably suffering the same financial privation the rest of the country was enduring, but were refusing to let the town look down-and-out. Only a few of the shops appeared to be permanently closed and even they were in good condition, as if merely awaiting a new tenant.

Several well-groomed ladies were sweeping the stoops of their homes. An elderly gentleman was painting his front door. A red-faced middle-aged woman was tending her garden and waved at them cheerfully with a muddy-gloved hand.

These were, Lily decided, proud, good people living in an old town they cared about.

For the first time, it really came to her in full force that this was now her hometown, too. And she was glad.

Chapter 11

As Lily and Robert explored the town further, they discovered several churches, a school and a number of other small, front-room businesses outside the town square. They got sandwiches from Mabel's Cafe, where their presence elicited a mixed reaction. The waitress, presumably Mabel herself, was friendly but not effusive. Two ladies in the corner booth stared at them with frowns and whispers. The rest of the patrons either ignored them entirely or showed only vague curiosity about the outsiders. The food was adequate and cheap.

They'd only half-finished their sandwiches when they spotted Mr. Prinney's pristine, well-kept old black Ford chugging down the street. They wrapped what remained of their sandwiches in oiled butcher paper sheets Mabel supplied and hurried to catch Mr. Prinney before he could run another errand.

The pin-curled secretary showed them into his office and he greeted them with surprise and a little alarm. "Come in. Come in. There's nothing wrong, is there?" They hadn't changed their minds about sticking out the ten years, had they? He'd already grown somewhat fond of them and hated the idea of handing anything over to Claude Cooke.

"Nothing's wrong," Lily said, sitting down in one of the visitor chairs and looking straight at him. "But we need some information. About our uncle's death."

Mr. Prinney burst into speech. "I should have told you sooner. I know that. But I didn't want to alarm you."

"We've heard that he didn't just die in the boating accident. We hear he was murdered and would like to know the truth."

Mr. Prinney nodded. "I'm sorry to learn that it's common knowledge, and sorrier yet to tell you it's almost certainly the case."

"Then why is it an open secret? Why hasn't someone been arrested?"

"Because, while there appears to be proof that it was murder, there's no way of knowing who the perpetrator was."

"What proof?" Robert said.

Mr. Prinney looked uncomfortably at Lily. "I'd rather not say in front of Miss Brewster."

"Nonsense," Robert said. "My sister reads every mystery story she can get her hands on. She's not going to faint dead away."

"Very well," Mr. Prinney said doubtfully. "It was the wound to the head that killed him. According to the coroner, it was an extremely heavy blow to the top of his head. If he hadn't been rather bald, the coroner said he wouldn't have noticed that it was from some distinct object. Not to mention that it's almost impossible to sustain a hard blow to the top of one's head unless one is dropped headfirst onto something."

"Distinct in what way?" Lily asked.

Mr. Prinney hesitated for a moment. "It was a perfectly round blow and compressed the skull in a concave pattern. There was nothing in the galley where he died of that shape and size."

"What could it have been?" Robert asked.

Mr. Prinney lifted his narrow shoulders. "No one knows. The police searched the wreckage thoroughly. They sent people to the island to see if anything of the sort had washed to shore and found nothing."

Lily nodded. "They wouldn't have. Skulls are very hard. It would have to be a very heavy object, which was probably either thrown or swept overboard and sank."

Mr. Prinney looked astonished at how calmly this apparently well-bred girl was taking this information. "You're quite right, of course."

"And it had to be someone on the boat who brought it along," Robert said. "Some common object that could be concealed in a pocket. A billiard ball or something."

Lily arched an eyebrow. "Could you carry around a billiard ball in your suit jacket and not have the bulge noticed?"

Robert laughed. "I couldn't. I'm too trim. But somebody like Claude, who bulges anyway, could. The problem is, was it brought on board as a weapon? Nobody could have predicted a terrible storm and the opportunity to knock off someone without it being noticed."

Lily changed the subject. "How commonly known is this information?"

"The police know. The coroner. Mr. Kessler. And me. But anybody might have told someone."

"And nothing's being done?" Lily asked.

"What *is* to be done?" Mr. Prinney countered. "Unless the object is found and can be laid clearly to someone's ownership, there is no proof of guilt. And even if that were the case, the person who owned it could say he or she had lost it in the turmoil of the shipwreck and someone else used it."

"But someone killed our uncle. They can't go free!" Lily exclaimed.

"I share your regret," Mr. Prinney said. "But without clear proof . . ." His voice trailed off.

"You were on board," Robert said. "And you saw nothing that could have been the weapon?"

"I wasn't looking for weapons. I was studying the scenery at first, and when the wind blew up and the boat came into danger, I was looking only at getting myself and others to shore."

Lily stood. "Thank you for telling us this, Mr. Prinney. I have only one more question. What was the purpose of the trip? Or was it merely social?"

Mr. Prinney became wary. "I don't know that I should say."

"I think you must," Lily said firmly.

"Your uncle merely told me that he had something to say to someone and wanted witnesses."

"Witnesses?" Robert said. They had headed back for the automobile and discovered that it had sunk into mud.

"It sounds to me as if whoever it was might have gotten some advance warning of Uncle's intent," Lily said. "Or perhaps had a very guilty conscience." She looked around. "How could it be muddy here?" she asked. "It hasn't rained recently."

She got her answer when Jack Summer bicycled by. He stopped and said, "I was on my way up the hill to see you. Let me help you push. This old barn is the town icehouse. You don't want to park near it at the end of the summer."

"Icehouse?" Robert said blankly.

"Ice farther upriver in the clear lakes is cut into blocks in the winter and brought down here," Jack said, then went into the barn and brought out a tarp to put under the back wheels for traction. "It's stored in this barn and by high summer, it melts so fast that the ground around it gets muddy. There. Try backing again."

When they had the automobile free and Robert was wringing his hands over how dirty it had gotten, Lily asked Jack, "Why were you heading for Grace and Favor?"

"I wanted to tell you I've found out the boat your uncle died in is still at a salvage yard a little ways out of town."

"Have you seen it?" Robert asked.

"Not yet," Jack replied.

"Could we go look it over?" Robert asked.

"I don't see why not, but I'm not sure it'll tell us anything."

They all piled into the Duesie and Jack directed them to a spot about five miles along a dirt road that ran north beside the railroad tracks next to the river. Just before they reached the salvage yard, they passed the city dump. There were people there, not disposing of trash, but picking through it. A man, a woman and two small children were walking about, bent over and carrying small bags into which they could put anything salvageable. A beat-up truck sat to the far side of the dump. It had a patchwork quilt suspended over the bed and was apparently their home.

Robert had slowed down for the potholes and Lily couldn't tear her eyes from the dreadful sight of the family living at the garbage dump. She'd had the vague idea that the worst of the Depression was in the cities. But here, in the country, where life should have been easier, it was just as awful. She watched the little girl, in her tattered dress, bend and pick up what looked like a couple of filthy bread rolls. Lily's stomach turned. If she'd had food along, she'd have flung herself out of the car and given it to them.

Uncle Horatio's boat had pride of place among the battered and rotting rowboats that populated the salvage yard. The boat was much larger than Lily had expected and very handsome. And except for the hole in the hull, it looked to be in good condition. It was resting upright, supported by an arrangement of wooden stilts and scaffolding.

"Why isn't it being repaired?" she asked.

"The keel was damaged," Jack said. "It would have to be completely dismantled to replace it. That would cost more than the boat is worth."

"Here! What are you three doing?" a voice called from a shack. A very dirty, wizened old man emerged. He was wearing hip waders that came clear to his armpits and a hat and plaid shirt that must have been generations old.

"Mr. Bond, I was just showing the Brewsters their uncle's boat," Jack said.

The old man's expression softened. "A real pity. She was a beaut. Forty-five-foot Cris Craft. Solid wood clear through. And fine appointments. Hate to see her like this, but there's nothing to do but strip her for parts. Mr. Horatio loved that boat like some men love a beautiful woman. So, are you Mr. Horatio's kin?"

"Niece and nephew," Robert said. "Could we climb up there and look it over?"

"It'll just break your heart," Mr. Bond said, "but go ahead. If there's any of his personal stuff in there, I reckon it belongs to you. It's real stable."

This last remark turned out to be something of a falsehood. The boat rocked gently as Robert and Jack climbed the scaffolding. Lily, who was wearing a skirt, decided she'd rely on their observations rather than attempting to follow them. She got out a handkerchief to put over a dirty stump nearby and sat and waited. She knew very little about boats, but enough to know the keel was like a person's spine—the most vital part of the whole structure.

She could barely hear Jack and Robert talking to each other. "What's this?" and "Where does this go?" and "How does this work?" The questions were Robert's. Jack's answers weren't quite audible. Lily wished they'd hurry up. The ground was dry and dusty, littered with bits of metal that threatened the already thin soles of her shoes. The air reeked of rotting fish and mildewing wood.

When the two young men had left the boat without seriously hurting themselves, though Robert was complaining loudly about a splinter in his hand, Lily asked, "Could you learn anything?"

Robert shook his head. "Nothing that looks like evidence of any kind. All the furnishings are waterlogged and molding. The galley's a mess, with pots and pans and broken dishes everywhere. We opened all the cabinets and drawers and there didn't seem to be anything of interest or importance in them."

"Lots of things that could serve as weapons though," Jack said. "But it was underwater for more than a week after the divers found your uncle. There wouldn't be bloodstains," he added bluntly.

"I didn't see anything round and heavy," Robert said, then glanced at Lily. Brother and sister exchanged a quick look. They hadn't had time to discuss whether they'd share the information Mr.

Prinney had given them. Jack Summer was, after all, a reporter.

"Round and heavy? What does that mean?" Jack asked suspiciously.

"We'll tell you later," Lily said firmly. "Let's get away from this awful place."

They shouted goodbyes at Mr. Bond, who was sitting on the stoop of his shed, scratching at the dirt aimlessly with a stick, and drove slowly back to town. Lily made a point of looking away when they approached the dump, fearing she'd see something else that ripped at her heart.

"Why would Uncle Horatio have gone below when it was obvious the boat was sinking?" Lily said, when the garbage dump was safely behind them.

Robert shrugged. "He must have left something in the cabin that he felt had to be saved, I suppose."

"What could have been important enough to risk your life for?" Lily asked.

"Maybe he just panicked, and tried to save something trivial," Jack Summer said. "People can do that in a crisis. More likely, he'd lost track of where everyone was and wanted to make sure nobody was left behind."

Lily nodded. "I guess either might make sense under the circumstances."

They rode in silence for a mile and Jack finally spoke again. "I've been asking a lot of questions."

"And getting answers?" Lily asked.

"A few," Jack said reluctantly. "But nobody seems to know the whole story and the accident wasn't investigated much. Too many authorities involved and trying to pass the work to someone else."

"Authorities?"

"The island itself is privately owned by the Ban-

nerman family. Nobody was quite sure at first which
side of the river has jurisdiction, though it's much
closer to the east side. The Coast Guard didn't want
to be stuck with investigating because they're not
primarily an investigative body and didn't have staff
to spare. And the Corps of Engineers, which main-
tains the safety of the river, were only concerned
with the Coast Guard raising the wreckage so it
wouldn't break apart and endanger shipping. Your
uncle lived in Voorburg and if he'd died here, the
local police or county sheriff would have been responsible, but since he died elsewhere, neither of
them felt they had the authority to closely question
the witnesses."

"So the whole incident fell between the cracks?"
Robert said.

"Officially," Jack said.

"What does that mean?" Lily asked.

"Just that the local police—well, they're local, you
see. They had their suspicions, but they have to live
here."

"I don't get what you mean, old boy," Robert said.

Jack thought for a moment, wanting to be careful
in framing his reply. "There were important people
on that boat. My editor, as an example. If he'd felt
the police were being too nosy and implicating him,
he could have run an editorial that made them look
bad and maybe get them fired. I know him pretty
well and feel sure that wouldn't have happened, but
everybody who has the good fortune to have a paying job these days doesn't want to risk losing it."

He ran his hands nervously through his mop of
hair. "And there's Mr. Prinney, too. He's on the
town council. The council is their boss."

"Mr. Prinney wouldn't get an honest cop fired for
doing his job!" Lily said.

"You feel that way, and you're probably right. But

people are scared to death of being out of work. And this police chief is a rotter, anyway, who's hanging onto the job by the skin of his teeth."

"How do you know all this?" Robert asked.

"My second cousin Ralph is a part-time deputy. Fills in when somebody's sick," Jack said, thinking as the words spilled out that he shouldn't have revealed his source. But oddly enough, he was— against his better judgment—coming to *almost* like and trust Lily and Robert Brewster.

"Who were the police suspicious of?" Robert asked.

"Billy Smith was at the top of the list, of course. He's been the bane of the authorities since he was eight years old. The police would love to get him for almost anything, just to put him away."

"Surely he doesn't carry any political weight, does he?" Lily asked. "Didn't they question him?"

"Oh, they did," Jack said. "Until they were blue in the face. And couldn't get anything out of him. Apparently he went on the dinghy and although he was the last to get on, he'd been the one who put it into the water and helped others onto it. Everybody else stated that they'd believed he was there the whole time. Not with great conviction, but no one could openly dispute it."

"So he couldn't have gone below and bopped Uncle Horatio over the head?" Lily asked.

"Oh, he could have, if he'd been real nippy about it. But no one noticed if he'd disappeared."

"You said he was top on the list as far as the police were concerned," Robert said. "Who was next on the list?"

"Claude Cooke."

"Oh, how saddening," Robert said sarcastically. "How he get off the hook?"

"Two ways. First, he did so much yelping about breaking his finger that everybody else assumed he'd been trying to get on the dinghy first. And secondly, because he was assumed to be your uncle's heir—a rich, powerful outsider who'd probably take an important role in town business when he inherited. Of course, they know now that he didn't inherit. You two did."

"Sounds to me like a good motive to bump off Uncle," Robert said. "Not that I find it easy to believe he'd have the nerve."

"I think Claude has a lot more nerve than you realize," Lily opined. "He's always scared me and I don't scare all that easily."

"But Jack said the others thought he was trying to be the first on the dinghy," Robert reminded her.

Jack said, "They thought so. But nobody would swear to it. It was all too fast and chaotic."

"So, is there anyone else on the list of suspects?" Robert asked.

Jack hesitated for a little too long before saying, "Yes."

"Who?" Lily inquired.

"You two," Jack said.

Robert slammed on the brakes so hard he nearly flung them all over the hood.

"Lily and I?" he exclaimed.

"Afraid so," Jack said. "After all, *you* turned out to be his heirs, not your Cousin Claude. That gives you the best motive."

"But we didn't know we were his heirs and didn't even hear about his death until much later," Lily said.

"There's nothing but your word for that," Jack said, slightly apologetically.

"Not to mention that we weren't on the boat," Robert said.

"No, but you could have hired someone to do the actual deed."

Lily laughed. "Oh, sure we could." She was about to add that they couldn't have paid for a newspaper, much less a hired killer, but thought better of it.

"Or you could have come to the boatyard and done something to the boat that would weaken the timbers, making it possible the boat would have sunk under even the slightest stress," Jack said.

"You can't possibly believe that," Lily said, near to tears of outrage.

"I don't believe it for a minute," Jack said, blushing bright red. "But you wanted to know what I found out and it didn't seem right not to tell you everything I've heard talked about."

"Are we still suspects?" Robert asked.

"I think so," Jack admitted.

"But nobody's questioned us," Lily said. "We haven't had a chance to clear ourselves."

"The police chief will get around to you once you're settled in," Jack said. "You can prove you weren't ever here until Mr. Prinney located you, can't you?"

"How can anybody prove they *weren't* somewhere?" Robert snapped. "You can only prove where you *were*."

He restarted the Duesie and they rode in utter silence back to the ice house where Jack had left his bicycle.

Jack got out of the automobile, mumbling vague apologies which neither Robert nor Lily could manage to respond to. "Listen," Jack said, "if—I mean, *since* you didn't have anything to do with your uncle's death—"

He quailed at the furious look Lily gave him, but bravely plowed on. "There can't be any proof. And nothing bad could happen to you."

"Except we'd live here among people who'd point at us as the niece and nephew who might have killed their uncle and got away with it," Lily said.

"But you don't have to stay in Voorburg," Jack said. "Sell the place or rent it and go somewhere else."

Lily and Robert exchanged a look. "We can't do that," Lily said firmly.

Then with a sigh, she added, "You were right to tell us the truth, Mr. Summer."

She looked a question at Robert, who nodded and said, "Yes, tell him. Tit for tat and all that."

Lily repeated what they'd learned from Mr. Prinney about the nature of the injury and the lack of evidence.

Chapter 12

Robert pulled off the road about halfway up the hill to Grace and Favor, turned off the engine and looked at Lily.

"So?" he said.

"So what?"

"We've been trifling with Uncle Horatio's death, thinking it was sort of a lark," Robert said. "Something to contemplate during the long boring evenings. Now it suddenly looks like we're suspects."

Lily nodded. "I hate this. Small towns are even more gossipy than big cities. If Jack's cousin, the part-time deputy, will shoot off his mouth to Jack, he'll tell everybody. We'll be the local Lizzie Bordens. We'll never make any friends or be trusted here."

"You want to give it up? Go back to the City and let Claude and the animal lovers have Grace and Favor?"

Lily glared at him. "I certainly do not! I'd throw myself in the river before I'd go back to the job at the bank. Even if I could get the job back, which is impossible anyway. No, Robert, we have to start taking this seriously. We have to prove who killed Uncle Horatio before he goes after someone else—like us, for example."

"And how do you propose doing that, my dear Lily?"

"I don't know . . . yet. We don't know enough. But lots of other people do. Mimi knows something and isn't talking. I'm sure of it. And Cousin Claude was suspiciously vague as well. We have to pry more information out of all of them. There's some reason they're all being so secretive."

"How do we go about making them spill the beans?"

"Oh, Robert, with all your charm, you could get anything out of anyone. You work on Cousin Claude and I'll keep asking Mimi questions. I hate to do it because it upsets her so, but we have to know what she knows."

"I guess it's a start," Robert said.

"And there's something else," Lily said. "I want to see this place where the boat sank. How can we do that?"

"Why do we need to?"

"Just to get the feel of it ourselves. I don't think you can solve a mystery without even seeing the scene of the crime."

"You've been reading those silly crime novels again, haven't you? Lily, we just went to the salvage yard to 'get the feel' of the boat and it wasn't any help at all."

"Still . . . I want to see the island. We don't have to get close to it. Just look at it."

"Okeydokey, I'll see what I can do."

When they got home, Mimi had taken it upon herself to haul all the rugs outdoors and beat them that day and Lily didn't get a chance to chat with her.

Mr. and Mrs. Prinney had a guest they insisted on her meeting. It was one of their son-in-laws who had dropped by to fetch a recipe his wife needed from her mother. He was a stork-like man with a big, gap-toothed grin under a shaggy moustache. "Charles Locke," he introduced himself.

"Charles is a teacher," Mr. Prinney said. "At Columbia University," he added proudly. "He and our daughter Rosalyn are thinking of moving into our old house in Voorburg. Charles would stay in a boardinghouse at Columbia during the week and Mrs. Prinney and I would have a daughter and the kiddies close by."

"What do you teach, Mr. Locke?" Lily asked.

"Economic theory."

"Then can you tell us what has happened to our country?"

"I probably could, but the important thing is what to do about it. Which isn't being done."

Lily sat down at one end of the library table and Robert sat at the other end, pulling a deck of cards from a little drawer beneath. Lily asked, "What should be done? How can this ever be fixed?" She thought of the family at the garbage dump.

"Are you really interested?" Charles Locke asked. Lily nodded.

"Then I'll explain it as I do to my freshman students. Picture a little square. Inside it is a family. Mother, Dad, the children. Dad loses his job. Mother has to take in laundry so the children can be fed and Dad, to save his pride, starts growing corn on their land. Around this little square are other little squares. Other families—relations and neighbors. And they all form a bigger square. And there are lots of these bigger squares, which form the various states. And it's all contained in a huge square that is the United States. But the border of the huge square is flimsy. Deliberately so. It can stretch and contract so the squares within squares inside it can shift and change, grow and shrink."

Lily could visualize what he meant, but couldn't see what he was getting at. "Is that bad or good?"

"Both," Charles Locke said, stroking his moustache. "Depending on circumstances. In good times it's good. The federal government stays out of the smaller squares' business except for necessities. Like keeping a standing army and navy for protection. And regulating with a light hand a very few industries which involve all the inside squares. This is the Jeffersonian theory of economics and government control. Horribly simplified, of course.

"But now we have bad times," he said. "Remember the original family square? Mother's taking in laundry. Father is raising just enough corn to use for the family and sell a bit to buy other necessities. Then some of the other families and relatives have bad times. They can't afford to send their laundry to Mother. She stops making money. And the price of corn has fallen so low that it's worth less than it costs to grow, so Father can't make money to buy more seed."

And they move to the garbage dump, Lily thought.

"Jeffersonian theory, of which President Hoover is a proponent, says the community and state must care for its own people. And private charities and industries are obligated to help. That it isn't the duty of the federal government."

"But . . ." Lily started to say.

"In good times, as I say, they're right," Charles rolled on. Private charities, funded by the wealthy and good-hearted, do a lot. It saves us all from having the federal government interfering in all our lives. But, the more liberal thinkers feel, the federal government, in a crisis like this, absolutely must step in. If they give Dad a good job and keep the corn prices down, Mother can send her laundry to someone else and give them part of the money. And if Dad makes money at his job and a little on the side with his corn crop, he can buy meat from the butcher, and clothes from the general store and help keep two more businesses afloat."

"Why can't President Hoover understand this?" Lily asked.

"Because he's a Jeffersonian. He's a good man who honestly believes that once the government steps into people's lives, it won't ever get back out of the business of butting in. And he wants to believe the terrible financial problem the country is in can cure itself."

"It can't?" Lily asked.

"It can't the way Hoover sees it. And if it can't, there's going to be anarchy and revolution. Even the farmers, the most independent, conservative element of our society, are starting to listen to the Communists, who say it's time for a revolution."

"You're scaring me," Lily said bluntly.

"I mean to," Charles Locke said. "We should all be terrified out of our wits. If Hoover is reelected next year, we're lost. Democracy will have failed utterly."

Lily glanced at Robert, who was playing patience and not appearing to be paying any attention to the conversation. "So what's to be done?" she asked.

"Elect a non-Jeffersonian," Charles said. "Oh, thank you," he said as his mother-in-law passed out glasses of fresh lemonade. He took a healthy slug of it and went, "Someone like your neighbor."

"Neighbor? Major Winslow?"

"Dear God, no. I meant neighbor in a general sense. Governor Roosevelt from Hyde Park, just up the road a bit."

"Is he going to run for president?"

"Not officially. He's being very coy," Charles Locke said. "But just this week, he's proposing a New York State emergency relief administration. The federal government has taken control of many aspects of society before—in the case of wars. Many of us feel this *is* a war. Or soon will be one. Even Foster and Eccles agree now."

Lily had no idea who Foster and Eccles might be and was afraid to ask for fear the lecture would veer off. She wanted some time to think over what the Prinneys' son-in-law had already said.

Apparently Mrs. Prinney felt enough was enough as well, and invited Charles to lunch.

"No, no, Rosalyn has made me promise to take the children for a boat ride and be home for a late picnic lunch."

Lily finished the lemonade Mrs. Prinney had given her, and used the change of subject as an excuse to go try to find Mimi, whom she found dragging rugs indoors. Lily didn't think it was an opportune time to interrupt her.

Robert disappeared on a mysterious errand in the mid-afternoon. He took Lily aside after dinner and said, "Let's take a walk."

They strolled out on the lawn behind the house, which overlooked the river, and Robert removed a couple pieces of paper from his shirt pocket. "Guess what I did this afternoon," he said. "I went to the town library. All by myself without anyone forcing me."

"There's a library in Voorburg?" Lily exclaimed, her eyes lighting up.

"It's a tiny one and rather dull. You won't find many of your lurid crime novels there. But I found out some things about this island you want to see."

He riffled through his scraps of paper. "It actually named Pollepel Island, but everybody calls it Bannerman's Island or Bannerman's Arsenal."

"Arsenal?"

"Yes, the Bannermans are a family who sell used war things to collectors and to other countries. Like cannons and swords, ammunition, guns and such."

"Yes, Jack Summer mentioned that."

"Jack was right. They had a big place in New York City, down on Broadway, but the city got very nervous about them having some sort of accident and blowing up half of Manhattan and asked them to move the arsenal. One of the family—I didn't take down his name—happened to be on a boat trip around the same time and bought the island, which had nothing on it, as a place to store a lot of the ammunition and firearms from the business and to build a summer house. This was about 1900. He'd come from some old important family in Scotland and started building a Scottish castle on the island. He died before it was finished, but the family still uses it to store things. The librarian said he didn't think any of them lived there anymore, though, only visit occasionally. But it's heavily guarded. Remember, the newspaper article mentioned guards that helped the passengers from Uncle Horatio's boat when they came ashore. Or maybe it was Jack Summer who told us. And Claude and Major Winslow also mentioned them."

"Where is this island?" Lily asked, still reeling from the fact of Robert's having gone to a library and done research. He'd never been an enthusiastic student of anything but living the Good Life. A few days of residing in the 'wilderness' was exerting a profound and surprising influence on him.

"That's the good part. It's just downriver about fifteen or twenty miles from here. And it's on our side of the river, about a thousand feet offshore. So we can take a pretty good look at it, if I can find some binoculars to borrow, without having to hire a boat. All we need is a little bit more gasoline money. The Duesie is a greedy old girl with gasoline."

"I could find another dollar somewhere," Lily said.

Robert was shuffling his paperwork. "Oh, get this! In 1776, the army or somebody stretched a thing called a 'chevaux-de-frise' from the island to Plum Point—I don't know just where Plum Point is though."

"A chevaux-de-frise? What's that?"

"I didn't quite understand it, but in English, it's a chain and boom. A chain of iron links and somehow big pointed logs come into the construction. It was meant to keep the British from sailing past the island to attack forts farther north during the Revolutionary War. I don't suppose there's any of it left, but if bits of the thing are still there, they might have caused the hole in the boat, if the tide was out."

Lily nodded. She didn't see how this was particularly useful information, but it was interesting and it was astonishing that Robert had hunted it down and recorded it—behavior she certainly didn't want to discourage. "Can we go there tomorrow?"

"Yes, let's do. But we need binoculars. Do you even have your old opera glasses?"

"No, I dropped them and smashed a lens last time I used them," Lily said. "That was back in the days when we threw broken things away. But I think I've seen a telescope somewhere in the house. Where was that?"

"Telescope! Oh! It's in my room, on top of that chest that's almost as big as the Duesie. I'd forgotten it, too. Uncle must have used it to look out at the river before the ivy took over the windows. This is good. I'll sneak it out to the garage tonight."

"Why sneak?"

"Because I'd just as soon nobody asked us where we're going with a telescope."

Dinner was excellent as always. There was a ham with a spicy sauce that went well with what Mrs. Prinney called *suppawn*, a rich, but bland sort of cornmeal mush that she explained was either a Dutch or Indian word. She'd never thought to ask her mother which.

"Mrs. Prinney is a descendant of Guilliam Bertholf, the well-known *voorleser* of Tappan," Mr. Prinney said proudly.

Lily smiled encouragingly, not having the faintest idea what he meant.

"A *voorleser* was one of the most honored members of the original old Dutch communities," Prinney explained. "You had to be a man of both learning and piety to hold the honor of the title."

"I'd forgotten the Dutch settled the Hudson River Valley," Lily said, feeling a bit ashamed of herself. She wanted to be part of the community, yet she'd made no effort to find out anything about it.

Mr. Prinney, who wasn't in a very good mood anyway, twitched his little moustache at her for this comment.

Lily decided she needed a trip to the Voorburg library as well.

*   *   *

They set out early in the morning, having break-fasted and told Mrs. Prinney they wanted to see some of the countryside.

"Do you have a map of where we're going?" Lily asked.

"It's downriver. How hard can that be?" Robert said.

Harder than he thought. The road didn't follow the river closely at all points. Several times Robert tried to get back to the river when it had disappeared by taking side roads that led west . . . usually to a dead end in a wooded area. Turning the Due-senberg around in a confined area was quite a challenge.

When they did come upon the island, it was so sudden it was startling. Robert had tried yet another steep side road that was hardly more than a footpath and stopped the automobile suddenly. "Through the trees," he said. "Can you see the top of the building?"

They couldn't go any farther in the automobile, so they got out and struggled through the under-growth.

"Isn't that just the cat's kimono!" he exclaimed when they could finally see the island.

Lily was awed, too. "The train tracks run so close. I can hardly believe we rode past that three times and never saw it!"

"We weren't exactly sight-seeing. What a place," Robert said.

The castle was indeed *A Castle*. Five to six stories high, bristling with towers, crenelations, turrets, bat-tlements, Bannerman's Arsenal sat at the low, north-west end of the island. There was even a flash of light reflecting off a tiny harbor which was outlined in the water by stone walls with squatty towers of the same construction as the castle. Taller towers of the same style, which had windows and were obviously guard towers, occurred at intervals.

The main building was a light gray-brown material, possibly cement or stucco, and probably backed with the red bricks that formed most of the excruciatingly elaborate ornamentation. There were a large number of smallish, sparkling windows on every level. The first three floors extended quite far, and there were two more floors, with an even more elaborate ornamentation covering only the front of the castle, as well as what appeared to be a flat roof with gazebo-type towers at the corners.

Other smaller structures sprouted around it. It looked ancient and wild and very, very Scottish. Lily could imagine tartan-clad warriors with painted faces and huge cudgel-like swords planning wars on this small island. The island itself was impressive as well. It sloped gently from the water at the end where the bulk of the castle sat, then rose in a wild tangle of trees and rocks and fell off steeply at the far end.

"The boat must have foundered on that end," Robert said, his imagination slightly more tame than Lily's. "The castle end doesn't look very dangerous."

"Remember, though, that there was a terrible storm," Lily said. "Blinding sheets of rain and horrible winds. Where's the telescope?"

They took turns examining the island with the telescope, which was a bit too heavy for Lily to hold steady. Robert knelt and let her crouch behind him, resting it on his shoulder. "Stop breathing for a minute, Robert. You're making the island heave up and down."

After Robert had also had a turn at studying the island, he proclaimed, "Given the bad weather, I think it had to be an accident. Just imagine the water in turmoil, maybe the tide coming in or rushing out, forcing the boat against the rocks, the wind tossing it out of control, nobody being able to see where they were. You can tell from the color of the water that some of it is quite shallow and who knows how rocky it might be on the riverbed underneath. Perfect conditions for an accident. And to take advantage of an accident to commit a murder without being caught at it."

Lily nodded. "Let me take one more look."

As she gazed at the castle again, noting the mild shoreline nearest it and the wild shore at the other end, she said, "Why didn't they head for open water when it started looking dangerous?" Lily handed the brass-barreled telescope back to Robert. "Wouldn't that have been safer?"

He stared out at the river. "I'm not much of a sailor, Lily, but the tides and winds may have been against them. Besides, if it were me, I'd rather head for land and say the hell with what happened to the boat instead of getting out in the middle of the river and risk drowning in deep water. Uncle Horatio might have not known how to swim or knew some of the others couldn't."

They stared out over the island for a little longer. "It would be an irresistible place to visit, wouldn't it? Especially if you wanted to show someone up in an impressive setting."

"Isn't that a tad Machiavellian?"

"We don't know that he wasn't," Lily said. "We don't know anything about him."

"Except that he gave us sweets," Robert said.

"That made us sick," Lily added with a smile.

Chapter 13

They'd started early and wasted a lot of time on dead ends on the way downriver, but returning to Grace and Favor was easy and fast. Robert left Lily at the house and went to put the Duesenberg in the garage. Lily had loved seeing the island, but, as Robert had predicted, it didn't seem to have 'told' them anything except that it was a dangerous place even on a mild day and horrendously dangerous in bad weather.

She took her handbag to her room and went to alert Mrs. Prinney that they'd returned. But she stopped short in the hall leading to the kitchen.

Mr. Prinney was in the kitchen and sounded upset. "I can't imagine how I forgot," he was saying.

"Anybody can forget, dearest," Mrs. Prinney said. This was obviously a private conversation, but Lily couldn't help herself. She shamelessly eavesdropped.

"I know. I know. And Mr. Brewster had a great deal of property that he was always buying and selling, but to forget I'd notarized a deed . . . it's just not like me. And the county clerk out there in California sure took his own sweet time returning it."

"Then it's their fault, not yours," Mrs. Prinney said. "Don't worry about it. Didn't you tell me he'd transferred a lot of property not long before he died? He was really keeping you busy for a while early last summer. Buying and selling and making partnerships and buying out other ones?"

"True. That's true." Lily could picture the way Mr. Prinney would be nodding like an elderly professor who was approving of a student's answer, even though she couldn't actually see him. "But I'm going to have to amend the probate filing I've already made. Such a nuisance."

Lily backed out of the hallway, then returned, making more noise so she would seem to have just arrived.

"We're back, Mrs. Prinney," she said as she entered the kitchen. "We didn't want you to fret about us being late for lunch."

"I wasn't fretting," Mrs. Prinney said. "Have you seen Mimi? I'm ready for her to set the table."

"I'll do it."

"You will not," Mrs. Prinney said pleasantly. "It's Mimi's job."

"Then I'll find her for you."

Mrs. Prinney patted Lily's arm with approval and turned back to adding some spice to an apple dish. Mr. Prinney had quietly disappeared.

Lily looked all over the house for Mimi, but couldn't find her. Perhaps she'd found yet another rug to beat. Lily went to the south side of the house, where a stout rope was tied between two trees at the front of the woods that concealed the garage, which was down a slight slope. There was a rug on the line, and the rug-beater, looking like an oversized snowshoe, was lying on the ground, but there was no sign of Mimi.

Lily called out for her and it was Robert who answered. "Right here," he said. He and Mimi appeared from the woods. He was holding her by the arm and she was crying. Lily hurried to meet them. "What's happened?"

"Nothing, Miss Lily. Really, it was nothing," Mimi said, pulling away from Robert and trying to hurry to the house.

Lily put out a hand and stopped her. "Mimi, it *isn't* nothing. Your eye is going all black and blue. How did you hurt yourself?"

"She didn't hurt herself," Robert said furiously. "She was smacked in the eye by some ugly hay-shaker. A hick. I saw it happen as I came out of the garage. He took off like a jackrabbit when he saw me."

"Billy?" Lily asked Mimi quietly.

Mimi nodded and put her hand over her swelling eye.

"That's Billy Smith, Mimi's husband," Lily explained.

"Husband? You're married to that sniveling cowardly bastard?" Robert asked.

"Robert," Lily said, "let me take care of this."

Robert stomped off and Lily took Mimi to the kitchen where Mrs. Prinney chipped off some ice from the block in the icebox, wrapped it in a clean dish towel and applied it to Mimi's eye.

"They say a silver knife is best to stop bruises, but I never believed it was as good as ice," Mrs. Prinney said. "What happened to you, Mimi?"

"I just ran into a branch," Mimi said.

Mrs. Prinney mouthed over Mimi's head, "Billy?"

Lily nodded. She needed to have a blunt talk with Mimi, but this wasn't the time.

"We'll put back lunch for half an hour," Mrs. Prinney said. Then she added, "Was that the doorbell?"

"I'll get it," Mimi said, starting to rise.

Mrs. Prinney pushed her back into the kitchen chair. "You will not. You look like something the cat drug in."

Lily didn't wait for the end of the argument. She went to the door herself and found Sissy standing there.

"I hope you don't mind me just dropping in, but there's something wrong with our telephone. Mummy and I want to invite you to dinner tonight. Terribly short notice, I know."

"I don't know if Robert has plans, but I'd be happy to come," Lily said graciously, stupidly and because she didn't have the wit to make up an excuse for herself on the spur of the moment. "Come in."

Sissy entered the hall and said, "Oh, my. You've certainly fixed this up nicely. Daddy and I came over one day before you got here—Daddy thought the house might be for sale—and took a look around. Everything was dusty and dark."

Snooping, Lily thought.

"Could you show me around?" Sissy asked.

More snooping. But Lily was pleased with how much nicer the house was looking and gave Sissy a tour.

Sissy gushed over almost everything—the library took her fancy, not for the books, but for the view. The sitting room was ever so nice, she said, with all those little tables and knickknacks. The dining room was so big and warm-looking. What grand dinner parties they could give here, she commented.

"Not for a while yet," Lily said.

"Oh, I know you must be ever so busy. Are you going to wallpaper the den? It's rather dark."

"Perhaps," Lily said. The den was Mr. Prinney's turf.

"*Do* tell me you took that dear little room upstairs with the cabbage roses!"

Lily thought Sissy was just a little too familiar with the house. Had they broken in and taken inventory? Still, she was unwillingly the hostess and took Sissy upstairs to see her bedroom. Sissy took root in the soft, squishy, pink grandmother chair by the window. "This is so lovely. So cozy. I'll be ashamed to show you my bedroom. It's terribly big and I feel utterly lost in it."

There was a crash and a muffled yelp from the hallway. "Just let me see what that was," Lily said.

Mimi was back at work, stripping bedsheets. She'd apparently come toward Lily's room with an armload of them and run into the fragile little chair, which was lying helpless and forlorn on its side.

"Oh, Miss Lily, I hope I didn't break it."

Lily picked up the chair, set it upright and gave it a jiggle. "It seems to be all right. Shouldn't you be resting?"

"I feel better working, Miss Lily. Can I do your room now?"

"That would be grand," Lily said. It would dislodge Sissy.

Sissy wanted to see Robert's room, but Lily refused. "I don't think it's been cleaned yet this morning," she said. "Maybe another time."

In a hushed voice, Sissy said, "What happened to your maid's eye?"

"She ran into a branch while she was beating rugs," Lily said as she headed for the stairs. Sissy had no choice but to follow her down and to the front door.

Mimi had gone down the back stairs to fetch a rug

for Lily's room and they could hear her squeal from around the corner. "Leave me alone! I don't want to lose my job."

"You don't need to work if you'd just tell the truth," Billy was saying. "Or maybe I should be the one to tell the truth."

"Fat chance," Mimi said.

"Listen, Mimi. I know what happened to the old boy and I just might talk to a certain person about it. Then we'd be rich enough to start over. Put this behind us and get back together. How about that?"

"You don't know nothing, Billy."

"I do. You know what I saw on that boat."

Lily had gestured at Sissy to stay at the door and rounded the corner of the house. "Mr. Smith, I'm going inside to call the police. You're trespassing and I'll call them on you every time you set foot on our land. Get out!"

Billy just sneered at her, but did turn and walk away.

"Go inside, Mimi," Lily said.

Mimi was so shaken, she actually ducked a quick curtsey and fled for the kitchen door.

"I'm sorry about that, Sissy," Lily said as she returned to her guest. "Just a little domestic dispute between our maid and her husband."

"Servants can be such a bother, can't they?" Sissy said. "We're really happy we've cut down on the staff. Dinner is at seven," she trilled. "I do hope Robert can come."

Lily went to alert Mrs. Prinney about the dinner plans before she launched into fixing another big meal.

"Why, how nice for you young people that you're getting out and meeting people. I'll just fix a cold supper for Mimi. Mr. Prinney and I were invited to some friends' house for dinner. I'll see if the invitation is still open."

"Mrs. Prinney! You don't have to give up your social life to feed us!"

"Then how would you eat?"

"We'd manage. Do you know the Winslow family well?" Lily asked.

"Oh, no, dear. They're outsiders. Very high-society New York people. Though they have spent a lot more time here, I think, in the last couple years. Mr. Prinney knows Major Winslow, of course. Major Winslow and your uncle had quite a few business dealings together and Mr. Prinney was involved in the legal side. But it was strictly business."

Lily smiled. Mrs. Prinney was a nice woman and if she was calling the Winslows 'outsiders' it seemed to imply that Lily and Robert weren't. This was surprisingly comforting.

What was *not* comforting was the thought of breaking it to Robert that they had to dine with the Winslows. She'd provided him with half an excuse, but realized she couldn't endure a dinner with them without Robert's presence. They were such boring people and Robert would be the only person who could save the evening and her sanity.

Lily found him in the garage, polishing the Duesenberg. "Lunch has been delayed a bit," she told him. "You'll wear the paint off that automobile if you don't quit polishing it three times a day."

"Have you had a talk with Mimi? She needs to make a complaint to the police. That husband of hers needs a good stint in the slammer."

"Not yet, but I will later. I thought I should let her calm down a little first. And I suspect Billy Smith has done a good deal of time in jail without any improvement. Umm, Robert, I have bad news.

We've been invited to the Winslows' house for dinner tonight. I couldn't think of an excuse fast enough.''

"Lily!"

"I'm sorry. But if we go now and get it over with, and then don't return the invitation for a good long time—say a couple years—they won't invite us again."

Robert grinned. "I'd almost forgotten about the old tit-for-tat rule. I'm losing my social skills."

"I'll say. You've got a smudge of wax on your forehead, too. Clean up and come to lunch. I just overheard a conversation I want to tell you about later."

Lily went back to the house and to her room to wash her hands and think about what she'd overheard Billy saying. Mimi had finished her room and left it sparkling clean and the freshly ironed sheets on the bed had created a sunshine scent. Lily sat down on the bed and drew a deep breath. There was a slight 'thunk' as her handbag slid off the foot of the bed. How was she going to tackle Mimi? Had she any right to interfere in the maid's dreadful marriage? she wondered as she bent down. The handbag had opened and spilled the contents everywhere. She started picking things up, still thinking about Mimi. Her compact, her house keys—which was silly, as nobody ever locked up the house—the little gold rouge container that had a bent hinge and never stayed closed properly, a cigarette lighter Robert had dropped in the hall, several coins . . .

Where was the paper money? She'd had a ten-dollar bill in her handbag. She got down and flipped up the bed skirt, thinking it must have gotten under the bed. But it wasn't there. She dumped the handbag back out on the coverlet. She must have put it in her wallet. But there was no ten-dollar bill in it. She searched the little side pocket where she kept extra hairpins. No, not there either.

How could she have *lost* ten dollars? That was a lot of money and they didn't have it to spare. She mentally went over the day, trying to think what she could have done with it. She'd put it in her handbag before she and Robert had gone to Bannerman Island in the morning, thinking if they had car trouble she might need it. But they didn't and she hadn't opened the handbag since then.

Had she lost the money or had someone taken it?

She'd left the handbag in her room as soon as they'd returned and the only people who'd been in the room since then—that she knew of—had been Sissy and Mimi and herself. Sissy wouldn't have taken it. Not because she was honest, but because the Winslows were rich.

That left Mimi.

Unthinkable.

But . . .

Lily had also lost her favorite scarf. When she got dressed this morning, she'd meant to wear it in the automobile as it went so well with her green patterned skirt and jade cotton sweater. But the blue and green paisley scarf had gone missing, too.

"You're being a fool," she said to herself out loud.

Was this cheeseparing attitude to do with being poor? Did all poor people imagine people were stealing things from them? Certainly not. Rich people might have cause to worry, though Lily had never worried. In fact, when she was rich, she'd been terribly lax about taking care of her belongings because it seemed there would always be money to replace things that got lost.

She went down to lunch, still upset as much with herself as the situation. She'd have to get together with Robert somewhere private this afternoon and talk to him about a lot of things.

Chapter 14

Late in the afternoon, Lily and Robert had walked out onto the grounds behind the house where the long lawn sloped gently toward the river. It had clouded up and storms were threatening. She repeated, as best she could remember, the conversation between Billy and Mimi.

"So they both have some Great Truth they're concealing? And both have to do with Uncle Horatio's death?"

There was an old teak bench set under a maple tree and brother and sister sat down on it, staring at the river. Robert was jingling the car keys in his pocket.

Lily said, "I'm not sure. Billy says Mimi should tell the truth and they'd both be rich. I can't imagine what he means by that."

"What did Mimi say? Did she deny it?"

"She didn't have a chance to say anything. Billy went right on about how he could tell the truth and said he knew what happened to the old boy. He must have meant Uncle Horatio. Who else would he say that about?"

Robert leaned forward and rested his elbows on

his knees. "But he didn't use his name. Could he have been talking about someone else? We have no idea what other 'old boy' might have had something happen to him."

"It had to be something serious, because he was threatening to blackmail someone about it." A bank of clouds was moving in and a light breeze had sprung up, making Lily think maybe this hot summer wouldn't last forever.

"Did he use the word 'blackmail'?"

"Oh, Robert, don't be so picky. Of course he didn't. But when somebody says there's a person he could talk to and then they'd be rich, that's what it means. He wasn't talking about applying for a job. Nobody in their right mind would hire him. And he said, 'You know what I saw on that boat.'"

"You didn't tell me that part before," Robert said, rubbing his hands together. "You're going to have to pry some information out of Mimi. She adores you. She'll spill the beans if you insist."

Lily thought for a long moment. Then said, "I know. But I hate it. Robert . . . there's something else. I took ten dollars with us this morning in case we had car trouble. Now it's missing. I put it in my handbag and never had reason to take it out."

"Have you checked the floor of the car? Maybe you took out a handkerchief or something and the money fell out."

"I haven't, but I will. My best scarf is missing, too. Robert, I'm terribly afraid Mimi's lifting things and I don't want to believe that of her."

"Then don't. You're one of the greatest Leaver-behinders-of-things I know."

"Not money. Not since Daddy died. I've become a miser. Sometimes I dream about counting our money because I do it so often for real. I could have lost the scarf, but not a ten-dollar bill."

Robert stretched, then suddenly leaped from the bench and removed a splinter from the seat of his pants. He paced, jingling keys again. "These secrets Mimi and Billy have—is it the same secret or two different ones? Did Billy just tell Mimi what he saw happen on the boat and expects Mimi to blackmail the person or he will?"

Lily ran through what she thought they'd both said again. "Two, I think. Because when Billy said the thing about blackmailing, she said he didn't know anything." She sighed and stood up. "We're going to have to dress for dinner, you know. I'll get Mimi to press your tux and I'll try on my old clothes until something fits."

Mimi's eye didn't look quite as bad as Lily had expected it to. And her spirits had improved as well. She was actually humming as she ran the carpet sweeper. Lily explained what she needed done. "I wouldn't ask except that I have no idea how to iron without ruining things."

Mimi pressed the tux while Lily rummaged for a respectable dinner dress that might not look too out of date and fit besides. Not an easily achieved combination. She finally found a short-sleeved emerald jacket and a long skirt that hadn't wrinkled too badly and when she tried them on, she realized she must have put on a little weight these past few days of eating Mrs. Prinney's excellent food. The jacket and skirt would just need a tiny bit of freshening up.

Mimi returned with the tux and took away Lily's outfit. When she returned to Lily's bedroom, Lily said, "Mimi, sit down for a moment."

Dread filled Mimi's features as she perched on the

front edge of the squashy grandmother chair. "Yes, Miss Lily?"

Lily drew a deep breath and said, "I'm mistress of this house. That means I have a responsibility for what goes on here. And to be responsible, I must know what's going on."

Mimi said, "Yes, miss."

"I heard your conversation with Billy. I insist on knowing what you two were talking about."

"Nothing really, Miss Lily."

"Nonsense. He was trying to make you tell something to someone that would result in you getting money. I told you I heard every word."

Mimi ducked her head, sniffling. "Oh, Miss Lily, it's so batty I'm ashamed to say."

"I'm sorry, but you must," Lily said.

"All right, but you won't like it. It was something my ma told me when I was getting fixed to marry Billy. She didn't like him one little bit. So, remember when I said I'd never met or seen Mr. Horatio before that day on the boat? Well, that was because of me. Or my mother. See, she worked for Miss Flora and lived in the house. When Ma got in trouble—you know, in a family way with me, she told Miss Flora."

Lily sat down slowly on the bed, half-knowing and fully dreading what Mimi was going to say next. "Go on," she said.

"Miss Flora really loved my ma. And she loved your uncle, too. But when Ma told Miss Flora that your uncle was the father of the baby she was going to have—that's me—Miss Flora was furious. She called Mr. Horatio to account and he said it wasn't so, that he'd never laid a hand on Ma, then he said some mean things about Ma. They argued and argued, my ma said."

"And that's why he left?"

Mimi nodded. "He never came back. He sent presents for Miss Flora's birthdays, nice things they was. Jewelry and nice perfume and such lovely handkerchieves with lots of embroidery and her initials and all. And he always sent presents to her at Christmas and a big wreath or a box of fruit or whatnot. But he never called, never wrote nothing but his name on the cards. And he never came here."

"And you told Billy this. That you were Uncle Horatio's child."

"No, not right off, Miss Lily. When your uncle left, my ma married a man in town who ran off and left her when I was two months old. Michael O'Hare, she said his name was. I never knew him, being only a baby. But I thought he was my real father. She had a picture of them getting married, see, and I fancied that I looked a little bit like him. So when she told me about Mr. Horatio, I didn't rightly believe her."

"When did you tell Billy? And why, if you didn't believe your mother?"

Mimi got tears in her eyes. "Not till a couple years ago. He'd been beating me and said he was going to leave me. And my aunts were being just awful as could be. It was plain terrible, Miss Lily. I had to make peace with Billy or my aunts or I'd of been sleeping in the woods, with no job and no money. So I told Billy what my ma had said. I told him I was really a rich man's daughter. And that he was old now and pretty soon he'd die, and I'd get all his money, so Billy better be nice to me and stay around and if he divorced me, he'd be sorry as sorry."

Mimi blew her nose loudly on a grimy handkerchief she pulled out of her apron pocket. "See, Miss Lily, I wanted to believe it, too. After my ma told me about Mr. Horatio, I started dreaming like. Of being rich. Having nice clothes. Living in this house.

I even wondered if I could change my name to Brewster, like yours. Anyhow, Billy was right nice to me for a long time after I told him. Then he got put in jail again for stealing some silver things from one of the big houses up here, and when he came out, he was mad at me again."

In spite of the heat of the day accumulating in the upstairs bedroom, Lily suddenly felt cold. The sky was getting more overcast.

"So—" Lily cleared her throat. "So you're really Uncle Horatio's daughter and should have inherited instead of us?"

"No."

"What do you mean, no?" Lily asked.

"It wasn't true, Miss Lily. When my ma was dying, I asked her if she wanted me to ask Miss Flora to let Mr. Horatio know. And she said, 'Why would I want that?' And I said because he's my father."

Mimi blew her nose again and went on. "Ma started crying and crying and said what an awful thing she'd done. Michael O'Hare *was* my real father. But she knew he was a bum. Good-looking and flashy, but a bum. So she up and lied to Miss Flora, thinking that Mr. Horatio might marry her if Miss Flora made him to, but mainly that Miss Flora would keep her on instead of throwing her out of the house for being a loose woman. And Miss Flora did keep her on, just like Ma wanted. Ma felt awful about it and took real, real good care of Miss Flora because she'd done such an awful thing to her. But once she'd told the story and driven Mr. Horatio away—Miss Flora really loved him—Ma couldn't tell the truth."

Lily unclenched her hands, which had become whitened claws. "But you'd already told Billy the story."

Mimi nodded. "I wanted to believe I was a rich man's daughter. But when Ma finally told me the truth, she said she'd only told me the lie to keep me from marrying Billy, see? She knew he was like my real father—a bum. She wanted me to have some hope of doing better, she said. But she was dying and couldn't stand to go to her reward with the lie in her heart—and mine, and Miss Flora's."

"Did you tell Billy the real truth?"

Mimi nodded again. "But he wouldn't believe it. He thought I was trying to get rid of him so I could keep the house and the money that I'd get when Mr. Horatio died. I told him and told him that I was really Michael O'Hare's daughter, but he never would believe it."

"Did you tell Miss Flora the truth, too?"

"I did. She said she'd figured it out as I'd grown up to look so much like my real father, but she was too ashamed to tell Mr. Horatio. But she didn't hold it against me, Miss Lily. She was a good lady."

Lily couldn't force herself to take much interest in Miss Flora's qualities. "But Billy still believes the first story?"

"Yes, miss. He keeps saying I should talk to Mr. Prinney about it. And I won't do that. Mr. Prinney's father before him was Miss Flora's lawyer and Mr. Prinney took care of Miss Flora's affairs when she was old. I'm sure she told him. No point in me talking to him about it at all."

"You do see what this all means, don't you?" Lily said.

"No," Mimi responded frankly.

"It means Billy had an excellent reason to get rid of our Uncle Horatio."

"Get rid of Mr. Horatio? Kill him, you mean?" Mimi exclaimed. "Oh, no, miss. Billy's mean as sin and he steals and he talks big and ugly, but he wouldn't do that. He wouldn't kill nobody. At least, not on purpose," she added.

"What makes you think that?" Lily asked. "He beats you. He has no sense of morality. He's probably learned a lot in jail about killing people from men who have done it."

Mimi's eyes opened very wide. "You think—?"

"I think you're in danger," Lily said, getting up and looking out the window. The sun was starting to set behind the hills across the river and the river itself looked murky and ominous. "And I think Robert and I are in even more danger."

Chapter 15

The two women were silent for a few minutes, neither looking at the other. Finally, Lily sighed and said, "Let's settle the rest of this. I guess you know that our uncle was murdered."

Mimi nodded. "I heard folks say that."

"What did Billy mean by saying he'd seen what happened?"

"He didn't mean anything, Miss Lily. He was just talking through his hat. Acting like he knew important things when he don't know nothing."

"But what did he tell you he knew?"

"That he saw someone go down in the cabin after Mr. Horatio did."

"Who?"

"He wouldn't say who. That's how I know he's making it up."

"Why would he do that? He was proposing to blackmail someone."

"He only acted that way to make me do what he wanted."

"Are you sure of that, or is it just what you'd *like* to think?"

Mimi didn't answer right away. Lily sensed that

she was still concealing something. "Mimi, you really must tell me all you know."

Mimi lowered her head and mumbled something. Lily just stared at her until Mimi looked up and repeated it. "I saw Billy go down into the cabin. He says someone else went down before he did."

"Was Uncle Horatio there then? In the cabin?"

"I don't know. I wasn't looking for him, I was looking for Billy. I was hitching up my skirt and one of those men was helping me into the boat and Billy wasn't there, so I looked around for him. Billy had these new shoes, see. They cost him a lot and he'd worn them to the boat dock, then changed on the boat to deck shoes. He left the good shoes down in the galley. I'm sure that's why he went down there. To get his shoes."

"And he claims he saw someone else go down there, too?" Lily asked. She was thinking, *Or he killed Uncle Horatio and just made up the story about someone else.*

"He might of done," Mimi admitted. "But I don't think so. He's just talking big. He always talks big, like he knows important things that he's keeping secret until he can use them."

"Did he get his shoes?" Lily asked.

"No, miss. He told me later that he couldn't find them and didn't want to drown for a pair of shoes."

"Is there anything else you know? Anything about the other men on the boat? How they acted? Odd things they might have said?"

"Most of them I didn't even know. Except for Mr. Prinney and Mr. Kessler. And Mr. Horatio, but I'd never even seen him before, so I didn't know how anybody *should* of acted."

It had been harrowing to both of them to have this conversation. Mimi hadn't wanted to talk about it and Lily, while she needed to know, hadn't liked hearing what Mimi had to say. She didn't think either of them would be able to cope with a further discussion of the missing ten-dollar bill and the scarf.

"Mimi, thank you for telling me this. If you think of anything else you even wonder if I might need to know, you'll tell me, won't you?"

Mimi looked surprised. "Then you're not going to fire me, Miss Lily?"

Lily patted her shoulder. "I wouldn't even think of it. Thank you for doing such a nice job on the dress," she said in dismissal. "And don't forget you're to stay in the house. Everybody else is going out for dinner, so please find some keys and lock up."

When Mimi had gone, Lily dressed and went downstairs to look for Robert. He was nowhere to be found and she wasn't about to venture outside on her own to look for him. She sat down in the front hall to wait for him and think about what Mimi had told her. Lily liked Mimi and felt sorry for her, but she didn't really know her. Was the whole story the truth? Mimi didn't seem to have the guile to make up such an elaborate fabrication. Or did she?

Robert finally arrived, breathless and with oil smudges on his shirt. "Sorry, I lost track of the time."

"We've got plenty of time. I was just ready early. But—" She drew close and whispered, "I have a lot to tell you, so get ready and we'll leave so we can talk."

Lily paced and kept looking at her watch, rehearsing how she could give the basics of what Mimi had told her while they were in the car. When Robert finally came down, spiffy in his tux and down at the mouth about having to go to the Winslows', Lily hustled him out of the house.

"Drive slowly so I can tell you what I've learned."

She ran through the whole story about Barbara O'Hare telling Miss Flora that Uncle Horatio was responsible for her "delicate condition."

"You mean to say that Mimi is Uncle Horatio's daughter?" Robert exclaimed, nearly running into a tree as he snapped his head around to stare at his sister in horror.

"No, listen to the rest."

By the time she'd finished, Robert had slowed the Duesenberg to a crawl and a huge black auto behind them was honking at him. Robert waved the other vehicle around, which sped past in a cloud of gravel dust. Robert stopped.

"Wasn't that—" Lily began.

"Lily, do you know what this means? Billy Smith had the best reason in the world to kill Uncle Horatio. If he believed Mimi was going to inherit Grace and Favor and the rest of his estate—"

"He wouldn't have left it to her even if the story of his being her father had been true. And it wasn't."

"But according to what you just said, Billy didn't believe her when she tried to take back the story. If he believed, for greedy reasons of his own, that she was Uncle's daughter, it would explain why he wouldn't divorce her and why he had the best motive to bump Uncle off."

"I know. Robert, we must get going, but there's one more thing. Billy claims to have seen something important happen on the boat that day. And he was threatening to have a talk with someone about it."

"Blackmail."

"Exactly. Mimi said he didn't know anything and was just pretending to be a tough guy. But when I prodded her some more, she admitted she'd seen him go down to the cabin while she was being hoisted onto the dinghy. She excused this by claiming he'd left his good shoes in the galley. But he never got his good shoes. And he claims he saw someone else go down there, too, but won't tell Mimi who it was. Mimi doesn't believe that part of his story and neither do I."

"But he *could* have seen something happen to Uncle Horatio," Robert said. "And more likely, Billy himself murdered him."

"I'll tell you all the details later. Right now, we'd better get on to the Winslows'."

As they stood at the front door, Lily and Robert were even more miserable than they'd have normally been about having to spend an evening with these boring people. All they both wanted to do was sit quietly, privately, and chew over what Mimi had told Lily. Instead Robert sighed and reached for the lion's head door knocker.

There was a long pause before they heard footsteps and the click of a cane striking the marble floor inside. Major Winslow opened the door, pointedly glancing at his watch.

"Nice timepiece, old boy," Robert said fatuously.

"Come in," Winslow snapped.

There were two other men in the sitting room. One of them was dreadful Cousin Claude. The other was a stranger.

"Claude!" Robert exclaimed. "You must be the batty driver who got my tux all dirty."

Claude lifted an eyebrow. "Perhaps that will encourage you to drive better in that great hog of an automobile of yours."

"Jealousy is most unbecoming," Robert said.

"She's not a hog, she's a steamship. The queen of the line. I think, in fact, she should have a name. 'Queenie' would be so vulgar. Maybe 'Countess' would be better. 'Countess Duesenberg' has a nice ring to it, don't you think?"

Claude was so stuffy that this trivial talk made him furious. Before he could go from red to purple in the face, Lily stepped in. "How is your mother, Claude?" she said pleasantly. "Still needlepointing?"

"She just finished a petit point set of dining room chair seats for the bishop's dining room," he said, glaring over his shoulder at Robert, who was being introduced to the other guest. "Museum quality, of course."

"Of course," Lily said mildly.

She turned away as Major Winslow approached her with his other guest in tow. "Miss Brewster, this is Mr. Kessler, the editor of the *Voorburg Times*."

Kessler was a stubby little man of about fifty with mouse-brown hair grown long and sweeping over his bald head. He was an inch or two shorter than Lily and shook her hand with his small, short-fingered one. Unlike the other men, he wasn't in a tux, but wore a blue suit.

"We've met your reporter, Jack Summer," Lily said.

"He's a good lad. Might turn into a good reporter someday," Mr. Kessler said in a gravelly voice. "It's nice to have met you, Miss Brewster. I don't mean to be rude, but I must be getting along."

"You're not dining with us?"

He stared at her for a moment with obvious surprise and said, "No, I just came to have a word with Major Winslow."

He was left to see himself out, which Lily thought uncommonly rude.

"Where are Mrs. Winslow and Sissy?" she asked.

"They're fixing dinner," Major Winslow replied. "They've found they enjoy cooking."

"More important," Robert said, "what is Claude doing here?"

"Your cousin is a friend of Sissy's." Major Winslow loaded his reply to this blunt question with all the haughtiness of many generations of gentlemen.

"Should I help in the kitchen?" Lily said, knowing full well this was an empty offer. She had no idea on earth how to function in a kitchen.

Just then, Mrs. Winslow entered the room and greeted them all. The underarms of her dress were sweaty and she'd doubtless be appalled if she knew that. "Dinner is almost ready. "Would anyone like a glass of wine before we sit down to table?"

"I would, very much, thank you," Robert said. "In fact, I'll be 'mother' if anyone else is joining me."

Lily had noticed Robert eyeing the liquor cabinet and knew he was just making sure he got the best there was to offer. If there was a wine cellar at Grace and Favor, they had yet to find it.

"Nice selection," Robert said, as Major Winslow opened the cabinet. "Where do you get it?"

"I have a 'connection' locally," Winslow said. "That would be the only good thing if Roosevelt wins this election. He would repeal Prohibition."

"Isn't he by way of being a local chum?"

"Oh, he lives quite near, but being as he's a Democrat," Winslow said, "we don't *socialize* with them."

"I'd vote for him on the strength of repealing Prohibition alone," Robert said.

Winslow looked like he was going to have a stroke. "You would? I'm shocked. Frankly shocked."

The men—Robert, Claude and Major Winslow—sat down to hash over politics and drink their wine. Lily accepted a tiny crystal glass of sherry and gingerly sat down in a chair next to a table covered with expensive knickknacks. China shepherdesses, little ivory bowls and a nest of silver ashtrays, which could have used a bit of polishing. She tried very hard not to listen to Robert expounding, since she knew for a fact that he took absolutely no interest in politics and was quite certainly making a great fool of himself. Possibly deliberately. Finally, there was no avoiding listening in.

"But even Eccles and Foster have come around to the liberal view," Robert was saying. "The government has taken things into its own hands before—during wartime, for example. And this is turning into a class war that can devastate the country. It could be the end of democracy unless—"

So Robert had been listening to Charles Locke. And had thoroughly understood the concept he'd propounded. Would Robert never stop surprising her?

Sissy finally appeared, her mass of curly red hair in some disarray. It looked as if it had all fallen down and been carelessly jammed back together. Her face was pink, sweaty and sullen. "Dinner is ready," she said.

This was a sad exaggeration. It might have been 'ready' in her eyes, but was a disaster. The jacketed baked potatoes were rock-hard on the outside and dried almost to powder inside. The peas had cooked so long they were virtually paste. The roast, on the other hand, was so undercooked that it was bloody and revolting. At least there was a salad. It was cut so finely it looked like confetti and swam in little individual bowls of dressing. Lily tasted it cautiously and discovered that the dressing seemed to be a very strong vinegar with a dollop of downright belligerent horseradish.

Her throat closed, her eyes watered and she was saved from disgrace only by the fact that Claude had tasted it at the same time and was having a violent coughing fit and had to leave the room to recover. Had he any sense, he'd have just kept going right out the door and home.

Everyone pretended to have extremely delicate appetites and picked at the food while aggressively discussing almost anything else that came to mind to avoid having to comment on the meal. Lily was seated facing the inside wall, upon which there was a truly vast portrait of the family. It had a lush garden setting and had probably been done about the time she and Sissy were in school together. Major Winslow was seated on a garden bench with a cane across his knees, not, Lily noticed, the one he carried now. A younger Sissy was standing to his right, and Mrs. Winslow was standing between and behind them, holding a bunch of flowers. Lily decided if she ever got money again, she'd hire the painter. He'd done a lovely job on the people, the flowers and the shafts of sunlight filtering through. Best of all, it saved her from having to eat dinner. She made small talk about the painting, which let Sissy complain about how the painter had gotten her hair all wrong and it had taken forever for them to pose for it.

Meanwhile, Major Winslow was loyally attempting to clean his plate, but got only halfway through a slice of almost raw beef before he excused himself and disappeared for quite a long while. It was assumed this was the result of a digestive upset that wasn't polite to talk about. Or perhaps he was only pretending to be ill so he could avoid eating any more.

At one point Mrs. Winslow, in her effort to contribute to the cover-up, blurted out that Claude and Sissy were engaged.

"No, Mummy. Not yet. Not officially," Sissy said, looking around for Claude to return.

"Then let's have a toast to making it official," Robert said. "Perhaps some champagne in the sitting room?"

Even Major Winslow, who had eventually returned to the table looking pale and a little wobbly, seemed grateful for the invitation to leave the table. But his wife exclaimed, "We haven't had dessert yet."

There were several almost imperceptible groans.

"Perhaps later, Mummy," Sissy said, still sullen. "I wonder where Claude has gone?"

Lily smiled to herself, wondering if Claude had made a break for it. She pleaded a terrible headache as soon as everybody had enjoyed one fine glass of champagne, which allowed Robert to become very solicitous of his sister and insist on taking her home immediately.

They drove back in miserable silence. "Worst meal I've ever had," Robert muttered.

"Robert, we need to talk. But I'm too tired tonight. I think we should consider discussing what Mimi told us with Jack Summer. Maybe he could fill in the blanks."

"In what way?"

"Let us know, for example, if this horrible Billy went around telling other people in town his belief that Mimi was Uncle Horatio's heir."

"Let's talk about it tomorrow. I need to take to my bed and forget this evening ever happened."

Lily said, "I'm going to starve before morning. Wasn't there an ice cream shop in town?"

"If there was, I didn't notice it," Robert said. "But it's a nice evening for a drive. We'll go see."

There *had* been an ice cream shop in Voorburg, but it was closed. Permanently. Another victim of the economic bad times. They gave up and went back home. Robert dropped her at the front door and went to park the automobile. The house was dark and Lily realized that it was later than she had thought. Everyone had gone to bed. She staggered upstairs, her stomach growling, and put on her nightgown. But before she could even turn down her bed, she realized there was no way she was going to get to sleep with her stomach roaring.

She put on a dressing gown and crept downstairs to the kitchen, stepped into the room, and turned on the overhead light.

Lying in the middle of the kitchen floor was a body with a butcher knife sticking out of its chest and Lily's missing scarf around its neck.

Lily screamed.

Chapter 16

Jack Summer was sitting in his tiny boardinghouse room, reading some old issues of the *Voorburg Times* that he'd borrowed from the newspaper morgue. He had the window wide open next to his small desk because the whole house always reeked of cabbage, even though it wasn't served very often. He'd have a roomful of moths, but the fresh air was great. He wondered idly whether the smell was ancestral, having permeated the building for so long that it was part of it.

He'd been looking through the old issues of the paper, trying to find any mention of Horatio Brewster or the other people on the ill-fated boat. He thought there might be some clue to their background or motives, but so far, he'd found nothing useful.

There was a sudden pounding on the door and his second cousin Ralph, the part-time deputy, burst into the room. "Jack, hurry up. I just got a call that your girlfriend has apparently murdered somebody. I've got my motorbike outside and I'll take you along."

"What girlfriend?"

"That rich girl up at the mansion you've been asking about."

"Lily Brewster? She wouldn't murder anyone!" Jack said, desperately cramming his bare feet into his shoes.

"Maybe not, but the chief says he got a call from someone up at Honeysuckle Cottage that she'd screamed the house down about a murder in the kitchen. Took a while to get it straight because whoever called said it was called something else. Gracie something. The chief told me to come up and guard the doors to keep nosy neighbors out and the people at the house in. Get a move on!"

The motorbike ride was harrowing. Ralph was in such a hurry to get to the actual scene of his first crime that he made no effort to avoid the potholes in the road. Jack, bounced like a dried pea in a can in the sidecar, was horrified both by the ride and Ralph's extraordinary news. Lily Brewster kill someone?

Ralph was pretty much of an idiot, but how could he have gotten something *that* wrong?

When they reached the house, Robert was standing at the front door.

Jack crawled, shaky-legged, out of the sidecar and Ralph dismounted from the motorbike. "What's happened?" Jack asked.

"We have a dead body in the kitchen. What are you doing here? How did you know anything happened?"

Jack waved vaguely. "Cousin Ralph. Does this body have a name?"

"Billy Smith," Robert said grimly. "If it weren't for the prospect of spending the rest of my life at Sing Sing, I'd like to claim credit for bumping off the bastard myself."

"Who did kill him?"

Robert shrugged. "No idea."

"Then it wasn't Miss Brewster?"

Robert reached forward and grabbed Jack by the front of his shirt, nearly lifting him off the ground. "You ask that again of anybody, and I'll—"

Robert looked at his hands as if they were someone else's and let go. "Sorry, old boy. Lost my head there. No, Lily and I had been out for the evening and had an awful dinner. Lily was hungry and went downstairs to find some food and found a murdered man instead."

"How do you know he was murdered?"

Robert rolled his eyes. "Go take a look and see what you think."

Jack entered the house. Ralph took over door duty, though he'd obviously have rather been part of the body-viewing party, and Robert followed Jack. There was the sound of Mimi crying in the library and Mrs. Prinney trying to comfort her. In the kitchen, the chief of police, a man of enormous proportions with a tiny bald head topping off his mass, was consulting with the town doctor, a plump little Dutchman with a square head and face, who lived just down the road a little way and had been summoned to pronounce death. The doctor was wearing a dress jacket over pajama tops and a fringe of matching fabric was ruffled around the ends of his trouser legs. The police chief had donned his uniform for the occasion, although it was dusty with neglect, too tight and was buttoned crookedly. Mr. Prinney, in nightwear with a flannel bathrobe over it, was standing quietly by the sink.

The chief was asking, "How long you reckon he's been dead?"

Jack was staring with horror at Billy sprawled on

the floor. The blade of a large butcher knife was embedded in Billy's chest up to the hilt, probably literally pinning him to the floor, and his eyes, above a blood-soaked scarf around his neck, were still wide open and staring at the ceiling. On the floor around him was a pool of blood. Jack gagged.

"A couple hours," Dr. Polhemus said. "The blood's congealed pretty well. Impossible to tell an exact time. Don't try to pin me down. Can't do it. Why isn't the town meat wagon here yet? We need to get this man out of here before he stinks up the whole place."

Robert and Jack left the room, neither wanting to see Billy being moved.

They went to sit in the hallway. Mimi was still sobbing faintly from the library. "Where's Miss Brewster?" Jack asked.

"Upstairs," Robert said. "I've got to check on her again in a minute. The doctor gave her something to make her sleep. She was really unraveled. She damned near stepped in the middle of him when she walked in the kitchen."

"What was Billy doing in the kitchen—besides being killed?"

Robert shrugged. "Sneaking in to beat up on his wife again? Nobody knows. Mr. and Mrs. Prinney were out visiting friends, came home and went straight to their rooms upstairs. Mimi was asleep, too, when Lily started screaming. She said she'd been in her room all evening, doing a jigsaw puzzle. Lily had told her to lock up the house, but she said she couldn't find a set of keys."

"Are you sure she was really in her room all evening?"

Robert drew himself up. "I'm not sure of a damned thing except that the bastard had the gall to come in our house and get himself killed."

They sat silently for a moment on the substantial chairs that flanked the small table in the front hall. Mr. Prinney passed through, going upstairs. He merely nodded to them grimly. A moment later, Mrs. Prinney came out of the library with Mimi, still crying, to lead her up the stairs. "I'll check on Miss Brewster," she said to Robert over her shoulder. "Mimi, you must get ahold of yourself. He wasn't worth making yourself sick with crying over."

"But he was my husband!" Mimi wailed.

"Not anymore, he's not." Mrs. Prinney's practical remark drifted down from the landing.

A moment later, Mr. Prinney came back downstairs in his street clothes. Jack got up and offered the older man his chair, an offer which was accepted. Mr. Prinney leaned toward Robert. "Tell me about coming home this evening."

"We left the Winslows' house in search of food," Robert said. "The meal was inedible. Drove to town. Not even Mabel's Cafe was open."

"What time was this?" Mr. Prinney asked.

"I don't know. Dinner at the Winslows' had seemed to last for days. What time does Mabel's close?"

"Whenever Mabel feels like it."

"I just don't know the time," Robert said. "We looked around for anywhere to get some food, then drove home. I dropped Lily at the door, then went to put the Duesie in the garage. Gave her a bit of a polish—the automobile, not Lily—then came inside."

"Through the front door?" Prinney asked.

"Of course. If I'd come through the kitchen door in back, I'd have been the one who found the body. I went to my room and as I was closing my door, I heard another door open. Lily's, I know now. A couple minutes later, I heard her scream."

"About this dinner at the Winslows' . . ." Mr. Prinney said. "Were both of you with the rest of the company the entire time?"

Robert opened his eyes very wide. "We need alibis?"

Mr. Prinney said nothing.

"All right. We were and we weren't. So to speak. What I mean is, we were both with someone or another the whole evening, but some of the others weren't. You see what I mean?"

"Not exactly."

"Sissy didn't appear for a long while because she was fixing the food—if you could call it food. And our Cousin Claude choked on something and was gone for quite a while later on. Major Winslow also got sick on the dinner and left the table for some time. But Lily and I stuck it out."

"Good. That's very good," Mr. Prinney said.

There was the sound of a vehicle pulling up to the front door and Mr. Prinney suggested they adjourn to the library to get out of the way of the removal of the body. Jack wasn't specifically invited, but trailed along anyway. He was wondering if he dared get out his notebook and pencil and take notes but decided it wouldn't be tactful and would probably get him sent away. He'd have to trust his memory.

As they sat down in the library, Robert said, "Oh, and there was someone else there when we arrived. Your editor," he said, turning to Jack.

"Mr. Kessler was at the dinner?" Jack asked.

"No, he was just leaving as we arrived."

"I wonder what he was doing there?" Jack said.

"I can tell you that," Mr. Prinney said briskly. "He also stopped by the home we were visiting this evening. There's a group of townspeople who want to have a festival of some sort in the fall. Just to perk everyone up a bit. He was out soliciting funds for it."

Robert hadn't been paying attention. "You can't honestly believe Lily and I are suspects in this murder," he said, still brooding about being asked for their alibis.

"I don't believe any such thing," Mr. Prinney said. "But the police are going to be asking a lot of questions in the morning. And I wanted the most important answer now."

Saturday morning Lily woke at dawn. Her mouth felt gummy, her mind fuzzy, her legs wobbly. She was brushing her teeth when she suddenly remembered what had happened last night. Fortunately, she was still so doped up from the draught the doctor had given her that she was more curious than alarmed.

Billy Smith was dead on the kitchen floor of Grace and Favor. She shook her head. That couldn't be right. It must have been a bad dream. She stumbled back into bed and slept for a few more hours.

When she next awoke, well after nine in the morning, her mind was working better and she knew that the horror she'd stumbled onto last night hadn't been a dream. She sat for a long time on the side of the bed, trying to work it out. She certainly wasn't grieved by Billy Smith's death. He'd frightened her, beat up his wife, possibly killed Uncle Horatio and she didn't regret that he was dead. But she hated that it was a violent death, and hated more than anything that it happened inside Grace and Favor. It was like an attack on the house itself, a desecration, somehow. Not just in a physical sense, but in a

moral sense. No matter what Billy had done to pro-
voke someone to such desperate means, it wasn't
right that it took place here.

There was a knock on the door and Mimi came in
the room. She was subdued, but no longer crying.
"Would you like a breakfast tray up here, miss?"

"Mimi, I hardly know what to say. I'm glad you're
free of Billy, but I know you must be sad. At least a
little."

Mimi set the breakfast tray, a nice white wicker
tray with a cutwork cloth and matching napkin, on
the bedside table after Lily had gotten the lamp out
of the way. "I guess you're right, miss. Billy wasn't
a good person, but nobody should die like that." But
as she said these practical words, her chin was trembling.

"Was he around last night? I mean earlier. When
we and the Prinneys had gone out to dinner."

"He yelled up at my window right after you'd all
gone. He must have been watching from the woods.
I hadn't locked up, but I said the house was locked
and he believed me. Told me to come down and let
him in to talk. I said no."

"Then what?"

Mimi looked out Lily's window and said quietly,
"He said he had some other folks to talk to and he'd
be back. That's what he must of done. And somebody followed him here."

"How did he get around?" Lily asked. "Did he
have an automobile or a bicycle or what?"

"No, he can't afford neither except when he steals
one. Then he always gets—got—caught. He walks.
He knows all the old paths."

"Paths?"

"Yes, miss. There used to be Indians hereabouts.

There was paths everywhere through the woods. When the Indians went away, the settlers used them. And the deers and such, too. Billy told me the dirt is so packed down that even though nobody much but the hobos uses them now, nothing'll grow on them."

"Are there paths around this house?"

"Sure. Lots. One starts across the road and goes straight down to town. The road winds all over the place, but the path makes a walk to the town real close. It's kinda steep, though. And another goes to the houses on both sides of here and a couple more back a ways from the river. We're much closer to them than you'd think from just going by the road."

"Does everybody who lives up here know about these shortcuts?"

"I s'pose so. The kiddies and the men, anyway. Ladies don't often use them because their clothes get caught on bushes and things. And folks from town come up here hunting sometimes."

Lily repeated her polite regrets and Mimi said, "There's men wanting to talk to you downstairs. But I told them they'd just have to wait until you're feeling up to it. Mrs. Prinney told them the same."

"Men? Who?"

"The police chief and the coroner."

Chapter 17

Lily bathed, and dressed slowly and carefully. She wasn't anxious to talk to anyone, least of all the police and a coroner. She put on one of her frumpy old dresses that she used to wear to the bank. The one that was least threadbare.

As she descended the stairs, Mr. Prinney popped up from a chair in the hall where he'd been waiting and met her. In a voice that was almost a whisper, he said, "Miss Brewster, a word with you."

They slipped quietly into his office. "I'm really the attorney for the estate, not your personal attorney, but I wish to advise you anyway. Say very little to Chief Henderson."

"I don't even know who that is."

"The police chief. Answer his questions politely and sparsely. He's not a very bright man and is easily led astray by extraneous information. And he's highly resentful of the rich, which he believes you to be."

"Thank you, Mr. Prinney. Have you told Robert this as well?"

"I have. Now, let's get your interview over with."

They went back to the library where Chief Henderson and the coroner were waiting impatiently. The coroner was the doctor who was at the house the night before. He was properly dressed now and introduced as Dr. Polhemus. There was another man, a young one who wasn't introduced and was sitting by the door with a notebook and pencil.

"Now, miss," Henderson said, smoothing a hand over his bald head. "Let's get to the bottom of this murder."

Lily merely nodded.

"I hear you and your brother were out last night."

Lily nodded again.

Henderson waited for her to be more forthcoming and when she said nothing else, he went on. "Where were you?"

"At the Winslow home for dinner."

And so it went. Lily followed Mr. Prinney's advice and Henderson grew more and more frustrated with her short, correct, terse answers. He tried to get her to gossip about the Winslows. He suggested that Lily and Robert might have stopped by the Grace and Favor before going to town to look for something to eat.

Finally he played his trump card. He pulled the bloody scarf out of an envelope like a rabbit out of a hat and waved it in her face. "Is this yours?"

"It is. Or it was. I don't want it back," Lily said, shocked and feeling faint at the sight of her favorite scarf, now stiff with blood.

"What was it doing around the dead man's neck?"

"I had no idea it was. I didn't study him carefully. I lost the scarf several days ago."

"Lost it where?"

"If I knew that, it wouldn't have been lost," Lily said.

Henderson finally asked, "Who do *you* think committed this crime with *your* scarf and *your* butcher knife?"

"I'm a newcomer to this community. I wouldn't have the slightest idea," Lily said, fighting back the urge to either slap the man or run away. She'd never been spoken to in this accusing tone in her life. "Who do you think it was?"

"You're not here to ask me questions!" he snapped. "I wouldn't be surprised if it was you and your brother."

Lily had to bite her teeth shut to keep from responding. She stared back at him boldly, but didn't speak.

Dr. Polhemus spoke up. "Now, Harold, that's no way to talk to a young woman. Miss Brewster, you can be honest with us. We've been told you threatened Billy Smith."

"I threatened him?"

"One of the workmen heard you saying you were going to call the police if he came on your property again."

"Which is precisely what happened," Mr. Prinney put in. "And he was dead by then. Miss Brewster has answered your questions to the best of her ability and I believe it would be in everyone's interest for you to move on."

"Look here, Prinney. You people had a man murdered in this house," Henderson said.

"There probably isn't a single person in Voorburg who will regret Billy Smith's death," Mr. Prinney said. "He was a violent, lawless man, which you well know. He came here several times to abuse his wife, who is Miss Brewster's employee. She warned him not to come back. That was not a threat."

"Still, he died in this house," Henderson said. "Miss Brewster is the mistress of the house."

"And she was at the Winslows' when Billy Smith was murdered. That's easily checked," Mr. Prinney said calmly.

"You bet I'll be talking to them."

"Then you had better get on with it," Mr. Prinney said in his most staid voice. "Meanwhile, Miss Brewster has her household duties to attend to and I have work to do as well." He rose and signaled to Lily to leave the room with him. They went back to the little den off the main hall that he used as an office and watched out the front window as Henderson, Dr. Polhemus and the young man, whom Lily later learned was Jack Summer's cousin Ralph, departed.

"Thank you again, Mr. Prinney," Lily said, severely shaken by the experience. "I now understand better why my uncle's death was never solved. That's a horrible man."

"Not as bad as the former police chief," Mr. Prinney said sadly. "Nor quite as stupid."

"Who do you think killed Billy?" Lily asked bluntly.

Mr. Prinney was no more eager to answer this than Lily had been. "I can think of half a dozen people who had good reason to. He's made a lot of lives hereabouts a misery. You mustn't worry about Henderson."

"How can I not? He all but accused Robert and me of killing Billy."

"That's his method of solving anything. He's too stupid to figure things out, so he makes wild accusations in the hope that someone will admit to them. He'll do the same with everyone he talks to."

"Why does the town tolerate him?"

"He was the only person to apply for the job when our last chief suddenly took off for California. Henderson won't be around much longer. This is confidential, but the town council is already quietly interviewing applicants from neighboring towns."

Lily sighed. "I'm glad of that."

Mr. Prinney shuffled some papers on his desk and said, "When this is sorted out, you and I need to have a good long talk. I assumed your brother would be taking an interest in the estate's holdings. As I told you earlier, you will both eventually have to handle these matters if you fulfill your . . ."

"Sentence?"

Mr. Prinney smiled thinly. "If you wish to think of it that way. Your brother didn't seem interested and suggested that you yourself were the more appropriate person."

"I suppose I am. And I'm interested. Does that offend you, sir?"

"I've had the good fortune to know a number of very intelligent, competent women in my life," Mr. Prinney said. "I suspect you may be yet another."

Lily didn't know if he was just being courtly or meant it, but she smiled and thanked him and said she hoped she could live up to his expectations.

Lily sat down on the window seat and was silent for a moment before saying, "Mr. Prinney, I think it's time you told me what you know about our uncle's death. Robert and I are unwillingly and ignorantly involved in all this. It appears to me that Billy Smith's death and my uncle's are connected."

Mr. Prinney had drawn himself up with closemouthed dignity when she started speaking, just as he had when she mentioned this before. But this time, he slowly deflated. "Yes, I suppose you are right."

He sat down in front of the small desk where he sometimes finished up his work from his office in town and stayed quite still, gathering his thoughts.

"What was the reason for the boat trip?" Lily asked.

"That's a perceptive question . . . and the heart of the matter," he said. "Your uncle invited me along, knowing full well I'm uneasy and uncomfortable on boats, saying it was vitally important that I join the group."

"Why was it important?"

"He was vague, but firm. He said he had something to reveal and especially wanted his attorney to be present as a witness. I had the feeling that he wanted a captive audience."

"And what did he 'reveal'?"

Mr. Prinney picked up a pile of untidy paperwork and tamped it on the desk to make it line up. "Nothing. I suppose he intended to moor the boat at the island and make his statement there. But the storm came up."

"That was all the information he gave you?" Lily said, leaning forward.

Prinney nodded. "He was angry. My feeling—and it's only my feeling, not fact—is that his anger was that of an honorable, unforgiving man who had been cheated by someone he trusted or had helped. And he was preparing to take full revenge. He was that sort of man. He was an honest man and expected honesty from others and was prepared to be dramatic about it."

Lily was thinking about what Mimi told her earlier. "That's why he left his Aunt Flora, wasn't it? He had been honest and she hadn't believed him."

"You know about that unfortunate incident?"

"More than unfortunate, I'd say. Tragic. Mimi told me about it. Uncle Horatio and his aunt were very close and devoted, it seems, until Mimi's mother came between them."

"It was nonsense, of course," Mr. Prinney said, gazing past her through the window. "Mimi is the image of her real father." He sighed and went on, "Horatio and I had been to school together. We were young, and good friends then. He came to me, terribly distraught over his aunt's accusation and her refusal to believe him that he had made no improper advances toward Mimi's mother. I was handling his legal affairs in those days. He said he was moving away and asked me to recommend another attorney. Later, when Flora was dead and he returned to Voorburg, he put his legal matters back in my hands. It had been so long that we were no longer friends, only mutually respected acquaintances."

Lily felt a wave of sadness for the elderly man. It was clearly unlike him to reveal his feelings and probably quite painful. They were both silent for a long moment, then Mr. Prinney went on more briskly, "We had a weekly meeting to discuss the legal ramifications of various properties and businesses he owned. It was he, in fact, who cleared this little den we're in now for my convenience. So that I wouldn't have to carry all the paperwork back and forth from town every week."

Was that why he was so eager to move to Grace and Favor? Lily wondered. Because it was already a home away from home?

"Did you have the impression that this revelation he was preparing to make had to do with someone in the boating party?" Lily asked.

"Oh, almost certainly so. He wasn't the sort to make accusations behind anyone's back. Very forthright man, he was. When he had a complaint, he went straight to the source."

"Tell me about the people on the boat," Lily said.

"I know who some of them were, but not others. There was a Mr. Winningham."

"He's a banker in New York. Winningham's father had advised Miss Flora on her financial matters. This Winningham wasn't as competent as his father and Horatio knew it, but put some very minor accounts in his bank out of old loyalty to the family."

"Was he a fit man? Could he have killed Uncle Horatio?" Lily asked bluntly.

"No. He's quite badly crippled with arthritis. Walks with two canes. Horatio ordered that he be the first one put on the dinghy because of his frailty."

Lily wondered if Horatio's intent in saving Winningham might have been to make sure he got another chance to make an accusation of some sort against him. But she didn't say anything. He was first on the boat; that and his affliction pretty much removed him from suspicion.

"And who is Fred Eggers?" she asked.

"How do you know these names?"

"I read the newspaper accounts."

"Fred Eggers had been Horatio's primary stockbroker back in the twenties. A bit younger than the rest of the guests. They had served each other well, Eggers and Horatio. A profitable business relationship for both of them. But in early twenty-nine, Horatio got out of the stock market almost entirely. Fred was upset by the decision. It meant the loss of significant commissions. He couldn't—or wouldn't—see the impending disaster, while Horatio thought the market was spinning completely out of control and was a dangerous investment. They had words."

"Why was he in the boating party then?"

"He'd gotten wind of it by way of Winningham and just showed up uninvited. I suppose he thought it was to be a purely social occasion and would give him the opportunity to mend fences with Horatio."

"He forced himself into the group? And Uncle Horatio allowed it?"

"To my surprise. Eggers was still hanging on by his fingernails. Perhaps Horatio felt sorry for him."

"Did it appear that Egger's ploy to ingratiate himself was working?" Lily asked.

Mr. Prinney smiled. An almost wicked smile. "Fred Eggers was the worst sailor in the world. He was turning green before the boat was fifty feet from shore. He spent the whole trip hanging over the rail, sick as a dog."

"But he was younger. Could he have pulled himself together well enough to make an attack on Uncle Horatio?"

"I suppose so. But keep in mind, Miss Brewster, that your uncle had not invited him along on the trip. So he probably wasn't in any danger from whatever Horatio intended to reveal."

"Unless secondhand," Lily said.

Mr. Prinney gave her a questioning look.

"If he was friends with the person Uncle Horatio was going to accuse of something illegal or dishonest, he might have been involved as well."

Mr. Prinney studied her for a moment, then smiled again. A much nicer smile this time. "Miss Brewster, you are much more cynical than I would have guessed. And much more intelligent."

Lily didn't know whether to be flattered or insulted.

Chapter 18

Lily was saved from having to respond by a knock on the door. Mrs. Prinney said, "I've been looking all over for you. Breakfast is ready. Though it's a good deal closer to lunchtime."

Lily suddenly realized she was starving. She hadn't eaten a decent bite since luncheon the day before. She'd been on her way to find something in the kitchen to eat last night when she nearly stumbled over Billy Smith. She'd have to go back in the kitchen to clear her mind of that vision. And the sooner the better.

She followed Mrs. Prinney. "Is there anything I can help with?" she asked, glancing warily at the wide wooden planks of the floor where Billy had died. She half-expected the pool of blood to still be there. But what she could see of that area was clean and someone had found yet another throw rug to cover the bloodstains.

Mrs. Prinney had gone to the opposite side of the room to pick up a tray with the sugar, cream and butter. Without turning around, she said, "It'll come out. I scrubbed most of the stain this morning. Might take me a few more days' work."

"Thank you, Mrs. Prinney. What an awful job. You should have hired someone to come in and do that."

"Oh, there, there. When I was a girl, we'd butcher hogs every November. I'd help my mother make blood pudding. Blood doesn't bother me a bit. It's all the same. Hogs, chickens or people. You have to think about it that way."

"I'll try. How is Mimi?"

"She's coming around. You wait and see, she'll be bright as a new penny in a few days. We just need to find something to cheer her up. In a way, it's like coming out of a cave. The light is sort of scary at first. But she's free of that awful man now and she'll come to appreciate that. I told her to take a little lie-down this morning. I didn't want her in the kitchen just yet."

Lily smiled. The contrast between Mr. Prinney's carefully measured and well-thought precision of speech and Mrs. Prinney's blunt pronouncements was strange. Almost like switching languages entirely. "And where's Robert?"

"Try to guess," Mrs. Prinney said with a smile. "He just ran down to the garage to have a chin-wag with that automobile he loves so much."

"And the Countess Duesenberg is doing fine," Robert said from the kitchen screen door. "As I hope we all are this morning. Lily, are you okay?"

"I'm still a bit stupid. Don't ever let that doctor near me again with his little black bag of drugs."

"You needed to sleep like a drunk," Robert said. "Everybody does, now and then. At least you did it in a bed. Remember the time we found Binky Silver sleeping it off in a rowboat out on the Cape? He walked like a crab for two days afterward."

"Robert, you do me a world of good," Lily said

with a laugh. "What was that?" she then asked, catching a view of something moving outside behind Robert.

He turned and glanced out the door. "It's a dog. It's been hanging around all morning. I tried to make friends with him, but he wasn't having it."

Lily looked out the door, but the dog had disappeared.

Breakfast was light by Mrs. Prinney's standards. Fruit, cheese, milk, apple juice, coffee, scrambled eggs and bacon. There was a huge plate piled high with fluffy biscuits and butter. Enough to easily feed a half dozen more eaters. How, Lily wondered, did the woman do it? Single-handedly clean up the blood of a murder victim and still fix biscuits?

Lily put away so much food that she feared she'd have to loosen the belt of her dress. She could use a little 'lie-down' herself, but didn't want Mr. Prinney to get a chance to clam up.

"Could we continue our conversation?" she asked him, as she finally finished her breakfast.

"Not for a bit. I have some letters that must go out. Later in the day?"

She didn't dare push him. "Robert, would you take me for a walk? I need some fresh air and I want to see those paths Mimi told me about."

"Best wear trousers, dear," Mrs. Prinney said. "There are some thorny plants in the woods."

Lily obediently went upstairs to change, took a quick peek into Mimi's room on the third floor where she was napping and went back downstairs. Robert was waiting at the back door. "Wait just a minute more," she said, and returned shortly with the last couple pieces of bacon wrapped in butcher paper.

"You're still eating? How *can* you?"

"It's not for me, Robert. It's for the dog."

"What's this about a conversation with Mr. Prune?"

"I finally got him to talk about the boat wreck and the people on it. And most important, the reason for the trip."

She started to explain as they strolled toward the woods where there was an opening in the dense growth.

"You mean Uncle Horatio planned this nice little boat ride to humiliate one of the guests? Not quite the 'done thing,' do you think?"

"Mr. Prinney accepted it as something Uncle Horatio would do. He went on about how honest and forthright he was." It was odd that Robert had developed this posthumous dislike of someone he didn't even know, while Lily's feelings were moving in the opposite direction.

"A stiff-necked prig, it sounds like to me. With no social graces," Robert groused.

"And probably a serious threat to one of the others," Lily said. "He told me about the two we didn't know. One of them, I believe it was Winningham, is a frail arthritic man who is a mildly incompetent banker. His father had handled Miss Flora's financial affairs and Mr. Prinney says Uncle Horatio had some loyalty to him."

"Or knew something to his detriment," Robert said. "People with money can get real mean about money."

"So can people without it," Lily said. "But this man had to use two canes to even walk and was the first to be put on the dinghy."

"Okay, count him out," Robert said, carefully holding back a branch of a vicious-looking shrub so Lily could pass safely. "Good Lord! Look at that!"

The back of a huge house loomed just ahead. It was surprisingly close to Grace and Favor.

"Is it the Winslows' house?" Lily asked.

"It must be. Isn't that Sissy in the lawn chair by the big windows?"

It *was* Sissy, sitting on a wooden chaise lounge, half-turned away from them and doing something in her lap. From her arm motions, it looked like she might be sewing something. "Duck back a bit, Robert. We don't want her to see us."

There was a sudden rustling noise from behind them. Lily whirled and caught sight of the dog. It was a big dog, mainly collie in heritage, she guessed. But it was very thin and very shy and its thick coat was matted and dirty. She crouched down, and tossed a little piece of bacon the dog's direction.

The dog approached gingerly and snapped up the food, then moved closer. She gave it another piece. "Who do you belong to?" Lily asked the dog, who didn't answer, but got close enough to be petted.

She gave the dog the last piece of bacon, showing it the butcher paper to prove there was no more. The dog tried to eat the paper as well. Lily stroked it and exclaimed, "Robert, this dog is starving. It's all bones."

Lily—" he warned. "Don't get any ideas about adopting a stray dog."

"Why not? It's a nice dog and needs a home."

"Dogs have to be walked and boarded and all sorts of nuisance things."

Lily sat down in the path as the dog nudged against her for more petting. She laughed. "Robert, we're country folk now. Dogs walk themselves. And where do you think we'd be going to need to board the dog?"

"Oh. Right. I keep forgetting we're trapped here. Ha! Would that I could!"

"You're not really hating this, are you?" Lily said. The dog had rolled onto its back and Lily was rubbing its neck, which was full of burrs.

"I'll never admit that," Robert said. "Let's see where the path goes from Grace and Favor in the other direction."

Lily got up to follow and the dog obediently fell into place on her left. "What shall I call him?"

"Who?"

"The dog, of course."

"Him? Oh, Lily! You'll never be a real country girl. It's not a him."

"Oh . . . Well, her then. Rover? Fido?"

"Too cliché," Robert said. "Too manly. Wait until she earns a name. I wish I'd left a trail of crumbs like Hansel would have. This path is harder to follow going this way."

"I wonder if Doggie saw who came to the house last night?"

"If you name this creature Doggie, I'll go back to waiting tables in New York. Just see if I don't."

They were suddenly back to Grace and Favor, which appeared as unexpectedly as the Winslows' house had. They took the other fork and soon found themselves looking at yet another house. One they didn't recognize. A path had branched off this one, but Robert was getting tired of traipsing around in the woods and Lily was anxious to take the dog home and feed it some more and brush the burrs out of its fur.

"We'll do that path another day," she said. "And Mimi says there's yet another that goes pretty much straight to town."

"So does the Duesie—well, not straight to town,

but you get to sit down while you get there. I'm going down to the garage to give her another coat of polish."

Mr. Prinney had gone to town to post his letters, so Lily couldn't question him more. Instead, she gave the dog a half dozen leftover biscuits, ate one herself and went upstairs, the dog following her and sniffing all the furniture along the way. She climbed to the third floor and tapped on Mimi's door. "Mimi? Are you awake? I need help."

Mimi opened the door, looked at the dog and said, "Oh, poor old boy. You're a mess!"

"Do you know this dog?"

"No, but I've seen it in the woods a couple times when I was beating on them rugs. Wouldn't come to me."

"You didn't give her bacon. Could you help me give her a bath? Do we have a big tub somewhere?"

"Only that one in Mr. Robert's room. And a wash-tub in the basement, but it's dark and nasty down there."

"Robert won't mind if we use his tub."

Lily knew this was a terrible lie.

The two women got wetter than the dog. Lily eventually discarded her shoes and got in the tub with it, whereupon the dog wagged its tail, slapping her in the face with soapsuds.

Mimi laughed and the dog wagged harder while Lily tried to dodge the tail. Bathing the dog had done both Mimi and the dog a lot of good. "What a mess we've made of this room!" Lily exclaimed when they'd gotten the dog rinsed and hauled out of the tub onto a pile of towels. "You start drying her while I get a big comb."

"What's her name?" Mimi said, wrapping one of Robert's best towels around the dog, who had shaken herself and flung water all over the room.

"She doesn't have one . . . yet."

"Then you're going to keep her?" Mimi said with a big smile.

"Certainly. Somebody's either abandoned her or neglected her. They don't deserve to get her back."

While Mimi cleaned up the bathroom, Lily took the dog down the back stairs and outside on the sunny part of the lawn overlooking the river. She combed and combed and a fairly steady warm breeze dried the soggy animal. She fell sound asleep and Lily suspected that if dogs could purr, this one would be doing so. Every now and then she opened soulful eyes and gazed adoringly at her.

"What's your name, dear?" she whispered into the full white mane, now clean and soft. The dog mumbled her pleasure. Lily smiled. "This is my house and my dog," she said happily.

Then the smile faded.

This was also where a man was murdered less than a day earlier.

Chapter 19

Lily's desire to continue her discussion with Mr. Prinney was further delayed by the arrival of Major Winslow and Sissy. Sissy was pale and upset. "Oh, Lily! The police were at our house, asking about dinner last night. They said someone had been killed at your house. Right *inside* your house!"

"That's true."

Major Winslow put a fatherly arm around Lily and gave her shoulder an affectionate squeeze. "We're horribly upset for you and your brother. I really should have seen you home!"

So he is human, Lily thought. *I don't dare tell Robert that Major Winslow said exactly what Dad would have.*

"That wasn't necessary. But I thank you for the thought. We—" She had started to admit they hadn't come right home anyway, but had gone to town to find food. She caught herself and said, "We took a little spin in the car. Robert thought it might help my headache."

"And you didn't see someone lurking around the house?" Sissy asked.

"Oh, no. The man—it was Billy Smith—had been dead for quite a while when I found him."

"*You* found him?" Sissy shrieked. "Oh, Lily, how utterly, utterly horrible. I'd have fainted right away. Did you faint?"

Major Winslow said, "Sissy, you would not have fainted, and I'll wager Miss Brewster didn't either. You sensibly called for help, I imagine."

"Oh, Daddy . . ." Sissy simpered.

"I rather screamed for help, I must admit," Lily said.

"Who is this person who was killed?" Sissy asked.

"Billy Smith was a local person. He was married to our maid Mimi. He was a despicable person. Greasy, sly, violent, with horrible teeth."

Sissy looked enlightened. "I think I know who you mean. Was that who we heard shouting at someone here yesterday? I saw him in the woods one day and he scared me to death. I called Daddy who went to run him off. Remember, Daddy?"

"I do. He claimed he'd come to ask for work. I told him he looked like he'd never done a day's work in his life. He was a river rat. In fact . . ." He paused to readjust the sentence he'd been about to speak.

But Lily finished it for him. "He was piloting the boat when our uncle died."

Major Winslow clapped his hands together. "That's *it!* I knew I'd seen him before and couldn't remember where. Only that I associated him with something unpleasant. Well, thank goodness I sent him on his way. I suspected him of having a part in your uncle's death, to be honest."

"Why is that?"

"I saw him go down to the cabin while I was helping people onto the dinghy. Looked around to see who was left on board and caught a glimpse of the man who'd been piloting the boat. Didn't even think about it again until the boat was brought up and I learned that Horatio's body had been found there. I told the police chief and he said he'd look into it. I expected the man to be arrested. But I never knew his name, I don't think. One doesn't introduce staff to guests."

"Not often enough," Lily said, her original bad opinion of his snobbism flaring up again.

"Well, no need to rehash old sorrows. Forgive me for bringing it up, if you would."

"The police asked us about your scarf," Sissy said.

"Sissy!" her father warned.

"I'm sure they asked Lily about it, too, Daddy. I'm not being a tattletale."

"What about my scarf?"

"They said that you said you lost it. That nice green paisley one."

"That's true."

Sissy looked confused. "No, you didn't. You left it at our house the first time you called on us."

Lily cast her mind back to that first visit. Robert had been on the brink of saying something very rude to Major Winslow and she had hustled him out in a great hurry, pausing but a second to pick up her purse from the hall table. But she couldn't remember having picked up the scarf. "I guess you're right," she said warily.

"And then I brought it back to you," Sissy added.

"No, you didn't. Not that I remember."

"Well, not directly. I went for a walk and decided to take it along to you, but I couldn't get anyone to come to the door and so I just peeked in to call you and still no one answered. So I just put it on this chair right here. When I came back later to invite you to dinner, it was gone, so I assumed you had found it."

"You brought it back?" Lily said dully.

Major Winslow reentered the conversation. "Sissy, are you certain you didn't lose it along the way? I saw you leave with it, but . . ."

"Daddy, I put it on that *chair*. Oh!" Sissy squealed again. "What is that thing?"

"This is my new dog," Lily said. "She doesn't have a name yet."

"Ought to get rid of her," Major Winslow said. "She's a killer."

Both young women stared at him.

"At least it looks like the same dog, just cleaner. We keep a dovecote and I saw that dog kill one of my doves the other day."

"She was starving," Lily said.

"So are a lot of people. That doesn't excuse theft," Winslow said.

"But people know better. Dogs don't," Lily said. "She was only doing what comes naturally to a starving animal."

"I must apologize again, Miss Brewster," Winslow said contritely. "I seem to be bringing up one unpleasant subject after another. It's not like me. We came to express our sympathy for your situation, not to upset you. Please forgive me."

"It's quite all right," Lily said politely. "I'm too easily upset anyway just now. It was my fault." She didn't mean this sincerely, but suspected her parents would have been thrashing in their graves if she hadn't said it. They had put such importance on good manners.

With more apologies, more expressions of sympathy and offers to be of any help or comfort that they could be at this difficult time, Winslow and his daughter finally oozed compassionately out of the house.

Lily closed the door, turned and stared at the chair in the hall. Had she ever seen the paisley scarf there? She couldn't picture it. Maybe Sissy had folded it up very small and she just overlooked it. But probably not. It was a combination of rather bright greens and blues and it would have stood out against the light pink of the upholstery. Maybe Mrs. Prinney or Mimi had picked it up and put it away on a random trip upstairs.

No, not Mrs. Prinney. She had seen the body when Lily screamed. She had come into the kitchen right behind Robert. If the police chief had asked her about it, and she'd said she put it back in Lily's room, the chief would have been thrilled to have accused Lily openly of having had it in her possession. He'd interviewed Mrs. Prinney long before he'd been allowed to talk to Lily herself.

It was more likely Mimi who moved it. That was much more along her line. She was always cleaning and tidying out of sheer habit. Every time Lily left her purse in the hall or a barrette on a side table or a mystery book on the sofa where she'd been reading, the item shortly turned up on the dressing table in her room. She felt a pang of guilt about suspecting Mimi, however momentarily, of having taken the scarf in the first place when it was Lily herself who had misplaced it.

So, if Sissy had brought the scarf back, where had it been until it ended up around Billy Smith's neck?

Lily hadn't seen it. She felt sure Mrs. Prinney hadn't seen it or she would have said something. Mimi hadn't picked it up and put it back in her room. Robert and Mr. Prinney wouldn't have even noticed it on the pink chair, much less taken the trouble to move it. But it turned up in the kitchen.

Could Billy himself have found it? Lily had as-

sumed he'd come in through the kitchen door and
had been killed there. But suppose he'd come in the
front door, prowled around the house looking for
Mimi's room and picked up the scarf for some reason. Nothing had been locked up because nobody
had been able to find keys to anything but the
French doors in the library. He might have latched
onto the scarf to strangle Mimi when he found her.
No, Mimi was his ticket to the money he thought
she deserved. He wouldn't have killed her. But he
might have pretended he was going to if she didn't
cooperate.

Lily shook her head. That was absurd. Had he
come to the house with the purpose of threatening
Mimi, he'd have brought the means of the threat
along with him. A knife or a gun or even a rope.

Lily was still standing in the front hall, pondering
the scarf mystery and only confusing herself, when
she heard a car pull up in front. It was Mr. Prinney,
back from mailing his letters. But he had two workmen with him.

"That's the tree," he was saying to them as they
got out. "I'm sure it's diseased and might be dangerous. Look at all the dead limbs up high there.
Start at the top, dropping the limbs carefully, then
take the trunk in sections so it doesn't fall toward
the house."

The workmen got their tools out of the trunk and
one started climbing the tree.

"Mr. Prinney," Lily said. "Might we continue our
conversation?"

"Not quite yet. I want to supervise this. I don't
want them putting a limb through a window. But
there is something I want to give you. Come to my
den."

Lily followed along and waited while Mr. Prinney

unlocked a drawer in his desk and removed a thick vellum envelope. He tapped it against his hand, thinking for a moment, then said, "Your uncle left a letter. He said I was to give it to you and your brother if and when I felt the time was right."

"A letter to us? Why didn't he mail it?"

"Because he lost track of where you were. You see, he had a bad spell shortly after your father died. The flu. A pretty bad case. The experience scared him into reevaluating his holdings and his will. He had originally left everything to your Cousin Claude and to charity. But, as with many men of his age, when he became ill, he started thinking about the rest of his family. He had a detective find you two."

"A detective! He *spied* on us?"

Prinney shook his head. "He wanted to know about you, but not directly. It was his way. He knew, though he didn't tell me until this letter was written, that you and your brother had been left in dire straits financially. He had you watched for a while, then you moved and the detective lost track of you. That's why I had to put an advertisement in the paper asking you to contact me."

"But why—"

"The letter explains it all. I'm not sure I should be giving it to you, but he did leave it to my judgment and I suspect this is the right time. Now I must get back outside to keep an eye on the men cutting down that tree."

Lily took the letter to her room to read it in privacy. The dog followed her and went to sleep in a spot of sunlight. Lily sat down at the dressing table and simply looked at the envelope for a long time, vaguely fearful of what it might contain. From what she'd learned of this virtually unknown uncle, she judged him to be a harsh, blunt man. And now, a sneaky one who had set a detective to spy on her and Robert. He knew they were destitute and made no offer to help—not that they would probably have been convinced to live on his charity. She wasn't sure she wanted to know what he had to say. It might be ugly. The letter might include even more restrictions on them.

She'd gone so far as to open a dressing table drawer to put the letter away, unread, when she realized it would haunt her until she faced up to its contents.

The envelope wasn't sealed. She pulled out two thick, expensive pieces of matching paper and was surprised at the boldness of the handwriting. It was spiky and done with a thick-nibbed pen. The letter was dated in January of 1931, six months or so before Uncle Horatio's death.

For Lily and Robert Brewster,

I'm sure if Elgin Prinney has been able to find you and explain your inheritance, you are wondering why I set things up for you as I did.

There were several reasons. The first was because Lily sent me Christmas cards with pleasant notes included. I was remembered with courtesy. This is a good quality in a young woman.

Second, because when your father left you penniless, I took care to see how you coped with the change in your lives. It appeared from the reports I received that you had both made the best of your limited resources and lack of knowledge of real work. While neither of you were educated to be of any benefit to society or to accomplish anything on your own, you didn't go on the dole. At least, not as far as I know.

Lily had to smile bitterly at this remark. It was so devastatingly true.

She went back to reading.

Thirdly, and most important, you seem to have made no attempt to get in touch with me. Relatives far more distant than you two, and far less needy, suddenly took a quite inappropriate interest in me when the financial tide turned for them. I left a forwarding address with the people in Connecticut who purchased my house there and quite a number of relatives attempted to take advantage of that to seek me out and pretend an interest and affection that they had never evidenced previously. But you two did not do so. You asked nothing of me.

I take this to mean that you have a certain amount of pride and honor, though how you might have come by it, raised in such useless and frivolous luxury, perplexes me. I could be wrong in my secondhand assessment of your more important qualities.

Therefore, I have bequeathed you my home and fortune with the restrictions with which you are already familiar. You will have a home and fuel to keep warm. Elgin Prinney will supervise, quite strictly I hope, any other vital financial needs, such as household necessities and reasonable medical care in case of accident or illness.

But, as you know by now, you must stay in the house, and you must support yourselves. I believe you can and will do this. I hope that you have the integrity, the ambition and the intelligence to become useful and self-supporting. And if you do, it will be a lifelong credit to your inherent good qualities—if, in fact, you have such qualities. I wish you well.

Your uncle, Horatio Brewster

Chapter 20

It was four in the afternoon. Jack was in the news-paper office, pounding out the story of Billy Smith's death on the battered old typewriter he shared with Mr. Kessler. Kessler had apparently, against all the odds, not heard about the murder. Jack had found his boss sitting in his office chair, feet on the desk, smoking a foul stogy and carving away at one of his stupid little animal figures.

"I know all about it, sir," Jack said. "I've been following the police chief and my Cousin Ralph around all day. Heard most of the interviews. I'll write it up."

"And I'll do the revisions," Kessler said. "The paper doesn't come out until Tuesday. Plenty of time to fix up your version."

Fix up my version, Jack thought angrily. *As if it'll need fixing.*

He'd put the two sheets of paper and the carbon (nearly a cobweb with age and overuse) into the typewriter and written:

A TRAGEDY IN VOORBURG

Last night a lifelong Voorburg resident, Billy Smith,

was killed at Grace and Favor Cottage (formerly Honeysuckle Cottage). The police have determined that his death was a murder which took place during the early hours of the evening when the house was almost vacant.

Residents and owners Miss Lily Brewster and Mr. Robert Brewster were at a neighboring home having dinner at the time. Mr. and Mrs. Elgin Prinney, who also reside at the house, were also away visiting friends. The only person in the home at the time was Mrs. Smith, the wife of the victim, who claims she was in her room the entire evening working a jigsaw puzzle and heard nothing alarming or untoward.

Mr. Smith met his demise either from strangulation or from a knife wound. The coroner has not yet determined which.

Jack chewed on his pencil for a moment. The coroner would probably know before the paper went to press. He could alter that sentence and fill in the actual cause of death later.

He went on:

Mr. Billy Smith was a lifelong resident . . .

No, he'd already said that in the first paragraph. He X'ed out the sentence.

Mr. Billy Smith, who is said to have been 34 years old, had been born and raised in Voorburg and married the former Miss Mimi O'Hare approximately ten years ago. Mrs. Smith is currently living at Grace and Favor Cottage as live-in help.

Mr. Smith had a long history of convictions for disorderly conduct . . ."

Could he get away with saying that? It was the truth. And who was there to object?

This paper has formerly noted his many arrests and jail terms. He was known to have made enemies of law enforcement officials and many of the populace.

Jack sat back and considered the last sentence. Just to be sure, he read it out loud in an undertone. Maybe he shouldn't mention law enforcement. That ass Chief Henderson might take it to mean the police were suspects in the murder. Jack X'ed out that section of the sentence. If he wanted to continue to be allowed to trail along with Ralph and eavesdrop, he'd better not offend the chief.

So far, no suspects have been identified, although many people are being questioned as to their whereabouts last Saturday evening. Billy Smith was last seen at Mabel's Cafe, telling a number of people he was going to have a long talk with someone and would be a "rich man before you can say Jack Rob inson." Several patrons heard this comment, but no one saw which way he went when he left the cafe

Jack read back over the piece, preening a bit. What a fool Billy Smith was. Jack hoped this statement would prove it to anyone who was in doubt.

There has been speculation that Billy Smith might have gone to Grace and Favor to see his wife and that a tramp or hobo—of which there are so many in Voorburg lately, owing to the presence of the train lines—might have overheard Smith's remarks about money and followed him.

Jack had worded this carefully. It was his own speculation, but he didn't want to attribute it to himself. If Kessler crossed out anything, it would be this. He didn't like words like 'speculation.'

This publication will continue to assiduously monitor the investigation and report further developments.

Would anybody in town know what "assiduously" meant? Probably not. He substituted 'thoroughly.'

The thing that frustrated him was that by the time the paper came out on Tuesday, everybody in town would already know all about it. Rumor would be rife and it would be old news. His only hope was that something dramatic, like an arrest, would happen late Monday night and he could add a grand finale to the article. If only he worked for a real newspaper. A city newspaper with lots of reporters, lots of contacts and daily publication.

Lily was starting to think she'd never get to finish her conversation with Mr. Prinney about the boat trip that killed Uncle Horatio. When the tree was successfully toppled and the limbs were being cut up for firewood, Mr. Prinney received a phone call saying his sister was ill. Mrs. Prinney made him a quick corned-beef sandwich for his dinner and sent him on his way.

"I hope she's not seriously ill," Lily said, when Mrs. Prinney informed her of the reason for his absence from dinner.

"Lord, no. She's one of those hypo people."

"Hypo people? Hypodermics?"

"No, that other hypo word."

"Hypochondriac?"

"That's it. Imagines herself a fragile little thing. Likes the attention, I suppose. Always complaining that people don't visit her often enough, so she stages these 'spells.' Naturally no one wants to visit her. She makes you take your shoes off to come in the house, if you can imagine. House-proud, that's what she is. Serves tea so sweet it makes your teeth hurt, though God knows how she affords the sugar—"

Mrs. Prinney rattled on a bit about her sister-in-law, not seeming to care much whether Lily responded or not. Finally, she finished up, ". . . and with Elgin gone, there will be extra leftovers for your dog's dinner."

"You and Mr. Prinney don't mind having a dog in the house, do you?" Lily asked belatedly. She should have thought to ask earlier if anyone was allergic or afraid of dogs. Though she couldn't have given the dog up no matter what.

"Lord, no," Mrs. Prinney said. "Elgin and I always had dogs when the girls were at home. It's safer to have a dog. If this dog had been part of the family yesterday and guarding the house while we were gone, who knows how things might have turned out."

They had a nice dinner of corned beef, cabbage and cornbread and a rhubarb cobbler for dessert. Mimi was back on duty, setting the table, serving the food and then sitting down to eat it with them. She was subdued, attending only to her meal, but had stopped looking so dreadfully sad.

Lily gave the dog the leftovers, let her outside for a few minutes and then she and Robert played pachisi at the library table for almost two hours, ending in a score of four wins for Lily and two for Robert.

"I don't know how you do it," Robert said. "You must be cheating."

Lily grinned. "You just don't bother to count ahead and plan. You're a grasshopper."

Mrs. Prinney had sat with them companionably, listening to the radio and darning socks. Mimi said she was tired and excused herself early. The dog had been sleeping through the games across Lily's feet, which soon became uncomfortable for Lily, but she couldn't bear to break the bond of affection.

Finally Lily put the board and markers away and yawned. "I'm going to bed, too. It's been a very long day. Robert, walk me upstairs. I have something to show you."

The dog stretched massively and raced them up the stairs, meeting them at the top landing with a wagging tail. "What have you got to show me?" Robert asked at the door to Lily's room.

She got the envelope with Uncle Horatio's letter and handed it to him.

"What is this?"

"A letter to us from Uncle Horatio."

"You've been communing with the dead? Lily, I didn't think you liked séances and such."

She smiled, but wearily. "Just read the letter. Tell me what you think tomorrow."

She took a quick, cool bath while the dog, big as she was yet barely tall enough to reach over the top of the high tub, drank bathwater. She put on one of her old-life nightgowns with the fancy tucks and lace insets. She gave the dog a last pet. "You must have a name by this time tomorrow," she told the dog, who licked her hand.

Turning off the light, Lily crawled into bed, folded the heavy bedspread at the bottom and pulled up only the light cotton sheet. Would it ever stop being so hot? It was almost September. Surely the heat would break soon.

She fell deeply asleep almost instantly, and woke with horror an hour later when something landed heavily on the bed. She sat up, stifling a scream, and got licked in the face. She cuddled the dog. "I shouldn't let you on the bed, but since you're so nice and clean . . . just for this one night."

When she woke again in the morning, her left arm was sound asleep and she was clinging, pillowless, to the edge of the bed. The dog had her arm pinned down, was taking up most of the bed and had her head on Lily's pillow, snoring peacefully.

Jack was livid.

He'd come into the newspaper office early Sunday morning to reread his article. He found it on his desk in the front room. Mr. Kessler had taken his legendary blue pencil to the piece and massacred it. He'd crossed out all the names in the article except Billy's. Jack stomped around, muttering, then picked up his chair and banged it on the floor in a fit of outrage.

"Who's there?" Kessler demanded from his own office.

"I didn't know you were here," Jack said. Kessler's desk was littered with little shavings of wood. "Why did you do this to my work?" Jack demanded.

"This is a family newspaper, not a scandal sheet. It's enough for people to know Billy Smith's dead and he died in one of the big houses up on the hill. No point in hinting at people's guilt or innocence. And all this stuff about people's alibis is hearsay, not facts. And this paragraph about speculations . . . well!"

Jack ran his hands through his hair, making it stand up like a lion's mane with a very bad permanent wave. "But people want to know what's going on and who it involves."

"People don't have to know everyone else's personal business."

"Dear God! I never thought I'd hear a reputable newspaperman say a thing like that."

Kessler scowled and his face got ugly and pink. "You've heard it now. We deal in facts, not gossip. That's reputable journalism. The Brewster brother and sister have a right to their privacy, even if the crime took place in their home. Unless and until the police determine someone's guilt."

"It isn't gossip to say where a crime took place."

"Nor is it necessary."

"It could be." Jack heard his voice getting shrill and couldn't help it. "What if somebody passing on the road, or walking those paths saw something relevant? If we don't report where the crime took place, a valuable piece of evidence might be lost."

"Our job is to report. Not solve crimes," Kessler said, getting even redder in the face.

"I guess we have different ideas about *that!*"

"And my ideas prevail, boy. Don't you forget it. I'm the big bear and you're just the cub. Keep that in mind if you want to keep your job."

Jack barely managed to refrain from making a vulgar comment, slammed out of Kessler's office, through the outer room and onto the street, where he stood cursing under his breath and attracting frowns from two elderly women who passed him in their full church regalia and caught a few choice words of his soliloquy.

Kessler sat at his desk, shaking his head miserably. Jack was a good kid, but he just didn't know what the situation really was.

And Kessler hoped to God Jack would never find out.

Chapter 21

Lily could hear church bells ringing. It must be Sunday. She had just finished donning suitable church clothes and her favorite white-veiled hat when Robert knocked on her bedroom door. When she opened it, he was flapping around Uncle Horatio's letter.

"The old reprobate! How dare he spy on us! I'm outraged that we didn't know. If I *had* known, I could have really entertained that detective."

He grinned.

Lily had feared for a moment that he really was in his rare angry moods and was relieved. "I've thought about it a lot," she said seriously. "Trying to imagine what I'd have done if I'd been Uncle. And I think it would have been roughly the same thing."

"But why a detective?" Robert asked. "If he knew where we were, why didn't he come see us for himself? Didn't he trust his own judgment?"

"I think he didn't want to attract our attention. If we'd remembered him, and known he was rich, we might have just been among the hordes of other relatives asking for money."

"No. We wouldn't," Robert said.

Lily gave him a quick hug and said, "You're right. We wouldn't have. It would have been too humiliating. Working at the loathsome bank was bad enough. Begging a rich uncle for a handout would have been infinitely worse. Robert, are you wearing that to church?"

Robert was in an old pair of baggy gray trousers and a slightly dingy white shirt that Lily had hand-washed for him more times than she cared to remember.

"We're going to church?"

"I think we should."

"Okeydokey, kiddo. Give me a second to change. Lily, did you ever sense that we were being watched? He must have gotten a pretty darned good detective."

Lily thought for a moment. "I did. But not by a detective. I thought practically everybody who saw us was either thinking 'poor Brewsters' if they were former friends or 'a deserved comeuppence' from the people in the apartment building and at the bank. We didn't fit in either group. But I want to fit here, Robert. We have to if we're going to be here for the next ten years. That's why we're going to church. Now, go change."

"I guess we're not driving the Duesie?"

Lily smiled. "Why don't you drive Mrs. Prinney in it? Let her do a bit of swanning about escorted by a handsome young man. I'll either get Mimi to show me the path to town or ride with Mr. Prinney."

"I like the idea!"

So did Mrs. Prinney. "Elgin's sisters will be so flummoxed!" she laughed when Lily suggested the plan as she fished her boiled eggs out of the big pot in the kitchen.

"I'll walk to town with Mimi, I think," Lily said.

"She's already at the early service," Mrs. Prinney said. "We better hurry with breakfast."

"Is it those eggs?"

"No, they're for lunch. We're having *sla stamppot*. That's hot lettuce salad."

"Oh," Lily said, unable to think how else to respond. *A hot lettuce salad?*

Mr. and Mrs. Prinney, Robert and Lily ate a hurried breakfast of toast and plum jelly and hot, sweet tea, a remarkably light meal considering Mrs. Prinney's considerable cooking skills. Perhaps, Lily thought, Mrs. Prinney's good Dutch upbringing taught her it wasn't fitting to praise the Lord on a full stomach.

Robert brought the Duesie to the front door and escorted Mrs. Prinney with flourishes, opening the passenger door with a bow. Mrs. Prinney giggled. Mr. Prinney was enjoying the scene, too, and tried the same thing with Lily and his old black Ford. It wasn't quite the same, but Lily thanked him with a proper curtsey before she ducked into the automobile.

The town square was crowded with late service attendees, most on foot, drifting toward the three churches—Dutch Reformed (the largest and oldest), Catholic (the prettiest) and Episcopal (the smallest). Robert parked the Duesie in front of the Dutch church and elegantly disgorged Mrs. Prinney and took her arm, which created quite a stir among her friends. Mr. Prinney and Lily followed along much less ostentatiously and joined them in a pew toward the back.

People were chatting quietly before the service began. Lily looked around, wondering if she'd see any familiar faces. She spotted Mabel from the cafe, sitting by the very back, no doubt in order to leave halfway through to prepare for Sunday diners. There was, of course, no sign of the Winslows or Claude Cook. They'd be firmly, formally seated in the Episcopal church, probably in a pew of their own right up front that might well have the Winslow name on a suitably small brass plaque on the end. She also spotted a man she thought was Mr. Kessler. But she'd met him so briefly that she couldn't be sure.

Mrs. Prinney whispered introductions to some of the ladies sitting near them. There was a mixed reaction. Two of the women smiled and nodded, the third merely gave a curt, resentful nod to Lily and a wary look at Robert who probably appeared to her to be too young and dashing to belong at a church service.

Part of the service was in Dutch, which had just enough words that sounded vaguely German or English for Lily to understand the gist. She let the minister's rich baritone voice wash over her comfortingly, and gave Robert a sharp nudge in the ribs when he started looking sleepy.

When the service was over, they discovered that a lot of socializing went on afterward on the village square. Most of the women were talking rather fast, fretting, no doubt about getting home and putting the final touches on hearty Dutch lunches. The men, however, didn't seem to be in any hurry and a small crowd of them and a cloud of small boys were looking over the Duesenberg, which Robert was all too happy to show off. A few young women, most with babies on their hips, approached Lily shyly and introduced themselves. She wasn't sure if they were especially friendly or simply curious about the new neighbors, but was glad of the amiable reception of her contemporaries. She was invited to a canning get-together on the next Friday and a quilting party held the first Wednesday night of each month and accepted both, giving fair warning that she knew nothing about either, but was eager to learn.

It was a lovely morning and Lily found herself thinking back to the after-church chats in her old life. Invitations extended there were usually for polo matches, house parties at Newport and dinners at Sardi's.

The hot lettuce salad turned out, to Lily's great surprise, to be a remarkably good, hearty meal Boiled eggs, boiled potatoes, lots of celery, cucumber and onion slices mixed with lettuce and finished with a hot bacon and vinegar dressing. Lily ate rather quickly, determined not to let Mr. Prinney get away from her again. They hadn't finished discussing the other people on the boat with Uncle Horatio.

She was certain their uncle's death and Billy's were closely connected. Though Mimi had said that Billy was just showing off, claiming he'd seen something suspicious on the boat that could provide a blackmail victim, Lily had come to believe it was quite likely true. Billy had been a fixture in Voorburg all his life and had probably seriously upset a lot of people with his criminal activities and ugly nature. But nobody had gone so far as to kill him until he started mouthing off about knowing something that endangered someone on Uncle Horatio's boat.

Elgin Prinney was eager to get the interrupted conversation over with as well. It was a shame that Horatio hadn't made the effort to meet Lily in person, relying instead on secondhand information about her. In a few short days, Elgin had come to have a good deal of respect for the young woman. Had

Horatio known how sensible she was, he might have just turned the estate over to the brother and sister without all this elaborate nonsense of the ten-year residence requirement.

But then, there was Robert to consider. Elgin himself couldn't quite figure out Robert. Could he possibly be as silly and shallow as he seemed to be? Or was it all an act? Robert was certainly likable, and pleasant to have around. And Elgin had thoroughly enjoyed the way Robert had treated Emmaline to a grand entrance at church this morning. But Elgin had a slightly more tolerant view of young people than Horatio did. Had Horatio spent a couple days with Robert, with his breezy attitude and slangy expressions, he might well have failed to even notice Lily.

Oh, well, he thought as he polished off the last of his hot lettuce salad, there was no going back and redoing the past. And having started telling Lily about the guests on the boat, he had obligated himself to provide an honest account of the rest of them as well. Frankly, he didn't believe either murder would ever be solved because the current chief of police was such a complete idiot. But Lily, and by extension, Robert, deserved to know as much as a lot of other people already did about the background.

"Miss Brewster, might I have a bit of your time after luncheon?" he asked.

Lily took Robert aside and said, "Do you want to hear the rest of what Mr. Prinney has to say?"

"I haven't even got the full lowdown on what he's already told you," Robert said. "I'll wait for the summary and translation of the whole thing, if you don't mind. Besides, I think I make Mr. Prinney nervous."

Lily's as yet unnamed dog was patrolling under the dining room table for any piece of food that might have been dropped. Lily gave a low whistle and told the dog to come along.

"I feel like this is one of those continuing movies," Lily said, as she sat down across from Mr. Prinney. "The ones that end with someone in the lion pit and you have to wait until the next week to see how he gets out."

Mr. Prinney smiled slightly. "I'm not quite certain why I'm telling you all this, you know."

"I'm not either," Lily admitted. "But I have a great need to know. What about Major Winslow? He was on the boat, too. Could he have been the person Uncle Horatio was angry with?"

Prinney shook his head. "I wouldn't suppose so. Most unlikely. Your uncle was a very . . . let us say 'restrained' individual. But if such a man can have a 'best friend,' Winslow was his."

"That's hard to imagine," Lily said.

"You don't like him?"

"He's a—a pontificator. Always making pronouncements instead of conversation."

"Much like your uncle. That may have been why they got along so well," Prinney said. "They were both highly successful men and appeared to hold similar opinions on property. Later on, I'll start going over all the properties with you. Your uncle was in various partnerships with a number of other wealthy men, but he always insisted on being the majority owner. With Major Winslow, he didn't always follow that rule. I think that indicated a great trust on his part."

"But all the worse if Major Winslow had done something he didn't like."

"That might be true, except that after the Crash, they had far fewer dealings with property. Your uncle felt it was the best time to invest in land and buildings. So many of them were going so extraordinarily cheaply due to the owners' misfortunes."

Lily considered whether to pass this information along to Robert. She didn't care for the theory of shortchanging people who were in bad circumstances. "Major Winslow didn't agree?"

"Apparently not. I'm not in his confidence, of course, so I don't know if he found the practice distasteful on moral grounds or whether he just felt it was a good time to hang onto what he had and not go into more speculative investments with partners until the economy of the nation improved. If it ever will."

Lily was tempted to pursue this question. She'd been vaguely wondering if, after serving their ten years at Grace and Favor, they'd find that neither the house nor the other investments would be worth anything at all. If Charles Locke was right about the necessity of a new Democratic administration and it didn't happen, she might be wearing a babushka and learning Russian in ten years.

But this wasn't the time to discuss that. Nor would Mr. Prinney be likely to have a helpful opinion.

"What about Cousin Claude?" she asked.

Mr. Prinney leaned back in his chair and sighed. "Your cousin . . ." he said, clearing his throat. "Your cousin is not someone I enjoy talking about. He had visited often over the years after your uncle moved here. And presumably before that as well."

"You don't like Claude, do you?" Lily said bluntly.

Mr. Prinney thought for a moment. "No, I have to admit I don't. But I try to be fair. Though I don't know him well, he's basically a rather stupid man, and a greedy one."

"That sounds like a fair assessment to me," Lily said with a smile.

"He must have his good points. I just never observed them. I think your uncle was flattered by his attentions. Mr. Cooke would come for weekends and ask your uncle's advice on stocks. Horatio liked being the font of knowledge for an aggressive young relative he imagined could follow in his footsteps. At least, that was my impression. I could have been quite wrong. But Horatio gave him good advice, which Mr. Cooke faithfully followed. Until just before the Crash. I told you that Horatio had advised me to get out of the stock market, which I did. He must have similarly advised Mr. Cooke."

"And Claude didn't agree?"

Prinney shook his head. "Mr. Cooke seemed to have forgotten that Horatio had always been right before. They had a falling-out. I wouldn't have known except that Horatio was so angry that he made several offhand remarks that were suddenly quite critical of Mr. Cooke."

"Did Claude lose his money?"

"Most of it, your uncle told me."

"So Claude became one of the needy relatives."

"He did. He continued to visit, acting very penitent. But once Horatio had turned his face away from someone, he never looked back."

"Just like with his Aunt Flora," Lily said.

"Precisely. He remained fairly cordial to Mr. Cooke, but informed me that he wanted to expunge him from his will. That's when he started investigating you and your brother."

"Does Claude know this?"

"I very much doubt it. In fact, after Horatio's funeral, Mr. Cooke came to see me a mere hour later to inquire about the will. I had to tell him he was not named in the will as a primary beneficiary and that I couldn't reveal the contents until I found the heirs."

Lily laughed. "You must have enjoyed that."

Mr. Prinney smiled, somewhat shamefaced. "Of course, the will was public record, so I'm sure he found out the truth soon enough."

Lily suddenly thought back to the dinner at the Winslows'. Mrs. Winslow had said that Sissy was engaged to Claude and Sissy pooh-poohed the idea. Claude was obviously the one pushing along the idea in the hopes of marrying into the Winslow money.

"So Claude is a good possibility as First Murderer," Lily said. "In spite of everything we both know about him, I find that a little hard to believe."

"So do I," Mr. Prinney admitted. "He's not a man of courage and it takes a certain sort of rash courage for a law-abiding person to decide to kill for what he wants."

"Who, then, does that leave us with?"

"Mr. Kessler," Prinney said. "And me, of course."

Chapter 22

"Mr. Kessler," Lily said. "I'd forgotten him. He publishes the local newspaper. Why would he have been invited along?"

"He's the editor. Not the publisher."

Lily looked at him questioningly. "What's the difference?"

"The editor is an employee. The publisher is the owner," Mr. Prinney said. "The publisher puts up the money, pays the bills and takes the profit or loss."

"And who is the publisher?"

Mr. Prinney folded his hands on his desk and said, mournfully, "Me, in a sense. On behalf of Horatio's estate. And someday you and your brother. That's if the paper survives, which is unlikely."

"Why?"

"Oh, a number of reasons. Kessler just hasn't got a feel for what people want to read about. He's too conservative. Not politically, just personally. Afraid of offending anybody."

"How did he get the job?"

"Your uncle bought the paper from a man who was both editor and publisher and had gotten a much better job in New York City. Deservedly so. He was good. People used to actually line up outside the office on the two mornings the paper was published to get an early copy. Horatio enjoyed the paper as well as anyone. It made him feel, he said, as if he knew the neighbors. So he found himself with a thriving newspaper, but no editor. I'm not privy to how he found Kessler or Kessler found him, but Kessler presented a fine proposal. He'd been a college professor of journalism, had lots of fresh ideas, excellent recommendations."

"What happened then? I've only seen articles from one issue. Is it not any good under his guidance?"

"It seems Kessler was a firebrand in theory, but a marshmallow in reality. The responsibility of actually deciding what went in the paper seemed to scare the stuffing out of him. The paper's just gotten duller and duller. People can hardly afford to subscribe to any local paper anyway, and when it's not interesting besides, well—"

"Does Jack Summer know this? About the legal ownership, I mean?"

"I hope not. It's none of his business or anyone else's in town. Horatio didn't want to be known as the owner of the paper. He was worried that people would think he was using his power and money to his own purposes. He preferred to keep behind the scenes in many of his financial dealings. And in this case, he simply felt that the community needed and deserved a good twice-a-week paper to keep them informed. Had he not purchased the paper, it would have ceased to exist."

"The previous owner would have abandoned his investment?"

Prinney nodded. "As I said, he was fortunate enough to get a very good job elsewhere."

"So the paper is really losing money?" Lily asked.

"A great deal, I'm afraid. The paper, ink and type-setting are still expensive. There's Mr. Kessler's salary, Jack Summer's salary and three delivery boys, one of whom only has seventeen subscriptions left on his route. It's making about half what it costs to produce."

"What do you propose to do with it?" Lily said.

"I was rather hoping you might have a suggestion, since you have a concern with this, too."

"Me? I wouldn't have any idea. This Mr. Kessler..." Lily thought for a moment. "Is Kessler a man capable of murder?"

"I shouldn't think so, Lily—er, Miss Brewster."

"I'd rather you'd call me Lily."

"Very well. I think the only person I've met in my life that I believed to be capable of killing another person for gain was Billy Smith. And he's the one who was killed. In my profession you get to know greedy people and selfish ones who don't mind who gets hurt or financially embarrassed, but in my experience normal human beings simply don't murder each other for reasons other than war or self-defense."

"Did Mr. Kessler know that Uncle Horatio was unhappy about the situation?"

"I'm certain he did. Your uncle didn't mince words. He was a private man, but not a shy one."

Lily pondered for a moment, pleating the folds of her skirt between her fingers. "Suppose..." she said, "that what Uncle Horatio intended to tell the group aboard the boat was that he was firing Mr. Kessler and wanted the others to help him find a good editor?"

Mr. Prinney shook his head. "No, he wouldn't

have needed a witness for that, and he said that was his purpose in inviting me along."

"That's right. I'd forgotten for a moment. But Mr. Kessler wouldn't have known that. Imagine if he'd feared that was going to happen and couldn't face the humiliation? Could he have killed Uncle to keep from being fired? In hopes that the heir or heirs wouldn't know for a while how awful the paper was and he could find another job?"

Mr. Prinney cocked an eyebrow. "The possibility seems rather remote."

"I guess so. Is there any way of helping him find another job instead of just leaving another person without work?"

"I don't know. The only thing he's good at is that whittling he does. Not much market for that, you know."

"Whittling?" Lily almost laughed.

"Does these little wooden figures. Animals and children and such. Clever, really. They just look like lumps of wood at first glance. Real rough. But you look again and it's like a figure sort of jumps out of the wood. Quite startling. Mrs. Prinney likes them and he's given her a few."

"Oh, I know what you mean. She has some on the kitchen windowsill. They are quite wonderful. I appreciate your having been so frank with me about the men on the boat with Uncle Horatio."

"It's probably useless information. But eventually you may have to have dealings with some of them. Your cousin, perhaps, and certainly Mr. Kessler. It might help you to know in advance what sort of people you're dealing with. In fact, Fred Eggers, the seasick man who was Horatio's stockbroker until Horatio pulled out of the market, has been nagging me with notes every week asking if he could come up here and talk to you and your brother about investments. He probably has no idea of the conditions of the will and sees you two as impressionable young people who would be happy for his advice."

"I'm happy for *your* advice," Lily said, "and need no more at this point." She stood, almost stepping on the dog, who had been sleeping quietly at her feet. "Thank you again for your explanations. Do you think there's any possibility of Chief Henderson accidentally coming to discover who killed Billy? Or even Uncle Horatio?"

"I wouldn't count on it."

"Well, we have to count on *someone* figuring it out," Lily said. "Otherwise, Robert and I remain suspects and a murderer is free to go his own way and possibly kill someone else."

She found Robert sitting on the bench at the far end of the lawn. He had the telescope and was studying something on the river below. "I've had that talk with Mr. Prinney about the people on the boat when Uncle Horatio died," she said, sitting down beside him.

"Speaking of boats and their passengers, take a look at the platinum blonde on the boat down there," he said, handing her the telescope.

Lily's telescoped and bobbing gaze wandered all over the landscape before locating the boat. It was a sailing yacht and a girl was standing at the front end (*Is that pointy part called the bow?* she wondered), posing as if she were the figurehead. "So?" Lily asked.

"So she looks good to me," Robert said with a leer.

"Oh, Robert!" Lily said, giving back the telescope.

"What did Mr. Prinney have to say?" he said, giving the girl yet another longing look before the yacht below them passed behind some woods and disappeared from view.

Lily recounted both the first and second conversations.

"So Uncle and that bastard Winslow were chums?" Robert said.

"It seems so. They did a lot of business together. Mr. Prinney said they were much alike."

"That doesn't surprise me," Robert said. "So Prinney thinks Winslows' out of the running? What a pity. I'd have loved to have a reason to pin it on him."

"Mr. Prinney did say that in the past couple years they hadn't done as much together, but suggested that it might have been over slightly differing theories of investing in land now that things are so bad. But there hadn't been any outright tiff between them."

"Differing theories? Why are you fidgeting like that, Lily?"

"Fidgeting? I never fidget! Oh, all right. He said Uncle Horatio had been buying up land that had been abandoned by those who lost their money and that Major Winslow might not have liked the idea."

"He's exactly the sort to love that idea."

"Mr. Prinney didn't claim this was true, simply that it was one explanation."

"Okay, let me get this straight. According to Mr. Prinney, and with no knowledge on our part, he says Mr. Winningham—that's the incompetent banker from New York City, right?—Winningham is out of the running because he's physically too feeble."

Robert raised a finger of his left hand. "And Fred Eggers is out because he wasn't even invited along and was violently seasick the entire time."

"Right," Lily said.

Robert raised another finger. "Jonathan Winslow, the next-door neighbor, is out because Uncle Horatio and he were bosom friends with a lot of mutually profitable property and attitudes." Robert raised a third finger.

"I presume Mimi is out, or Mr. Prinney wouldn't have hired her to work in the house if he'd thought she was a murderer."

"Mimi! You can't even consider Mimi," Lily said.

"Why? Because she's a woman? Lily, think about it. She's strong as a horse. You've seen her beating the stuffing out of those rugs and hauling tons of laundry up and down the stairs. She could easily have coshed Uncle. And she thought for quite a few years that she was Uncle's illegitimate child and might inherit."

"But she got over that," Lily objected.

"So she says. But even if she did, Uncle Horatio's death gave her what she wanted. She got away from Billy and the Dreadful Aunts, got to go back to living in what she'd always considered her home, even if it was as a maid, not the owner. She likes her job, it seems. She cleans stuff that doesn't even need cleaning, just for the joy of it. And now she's rid of a husband who made her life a misery as well. And don't forget the matter of the missing ten-dollar bill."

"Robert, I don't like this. And I still maintain that if Mr. Prinney would hire her to work in the house, he must trust her entirely to be innocent of any wrongdoing."

"But that's Mr. Prinney's view, Lily. It's good of him to share what he knows and thinks of these people, but it doesn't mean he's right about all of them. We have to eliminate Billy, too, since it's unlikely he killed Uncle and someone killed Billy for revenge. Uncle wasn't all that well-liked. I can't imagine his death causing such passion." He raised one finger of his right hand. "Then there's Cousin Claude, whom we do know and dislike and Mr. Prinney feels the same way."

"He said Claude was both stupid and greedy. And probably expected to be Uncle Horatio's heir."

Robert raised another finger on his right hand. "So we have Mimi and Claude to consider, as well as the newspaper editor, who was about to be out of work." Another finger of the right hand went up.

"But Mr. Prinney said—"

"Enough of Mr. Prinney for the moment," Robert said. "In these days a middle-aged man with a job has to hang onto it for dear life. Especially if he has a family. Does he have a wife and children to support?"

"I didn't think to ask," Lily said.

"We know *we* didn't commit either murder, so that eliminates seven people from consideration, with three still in the running—Mimi, Claude and the newspaper editor—and leaves only one more to consider."

"Who?"

"Mr. Prinney himself."

"Robert!"

"Lily, think about it. Almost everything we know about most of these people comes from him. But he was on the boat, too, and he and Mrs. Prinney came home from dinner before we did the night Billy was killed."

"But they went straight upstairs and not to the kitchen."

"I repeat—according to him. And Mrs. Prinney might either be lying on his behalf or she fell straight to sleep and didn't know he went back downstairs."

"And you claim that I'm the most cynical! I would never consider Mr. Prinney as a murderer."

"But you have to, Lily. Horatio's death solved his problems, too. He and his wife managed to unload their house and live at Grace and Favor. And he gets to handle all Uncle's considerable fortune without asking anyone."

"I refuse absolutely to listen to more of this," Lily said, springing to her feet.

"But you have to think about it," Robert said calmly. "You're the one who reads the murder mysteries and fancies yourself quite a sleuth."

"Come, dog," Lily said sharply, marching hard on her heels back to the house.

The dog ambled along behind obediently, but stopped at the bench for a pet from Robert.

"I sure rattled her cage, didn't I," Robert said with a grin.

Chapter 23

Lily was furious.

How dare Robert accuse Mimi and Mr. Prinney of being killers and Mrs. Prinney of covering up a murder. Okay, not *accuse* exactly. Just suggest the possibility. That was bad enough. Yes, his arguments about their motives were as good as the other motives they'd talked about. But it was impossible.

Or was it?

Rats! Now that Robert had put this treason in her head, she couldn't help but consider it. But not for long. All silly motives aside, Lily was convinced that Mimi, Mr. Prinney and his wife were all thoroughly good people. Yes, she'd thought for a while that Mimi might have taken her scarf and the ten-dollar bill, but the scarf accusation had been dismissed by the fact that Lily had left it at the Winslows' and Sissy had brought it back to Grace and Favor. And Lily had come to think she had simply carelessly lost the money. It wasn't like her to lose something so important, but it had to be what happened. She was ashamed of herself now for having the least suspicion of Mimi.

Lily went to her room, sat down on the bed and

patted the bedclothes, indicating that the dog could come take a nap with her. The dog sprawled out beside her and Lily said, "We have to figure this out. We can be Agatha Christie." She stopped and thought. "Agatha. You look like an Agatha. Would you like that as a name?"

The dog licked her chin and thumped its tail.

"So, Agatha, who committed these murders? It's inconceivable that two people among the suspects could be killers. Billy was the best suspect—until somebody killed him as well. It had to have been the same person."

Agatha had taken up most of the bed. Lily eased herself around the dog and closed her eyes, determined that concentration and common sense would tell her the answer if she just thought very hard about everything she knew. But as her anger at Robert faded—she knew Robert too well to really believe he meant his suspicions, he was just making fun of her—she felt her eyes growing heavy and fell sound asleep.

When she woke, there was something niggling at the back of her mind. It must have been something she dreamed, but she couldn't quite pull it out of the dream part of her mind. It had struck her as important. But then, she'd once woken in the middle of the night with a Great Revelation from a dream and wrote it down on the notepad on the night table so she wouldn't forget. In the morning she read the note, which said: *Cats don't wear clothes.*

She went downstairs and found the house seemingly deserted. Everybody else must have been napping as well on this hot, lazy summer afternoon. She finally found Robert, who'd taken a blanket out to sleep in the shade behind the kitchen. "Robert, what are we to do about Mr. Kessler?"

"Jeepers, Lily! You scared me to death. We? Why must we do anything about him?"

"I told you. The newspaper is losing money. Our money."

"It's up to Mr. Prinney."

"But he doesn't know what to do either. I have sort of an idea. Would you like to use one of our few days we're allowed to be away to go to the City tomorrow?"

At that, Robert finally opened his eyes and sat up. "I'd love to! Gotta catch up with the chaps at the club. Can't go in anymore unless someone takes me as a guest, but I can waylay someone at the doorway. Let's go early. I might be able to work in a champagne brunch *and* luncheon at someone else's expense. I've got to find something decent to wear." He leaped up and headed for the house.

"Aren't you going to ask me what my idea *is?*" Lily called after him.

"No need. I'm sure it's great."

"I'm afraid we're on our own for dinner," Mr. Prinney said later. "My wife is having one of her headaches."

"I'm sorry to hear that," Lily said. "Is there anything I can do to help her?"

"No. She gets one every year or so and it lasts about a day and a half. She can't even stand up. Mimi's looking after her."

"Robert and I are going to the City tomorrow. I think I might have a solution to one of our problems. But I can't talk about it until I see an old friend."

Early the next morning, Lily tapped lightly at Mrs.

Prinney's bedroom door. Mimi opened it and Lily said, "How is Mrs. Prinney doing?"

"She's feeling real bad, Miss Lily. Poor thing."

"Do you think you could ask her one question for me? I want to borrow her little wooden figures on the kitchen windowsill for the day."

Mimi disappeared for a moment and Lily could hear Mrs. Prinney's weak voice saying fretfully, "Yes, yes, I don't care."

Lily and Robert took the eight o'clock train. Robert could hardly hold still, he was so excited about getting back to town. He had the train schedule in hand and kept marking off each station as they passed along the river. This time Lily made a point of watching for Bannerman's Island. It was a slightly closer view, but an extraordinarily fast one and didn't inspire her with any new ideas. When they got to Grand Central Station, Lily said, "You must be back here at three, Robert. I don't want to go back with the rush-hour crowd."

He bounced off, and Lily took her time. The streets were just as hot as she remembered and seemed incredibly dirty after only a few days in the country. There were distinguished-looking men selling apples on the street corners, which broke her heart. Thank God she and Robert had escaped. Then she recognized one of the apple sellers. He was her high school history teacher. He'd always been so prim and exacting and well-dressed. She greeted him by name.

"Miss Brewster, I hope you're well," he said with obvious embarrassment. "Or are you Mrs. Somebody now?"

"No, I'm not married. But I would like an apple, please."

She gave him one of her precious quarters and

refused the change. His expression grew angry. "I'm not on the dole, Miss Brewster." He slapped two dimes into her hand and turned his back on her.

Lily was offended, but as she walked away, she realized she'd committed a faux pas that deserved censure. She wouldn't have appreciated pity and charity. Neither did her old teacher. It was probably the last lesson he'd give her and it was a good one.

She continued up to Fiftieth Street, where an old friend had a gallery. The friend, who was named Jimmy Anderson, but called himself the Duke of Albania, greeted her effusively.

"My darling, darling Lily!" He grabbed her by both arms and bestowed elaborate air kisses. "What on earth brings you here? I heard you and Robert moved to the wilderness somewhere upstate. Oh, do come back to my office and we'll gossip ourselves to death."

"Is that a real Picasso?" Lily said, following along.

"As real as they come. Hate it myself. But I'll make a king's ransom on it."

Jimmy's private office at the back of the gallery was done up like a seraglio. Gauzy fabric swagged up on the walls, overlapping Oriental rugs, outrageous pictures of half-naked (and in several cases entirely naked) men on the walls. A harpsichord sat in the corner and a dim light came in the back window, illuminating the room pinkly through the swathes of filmy maroon curtains covering it.

"You're doing rather well, Jimmy," Lily said, sitting down on a very low silk-covered divan that nearly swallowed her up.

Jimmy nodded. "It's surprising how many people still have money and are just dying to spend it to prove they have good taste in art. They don't, of course, but I tell them what's good and what's not

and they shell out lovely amounts of hard cash. It's
the title, you know. Best trick in the book. Are you
here for a touch? I could spare you a bit."

"No, no. Not at all. But I wouldn't mind if you
gave me a very good lunch. I've come to show you
something." She fished in her large purse and pulled
out Mrs. Prinney's four wooden figures.

"Lumps of wood? How very quaint," Jimmy said
with his best fake Albanian accent.

"Look again."

Jimmy took one of the figures and his eyes wid-
ened. "Why, it's not a lump, it's a what-do-you-call-
it."

"A raccoon."

"Give me the others. Oh, oh! These are delightful.
Such a clever trick and so exquisitely deceptive.
Primitive, yet sophisticated." He'd dropped the ac-
cent. "Where the hell did you get these, Lily?"

"They're made by a man in Voorburg-on-
Hudson."

"Voorburg-on-Hudson," Jimmy groaned. "How
utterly rural. Has he an exclusive contract on them?"

"I don't think he has any contract. He gives them
away to friends."

"Holy God in heaven! Say it isn't true, darling!
Too, too good for words! Tell me his name. I'll rush
to see him."

"I think not. I'm acting as his agent. He'll get
seventy-five percent of the sale price."

"Lily, you've turned into a greedy bitch," Jimmy
said with a giggle. "I never pay that. No more than
twenty-five percent."

"Fifty-five percent. Not a cent less. And I'll come
to town at intervals to check your prices."

Jimmy clasped his long-fingered hands under his

chin. "I do love powerful women. Fifty-five percent."

"Done," Lily said.

"When can you have a dozen of them? I'll come fetch them."

"No, you won't. I don't want you talking to the artist."

"A man of mystery?"

"More than you'll ever guess." She was tempted to tell him that the artist might well turn out to be a murderer and have plenty of time in Sing Sing to produce his work, but resisted the impulse. "Now, Jimmy, where are you taking me to lunch? I'm starving."

Robert shrieked with laughter when they met at the train station and she told him what she'd done. "Good old Jimmy. I didn't think anyone could beat him at his own game. But will Kessler go along with it?"

"He's going to have to. He obviously likes making the figures more than he likes being a newspaper editor. And he's much better with wood than words. He can just whittle his heart out. Wherever he might end up."

"So we have Mr. Prinney close down the paper and quit losing money on it?"

"That's something I wanted to talk to you about. Mr. Prinney wants to keep the paper. And I think it's good for the town to have one. These are hard times for everyone and a really entertaining, informative paper is a good thing."

"How do you get an editor then? Neither we nor Mr. Prinney knows anything about finding one."

"I thought we could give Jack Summer a chance at it first. If he's no good, we'll have to figure out something else."

"Dear God, Lily. You're turning into Lady Bountiful."

"I am, aren't I?" she said smugly. "But I wish I could turn into Agatha Christie instead and get the murders solved. Oh, and I've named the dog Agatha."

"Agatha! Are you mad? That's a terrible name."

"Don't say so at Grace and Favor. I think one of the Prinneys' daughters is named Agatha."

"Oh! Well, a good enough name for a girl, but a dog . . . ?"

Lily put the wooden figures back on the windowsill when they got home and went to check on Mrs. Prinney. Mimi claimed she was recovering, but still too shaky on her pins to get out of bed. "And she even made a grocery list. I'd walk to town, but she needs me here."

"I'll go. Robert can drive me. Give me the list."

The list came with a twenty-dollar bill. She hunted down Robert and before doing their shopping, she asked him to stop at Mr. Prinney's office in town. Prinney was thrilled with the solution to the Kessler problem.

"You'll have to see if he's agreeable, of course," Prinney added. "He'd be a fool not to be."

"Shouldn't you talk to him?"

Prinney shook his head. "No, it's your excellent idea and your friend in the city. I trust you to handle it well."

"Isn't she a wonder?" Robert said proudly.

"She is indeed," Mr. Prinney said.

Shops were closing and Lily had to rush from the greengrocer to the butcher to the bakery to get everything Mrs. Prinney had asked for. She felt duty-bound to get receipts as well, so there was no question where the money had gone. As they drove back up the hill, Lily checked the receipts and counted up her change.

"Robert!" she suddenly said. "This is *my* ten-dollar bill in the change."

"Lily, don't be daft. All bills look alike."

"Not this one. Pull over. Look."

Robert stopped the car. "It's been folded like a tiny fan."

"I did that. I really did. When we were coming up on the train the day we moved here. I was so nervous and upset and I folded it that way when I'd finished double-checking how much money we had left. And look, Robert, there's the same grease spot on the corner."

"So you lost it in town and somebody found it and used it. You can't blame anyone for that."

"Or somebody stole it and used it. Go back. I want to find out who spent this money."

"The shops are closed by now, Lily. We'll go back tomorrow."

"We certainly will!" Maybe she couldn't solve a double murder, but Lily was determined to solve the ten-dollar bill mystery.

Chapter 24

By the next morning, Mrs. Prinney had recovered, though she was still pale and wan, and Mimi was free to show Lily the shortcut path to town. "Just don't take no turnings. Keep going straight as you can. Worst that can happen is that you come out at the icehouse instead of behind the church. Wear stout shoes."

The path was very steep, but wider and more used than the paths behind Grace and Favor. Someone had even put in some rudimentary stone steps in some of the most hazardous spots. Lily was surprised at how quickly she found herself in town. Sooner than she wanted, really. The shops weren't even open yet.

While she waited, she went to the newspaper office. Jack Summer was in the outer room, banging away at a beat-up typewriter. "Hello, Miss Brewster," he said cheerfully. "What can I do for you?"

"I came to see Mr. Kessler. Is he in?"

"Oh? Why do you want to see him?"

Lily gave him a long, blank look.

Jack grew a bit red in the face at her reaction to

his question and scowled. "In his own office." He
jerked a thumb at the door.

Lily tapped on it and Kessler called out, "Enter."
His office was a mess. Papers everywhere, newspapers and ordinary sheets with scribbled notes. The
file cabinets were so stuffed that they wouldn't entirely close. The windows were grimy, the paint on
the walls was water-stained and there were scratches
on the second- or thirdhand furniture. The floor was
littered with wood chips and on the one clean surface, a shelf behind the desk, was a good dozen of
his wooden figures.

"Miss Brewster, I believe."

"Mr. Kessler. I'm here on behalf of my brother,
myself and Mr. Prinney who is managing Uncle
Horatio's estate. I'd like to have a private talk with
you."

Kessler put down the figure he was carving. "I
guess you know, then, who owns the newspaper."

"I do." Thinking of Jack in the next room, possibly
with his ear against the door, she added, "Could we
take a stroll? Perhaps sit at the bandstand in the
square?"

Kessler nodded, looking grim, as if he knew he
was about to get his walking papers.

"I'm showing Miss Brewster around town," Kessler said to Jack, who was just sitting back down at
his typing desk as they came out of the back office.

They strolled across the grass to the bandstand
and sat in the shade.

"You're going to fire me, aren't you?" Kessler
said.

"I'm afraid so," Lily replied. "But I'm also going
to tell you something you'll like, I hope. I'm afraid
I've interfered in your life a little. Yesterday I borrowed some of your carved works from Mrs. Prin-

ney and went to an art dealer in New York City with them."

"Why?"

"Because they're very good. The art dealer agreed."

Kessler gawked at her. "You don't say! They're just a hobby."

"They can be more than a hobby, if you're willing. He wants to try selling a dozen of them. And I'm sure he'll want more. If he thinks something will sell, he's always right and he sells at very high prices. You can make a better living than you're making now. I also offered to act as your agent for selling them to him. He'll pay you fifty-five percent what he's selling them for and I'll take five percent for protecting you from him. You don't need to accept my offer, but . . ."

"But you don't think I know how to make money. I sure haven't with the newspaper. I just don't know where I went wrong."

"It doesn't matter anymore. You're fired from the newspaper," she added with a smile. "You have a new business now. If you want it."

Kessler nearly got teary. "I don't know how to thank you."

"I do," Lily said. "I want you to tell me about the boat trip our uncle died on."

Kessler's face seemed to shut down. "I don't know anything but what I printed in the paper. I can give you a copy."

"I've read your report. It only gave names. I want to know what you saw and thought."

Kessler fished around in his pocket, got out his penknife and opened and shut it a few times while he composed his thoughts. "All right. You did me a good turn. I guess I owe you one. We were going around the island, taking a look at all of it before docking. The storm came up out of nowhere—this huge, black cloud came over Storm King Mountain like a freight train. We were just coming down-stream along that west side that's so sheer when the rain started coming down in buckets. There was an awful wind and it raised terrific waves. The boat started bucking and scraping against the wall of rock. I saw Mr. Brewster heading for the cabin. I even took his arm and said, 'Get in the dinghy be-fore we sink.' And he just shrugged me off. Said he had to get something."

"Did he say what it was?"

"No, he'd gotten away from me before I could ask. And I wasn't in the mood to stand around arguing. By then it seemed we'd turned east and there was a terrific tearing, ripping sound below. I thought I could see one of those guard towers in front of us, but I couldn't be sure. I wanted on the dinghy before the boat went down."

"Did you see anyone follow Uncle Horatio?"

Kessler opened and shut the penknife again and nodded. "But I couldn't tell who it was. Just a dark shape behind the torrent of rain."

"Could it have been Billy Smith?"

He shook his head. "No. He was a little scrawny thing. This was a big shape. But nothing more than a shape."

"You didn't even have an impression of who it might have been?" Lily asked.

"I had an 'impression,' as you say, but nothing whatsoever to back it up. And I'm not going to ruin someone's life by giving you a name."

Lily thought for a moment. "If I were to give you a name, would you confirm it?"

"Maybe."

"Then when I have one, we'll give it a try."

They sat in uneasy silence for a while. Kessler finally said, "Who are you going to get to replace me at the paper?"

"I was thinking of letting Jack Summer try it."

She expected him to object, but to her surprise, he said, "He might do it well with a little reining in. You'll have to see to that. You or Mr. Prinney. If I were you, I'd insist on seeing drafts of what he's planning to print. He tends to want to liven up articles with his own opinions. He could get himself—and you—in trouble with that. When do you want me to leave?"

"I hadn't even thought about it. Tomorrow is the next paper, right? Let's talk to Jack first, then you can get in an announcement that you're taking a new job and the paper's getting a new editor—if he takes the job. Can you find a front-page spot for it?"

"Only if I move the garden club minutes to the back," Kessler said with a grin.

Lily went to the greengrocer first with her fan-folded ten-dollar bill. He claimed to have never seen it before. She went next to the bakery. The clerk there said they hadn't had to make change for anything over a ten for months. But the butcher recognized it. "I thought when I cleaned out the cash drawer Saturday night that it had sure had a hard life, that bill. Somebody had folded it into a fan sort of shape and creased it real tight."

"Who gave it to you?"

"Oh, lady, I have no idea. We were busy Saturday. I'm not even sure I took it myself. Might have been the boy who sweeps up and waits on customers when we have a rush of them."

"Would you try to think about who was in on

Saturday and let me know? It's really more important than it might seem, but I can't explain it right now."

"Dunno, miss, but I'll give it a try. Maybe my helper will know. I'll ask him when he gets in."

Lily hoped he'd remember, but thought it unlikely. She walked back up the hill, making a few stops to get her breath. It was a lot harder getting up the hill than down. She'd have to remember that.

When she finally crossed the road to Grace and Favor, Mr. Prinney was strolling around the front yard aimlessly. He spotted her and rushed to meet her. "How did your conversation with Mr. Kessler work out?"

Lily repeated it and Prinney nodded contentedly. "I was more worried than I cared to admit. And did you talk to Jack Summer as well?"

"I did. Mr. Kessler and I told him who owned the paper—I fudged a bit and told Kessler that you were 'managing' the estate, not that you were wholly in charge, so that's what he told Jack."

"Very wise. Nobody needs to know the exact details of the unusual situation here unless they're willing to take the trouble to go hunt down Horatio's will in the county courthouse. How did Jack take the news?"

"He was obviously surprised to learn that Mr. Kessler didn't own the paper, but we slipped by that. Mr. Kessler told him about how he had a new job which he anticipated enjoying a great deal more. Jack looked downright stricken for a moment. I guess fearing the newspaper was going to shut down and he'd be out of work. So I told him immediately that we were offering him the job under certain conditions on a trial basis."

"And . . . ?"

"He didn't like the conditions. Having to submit the articles to us first."

"He turned down the job?"

"No. Mr. Kessler went into his professorial mode and explained that the owner of the paper was entitled to set the tone of the paper since it was the owner who paid the bills."

"Rather silly of him," Mr. Prinney said. "Especially as that was exactly why Horatio was contemplating firing him."

Lily smiled. "He also jabbed at Jack that he wasn't supposed to give his own opinions of news stories. Jack took it like a man. I told him that the requirement wouldn't last forever. Just for a couple months until we were sure he was doing the job as we wanted it done. Then he agreed, but wanted a specific time limit set. I said I'd consult with you."

Mr. Prinney let out a sigh. "I'm relieved. We'll see how he does."

Mrs. Prinney came to the front door just then. "Oh, there you two are. Lily, you had a phone call from the butcher, but I told him I didn't think you were home yet."

"The butcher! Good. I'll call him right back. You're feeling better?"

"I'm fine now," Mrs. Prinney said. "When the headache stops, I perk right up."

Lily ran inside and called back from the only phone in the house in the front hall, telling the telephone girl she needed to speak to the proprietor of the butcher shop.

"Yes, ma'am. I'll put you through. You know he's got a nickel off on rump roasts today."

Lily grinned. "No, I didn't know. Thanks."

When she was put through to the butcher's shop, the man she'd spoken to earlier said, "I asked my helper about that bill. He said it was Miss Winslow who used it."

"Sissy Winslow? Was he sure?"

"Yes, he's got a bit of a crush on her and noticed for sure."

Lily thanked him and hung up.

So Sissy had stolen the bill, almost certainly while Lily had been out of her bedroom helping Mimi get the fragile little chair in the hall set back up. But why would Sissy need to steal money? Was she one of those weird people who couldn't help themselves from stealing?

Lily tried to think back to their school days so long ago. Every now and then one of the girls had claimed something of hers had been stolen, but it usually turned out that it had just been mislaid. On the rare occasions when the missing object didn't turn up, could Sissy have been responsible? Or maybe this was an aberration that had come to her later? Lily hadn't been in touch with Sissy for years until last week. Might Sissy have taken anything else?

Or . . .

Lily's thoughts took a sharp turn. And having done so went leaping along a whole new string of events.

This could be it. Maybe she'd solved more than just the mystery of the missing money. But how could anything be proved? She sat down in the chair where Sissy had said she'd left the missing scarf and just let her mind race. Images she'd ignored suddenly came to light. As well as a conversation she'd overheard and paid no attention to.

Then she jumped up and ran to find Mr. Prinney. If there was proof, he probably had it and didn't even know it.

Chapter 25

At the end of Lily's hourlong discussion with Mr. Prinney, he was convinced.

"But how can we prove it?" he asked.

"You have the proof of the motive. Or probably could with a single phone call. But we're going to have to get a confession. The weight of the evidence . . ."

"A confession?"

"A confession that's witnessed by a lot of people," Lily said. "I propose that we reassemble the people who were on the boat. Except for Uncle and Billy Smith, of course. We could call it a housewarming party."

"Won't that make everyone wary, to gather them together again?"

"We don't need to tell anyone who else is invited. And we'll invite Chief Henderson, Jack Summer and his cousin the deputy as well. And we couldn't leave out the doctor. Dr. Polhemus, isn't that his name? Will Mrs. Prinney be willing to feed that many people?"

"She'd love nothing better. But I don't see how this is going to work . . ."

"It may not," Lily said. "But we have to try. And we shouldn't let anyone but the two of us and Robert know what the real purpose is."

"The three of us could make first-class fools of ourselves," Mr. Prinney said.

"We could. But you know as well as I do that we're right."

"Oh, yes. There's no question. Everything fits." He sat back in the chair in his small office for a moment, his hands to the sides of his face, and after a moment, he nodded. "We'll do it. This Thursday? That will give everyone time to get an invitation and respond. If the right person begs off, it will just be a housewarming party and we'll have to rethink things."

"In what way?"

"Well, if we had a competent police chief, we could just present the information we have to him and keep ourselves out of it. We'll have to do that eventually anyway."

"I'll tell Robert everything and then ask Mrs. Prinney to start planning the menu," Lily said.

From Monday to Thursday seemed to last years. The only relief from the tension was that the weather finally cooled. Even Robert was edgy and paced around mumbling to himself. Lily took a number of entirely unnecessary naps, just to keep herself from thinking about what they were about to do and fretting about whether it would work.

The invitations went out on Monday afternoon by telephone to the city people and notes to the locals. And by Tuesday, the Winslows had responded favorably. Sissy came over to confirm to Lily that they would be delighted to attend the party.

"We were going to go back to our apartment in

the City if the weather stays nice, but Mummy said we couldn't miss your housewarming, being as we're next-door neighbors.'' Then she asked if Robert was around and Lily said unfortunately not, that he'd gone to town on an errand. Sissy found another feeble excuse to visit again on Wednesday, once again trying to latch onto Robert—who had seen her coming and was hiding in his room.

"She's got a crush on you," Lily said after she'd gotten rid of Sissy for the second time in two days.

"Anybody whose family was trying to marry them off to Claude would," he said. "It's not a compliment."

Sissy's visits were a horrible annoyance but Lily had to pretend to be friendly. She had to practically bite her lip to keep from tackling Sissy about the theft of the ten-dollar bill.

Both Mr. Winningham and Mr. Eggers replied that they would be happy to attend the housewarming, even though it meant a train trip from New York. Lily was pleased, but surprised.

Mr. Prinney said, "Of course they'll be here. They're both eager to meet you and Robert and try to rope you into dealing with them as Horatio once did. Winningham's bank has failed and, amazingly, he's got a new job at another. He needs desperately to bring in your cash. Same with Fred Eggers. Potential stock investors aren't thick on the ground anymore like they were in his heyday."

Chief Henderson was told by Mr. Prinney only that it would be to his advantage to remain until the end of the party.

"Why's that?" he asked belligerently.

"You might learn something interesting. Bring your deputy along, but leave him in the kitchen."

"You know who murdered those folks, don't you?

And you're withholding the information from the lawful authority—namely me!"

"No, no!" Mr. Prinney said with enormous affability. "We just have a suggestion you might want to investigate."

Jack Summer dropped by on his bicycle, the chain of which was still slipping badly. "I'm looking into a motorcycle like my cousin Ralph has. With a sidecar. Now that I've got the salary to afford one," he told Robert. "And I'm glad to come to the party. I need a good meal and I hear Mrs. Prinney is a fine cook. Am I supposed to bring a present?"

"Good Lord, no!" Robert exclaimed, dreading what sort of present Jack might think was appropriate.

Dr. Polhemus, the young, square-set Dutch doctor who had been at the house the night Billy died, sent a short note saying he'd be there, provided Mrs. Parker down the road wasn't having her sixth baby that night or old man Yaron wasn't having another of his spells.

Claude, who was still staying with the Winslows, stopped by to say he supposed he'd attend the party unless something more important came up in the meantime. Sometimes, however, he pontificated, important business matters came up rather quickly. Lily, knowing that he had very few business matters left to attend to, unless it was an urgent need to borrow money, didn't worry that he wouldn't show up.

The only person who turned down the invitation, but graciously, was Mr. Kessler. Mr. Prinney went to see him immediately.

"Prinney, I've got a job to do. This art gallery fellow wants a dozen figures by next week and I've only got nine I think are really good enough."

"And who, may I remind you, got you this job?"

Mr. Prinney said, laying on a thick layer of shame.

"Oh, I guess you're right. Thoughtless of me. I'll come."

"And you'll stay to the end of the party," Prinney said. "You can carve over a newspaper to catch the shavings."

At dawn Thursday morning, Mrs. Prinney went into a cooking frenzy. She'd even gone so far as to hire another girl from the village to help her and Mimi. Lily, Robert and Mr. Prinney woke to the sound of pans and crockery being crashed around. The dinner was to be extensive and set out as a buffet.

There was a huge ham with her secret glaze and an elaborate pattern of cloves on the surface, a turkey breast with stuffing and a gravy so thick you could stand a fork in it, stewed currants, stuffed potatoes, green beans with onions and bits of the ham. There were three pies—raspberry, banana and chocolate cream—and an unpronounceable Dutch pastry that had so many stages of preparation that Mrs. Prinney had started it the day before.

Lily offered to help and was sent to a storage room she'd never known about until that day to get down the crystal stemware, antique china and Miss Flora's silver service to clean. Mimi, instead of being underfoot in the kitchen, was assigned to open two more of the many bedrooms to air, clean and polish up for the New York overnight guests. Nobody mentioned to them that one of the guests might not be staying the night.

Agatha abandoned Lily to lurk in the kitchen in the hope of scraps. She got her foot stepped on twice, but stuck the course. Mrs. Prinney was too efficient a cook to drop much of anything on the floor, but too kind a woman not to share a few little scraps with the dog.

Robert and Mr. Prinney simply disappeared from the chaos. They never admitted to where they'd gone, but from the smell of them when they returned from lunch in town, Lily suspected that they'd spent the early afternoon in the openly secret back room at Mabel's Cafe. In spite of the peppermint overlay, she could smell the scotch on their breaths.

Mr. Winningham and Mr. Eggers arrived on the same train and Robert picked them up and escorted them to Grace and Favor in the Duesenberg. Eggers tried to get him aside to talk about reinvesting in the market, but Robert merely lit a cigarette, said he was a perfect ass about money and Eggers should save it for tomorrow and talk to his sister and Mr. Prinney.

At seven, the silver, china, glasses and linens were laid out on the enormous dining room table. Smaller tables and chairs had been set up in the reception room next to it in attractive groupings. Dinner was to be at eight and Mrs. Prinney went to bathe and dress and left the hired girl to do the last-minute details. Lily followed Mrs. Prinney up the stairs and went to her room to do the same.

Lily was nervous and having second thoughts. What if this *was* a catastrophe and Mr. Prinney had been right in his fears that they were simply going to make idiots of themselves? She put on her best gown, a slinky apricot concoction with sequins on the sleeve bands that were unfortunately starting to come loose in spots. She did her hair in an elaborate upswept style she hoped would hold. Agatha, who had finally been run out of the kitchen, watched the process.

When Lily finally left her room, Robert was coming down the hall in his tux. "Let the games begin!" he exclaimed cheerfully, taking her arm.

"Oh, Robert . . ."

"No fretting, dear. If we fall on our faces, we'll just pick ourselves up yet again."

"If we fall on our faces, we'll be sued for slander," Lily remarked. "Good thing we don't have any money," she added with a smile.

Mr. Prinney, in a dark suit, was in the reception room with Mr. Winningham and Mr. Eggers. They were sipping at crystal glasses of some drink that was clearly illegal to possess and discussing politics in a fairly amiable way. Mrs. Prinney was in the front hall, welcoming the other guests. She was clad in a stunning gown of peacock-blue with a big matching feather in her hair. Lily nudged Robert into polite silence.

Dr. Polhemus arrived in something of a flurry, warning them that he'd told the switchboard girl to call him at Grace and Favor if he were needed.

Jack Summer and Mr. Kessler arrived together. Each appeared to have bought a new jacket for the occasion. They were on the best of terms. Chief Henderson, stuffed as usual into a suit far too small for him, arrived next. He shooed Ralph around the back to the kitchen door. .

Major and Mrs. Winslow were the next to arrive, in full party regalia, and said that Claude and Sissy were coming along behind in Claude's car, which pulled into the drive only moments later. Sissy, too, had dressed to the nines in a long gown of a muted silver-gray with a fine white vertical stripe that was extremely flattering. The gown was a couple years out of fashion, but so were Mrs. Prinney's and Lily's. Sissy was clearly thrilled to be coming to a party, but Claude wasn't. He looked sour and cranky and became even more so as Sissy abandoned him to gush over Robert.

The whole party having assembled, most of them joined the others in the reception room while Mrs. Prinney went back to the kitchen to supervise putting the copious amount of food on the dining room table.

The guests drifted about, partaking of illegal alcohol. Chief Henderson, who was supposed to report such violations, was drinking the most. Conversation was general and pleasant—the delightful change in the weather, congratulations to both Jack Summer and Mr. Kessler on their new jobs, expressions of admiration for the way Grace and Favor was being improved. Dr. Polhemus lamented the fact that Mrs. Parker kept having children, being as the last two were simpleminded. The out-of-towners talked about the train journey. Mrs. Winslow, Sissy and Lily chatted about fashion. Claude tried to strike up a conversation with Mr. Prinney about automobiles and Jack joined in with questions about what motorbikes with sidecars ought to cost.

For a few minutes Lily was able to pretend this was merely a nice party with no ulterior motive and enjoy herself. All these people had known Uncle Horatio. A few had liked him and some had not. And all had known Billy Smith and disliked him. But no one mentioned either man. There was an unspoken conspiracy not to bring up any unpleasantness.

When Mrs. Prinney finally opened the double doors between the dining room and the reception room, there was a general chorus of approval. Everybody was probably hungry, but tried to outdo each other in courtesy by hanging back. Finally, it was Jonathan Winslow who said with unusual charm, "As much as we're admiring the sight and delightful smell of this food Mrs. Prinney has prepared so skillfully, I'm starving, so I'll go first."

There was a sudden rush for plates and silverware.

When everybody but Chief Henderson had finished eating, and the plates had been cleared away, Lily rose and stood at one end of the room. "I'd like to welcome our guests tonight. My brother and I hope that all but one of you will visit us again."

Her hands were trembling so badly she had to hold them behind her back.

Several people laughed nervously at what they assumed was meant as a compliment that had accidentally turned into a tactless remark.

Lily went on, "I have something to tell all of you. Something our uncle intended to say to some of you on the tragic boat trip and never got to reveal."

She glanced around the room. Most of the faces were merely interested. One looked alarmed.

Clearing her throat, Lily went on in a shaky voice. "I wouldn't have figured this out except that I learned that Sissy Winslow stole ten dollars from my purse last week."

Sissy made a little shrieking noise and buried her face in her hands.

"Which," Lily continued, "is how Mr. Prinney and I came to realize that Jonathan Winslow murdered Horatio Brewster and Billy Smith."

Chapter 26

Sensation!

For a long moment, everyone in the room fell silent and stared at Lily.

Jonathan Winslow broke the spell by rising suddenly and saying, "What utter rot! Prinney, has this young woman gone entirely mad? Dr. Polhemus, I recommend that you immediately remove her to an insane asylum. I'll be bringing charges of public slander, of course."

"Let's hear her out," Dr. Polhemus said with remarkable calm.

Robert came over and put his arm around Lily's waist for support. "Go on, Lily."

Chief Henderson's eyes were bugged out and he finally put his plate down and wiped his mouth on his jacket sleeve. Jack had pulled a notebook from the pocket of his jacket and was scribbling madly.

"When I learned that Sissy had stolen a ten-dollar bill from me—you can talk to the butcher in town to find out how I know this—I thought she was just a common thief, or stealing for the thrill of getting away with it," Lily said. "But after a few moments, I realized that was quite wrong. She stole the money because she needed it. The Winslow family needed it."

"What nonsense!" Jonathan Winslow snapped. He'd sat back down and was absently patting Sissy on the shoulder as she continued to sob. Mrs. Winslow was looking as though someone had slapped her in the face hard enough to addle her wits.

"Take the girl away, Polhemus," Winslow shouted. "And you take down every word she's said, Summer. I want it on the record."

Chief Henderson moved around behind Winslow and put a beefy hand on his shoulder. "I do, too. And I want to hear the rest."

Winslow shook off Henderson's hand and said sharply to Sissy, "Stop that damned sniffling."

Robert gave Lily's waist a squeeze, urging her to continue.

"Major Winslow told us that they'd let their staff go because it wasn't decent to act rich when so many people were poor. Robert and I found that a distasteful remark, considering that Major Winslow himself had contributed to the general unemployment, but we didn't question at the time that he might have fired them because he couldn't afford to pay them and his pride wouldn't let him admit it."

"This is ridiculous!" Winslow exclaimed. "We're not going to stay and listen to any more of this. And in front of my wife and daughter. Shame on you, you stupid girl."

Lily ignored him. "There was more. Much more. And I still can't believe we didn't see it at first. Major Winslow claimed that his wife and daughter were enjoying learning to cook and clean and take care of the house themselves. But that obviously wasn't true. They prepared an inedible dinner and looked as miserable as the guests. Robert and I later saw

Sissy sitting in the yard attempting to mend something, and making a hash of it. Major Winslow accused my dog of killing his doves, implying that he
was raising them as a hobby, when in fact, I think
they were being raised to be eaten to save money on
food."

"This is all speculation, isn't it?" Jack Summer put
in with a wicked grin. Mr. Kessler mumbled at him
in an undertone.

"Yes, but there's more that isn't," Robert said.

"At this dinner we attended at the Winslows',"
Lily said, "I was seated facing a family portrait. Major Winslow had his cane across his knees. I thought
nothing of it until I remembered that I'd been told
that Uncle Horatio had suffered a deadly wound in
the back of his head from a round, very hard object.
Chief Henderson, when you see the portrait, I think
you'll recognize the large, round, gold head of the
cane matches this description. It isn't the cane Major
Winslow is using these days."

"Daddy will pay the money back. It was only ten
dollars," Sissy burst out.

A dreadful silence fell as the rest of the group realized Sissy had completely missed the point of what
Lily was saying.

Lily said, rather more gently, "Sissy, tell us the
rest of the truth. You didn't bring my scarf back here
like you said, did you?"

Sissy shook her head miserably. "No, Daddy said
I was to say so. When the police came the next day
and asked about the scarf, he told them I'd taken it
back to Grace and Favor. He explained to me later."

"He explained what?" Robert asked.

"That Claude had been away from the table for a
long time during dinner. It might have been at the
same time that the horrible Billy person was killed

and we didn't want the police to get the wrong idea about Claude."

At this, Claude himself rose from his chair like an angry rhinocerous in bellowing indignation. "You old bastard! You were trying to pin this on *me!*"

"I was trying to protect you, for Sissy's sake. We wanted her to marry well," Winslow said. He was running out of steam.

"Marry a girl who has to steal from my cousins to buy food? You fool. You absolute blithering old fool."

Robert firmly waved Claude back to his seat. Claude sat down, seething and muttering to himself.

"Sissy," Robert said, "Claude wasn't the only person who was gone from the table for a long time."

Suddenly Sissy caught on to what was really happening around her. "No!" she screamed. "Not Daddy!" She collapsed in wracking sobs.

Mrs. Winslow finally got her wits together and whispered, "May I take her away?"

Chief Henderson nodded. Mrs. Winslow led Sissy out of the room, pausing to take a long, hard look at her husband before she closed the door behind them. He wouldn't meet her gaze.

Lily looked at Mr. Kessler. "Is Major Winslow the man you thought you saw following our uncle down to the cabin?"

Kessler nodded. "I was pretty sure it was he."

Jonathan Winslow ignored Kessler's remark and said with what he apparently meant as withering sarcasm, "Even if this were all true, which it isn't, it proves nothing. And my finances are my business. No one else's."

At this point, Mr. Prinney, who had been quietly sitting in a corner, opened a drawer in the table next to him and took out some papers, then came to stand by Lily and Robert. "That's not quite true, Winslow. I'm afraid you are going to have to provide a financial statement. You see, I received a letter last week that perplexed me considerably. Allow me to read from it."

Everyone who remained in the room, except Jonathan Winslow, was leaning forward in anticipation. Winslow was gazing about the room with poorly feigned unconcern.

Mr. Prinney said, "This is from the county clerk of Orange County, California, who says,

Dear Mr. Prinney,

I'm writing you in regard to the deed dated April 1, 1931, which was filed in this office. It came by mail from Mr. Horatio Brewster on April 10th of the same month. In checking the title records, I discovered that the deed, signed over to his co-owner, Major Jonathan Winslow—who, according to Mr. Brewster's cover letter, was to subsequently sell it to a local film company—had the property description incorrect. I immediately wrote to Mr. Brewster, asking if he and his partner Major Jonathan Winslow wished to file an amended deed and if he wished this one returned or destroyed. I never heard from him. The buyer is anxious that the title be corrected promptly so that he may pay the new sole owner and take title to the property. Since you are the attorney of record and notarized the signatures, I would appreciate it if you could consult with Mr. Brewster with all due haste."

Prinney folded up the letter carefully and looked at Jonathan Winslow. "The clerk enclosed the faulty deed. Mr. Brewster had made a great many property changes in March and April of this year and I originally thought that I had simply forgotten this one. That isn't likely, but it was possible. But when Miss Brewster came to me and said she'd overheard me mentioning my confusion to my wife and asked me to look into the matter more carefully, I realized that the notarized signature purporting to be mine was not in my handwriting, though it was a fairly good imitation. Nor did Mr. Brewster's signature look quite right. That was when I also remembered an incident a short time before the deed was signed when my notary seal was missing and later turned up just where I always kept it and had looked for it several times."

Somebody made a low whistling sound.

"So you see, Major Winslow, it appears that you forged my signature and Mr. Brewster's on the deed of sale, hoping he was too busy to notice that the property had been sold or forget that he had not signed the deed. That was unlikely as well, but perhaps you hoped to throw yourself on his mercy when he discovered what you had done."

Winslow was looking down at the cane across his lap and said nothing.

Mr. Prinney continued. "If you hadn't copied out the property description incorrectly and if the clerk hadn't been particular in checking it carefully, you might have gotten away with it. Mr. Brewster apparently received the first letter from the clerk and my guess is that he had it in the cabin of the boat and was prepared to flourish it when he announced to all present what treachery his best friend had attempted to perpetrate."

Mr. Prinney put the document back in the envelope, which he handed to Chief Henderson. "Horatio told me he wanted me to go along to serve as a witness. I didn't understand that at the time, but now I do. Perhaps he hinted to you that he was going to reveal something to your disadvantage. It may be that the clerk carbon-copied the original letter, which is probably on the bottom of the river or has floated out to the Atlantic, to Major Winslow as well."

Winslow made a deep, low, growling sound that made the whole room seem cold.

"So I think Chief Henderson needs to acquire your files and take you in for—"

Winslow suddenly jumped from his chair, both hands holding the lower end of his cane, and flung himself toward Lily with the cane upraised.

And just as suddenly, Agatha seemed to materialize from nowhere and leaped to intercept him. She sank her teeth into his left arm and Winslow fell into a screaming heap. He thrashed around for a moment, trying to get back on his feet and strike at the dog at the same time.

Chief Henderson waded into the fray and took hold of Winslow, who struggled violently until both Jack Summer and Mr. Kessler each took one of his arms in their strong grips.

Once Winslow was upright again, he looked at Lily with loathing. "You bitch!" he said. "You interfering bitch!"

Jack's cousin Ralph, in the kitchen as instructed, heard the commotion, and came running. He and Henderson escorted a raving, swearing Jonathan Winslow outside to the police car.

Lily felt around behind herself for a chair and collapsed into it. She could hardly breathe or see straight and was afraid she was about to faint or throw up.

As she leaned over, Agatha came to her ánd nuzzled her face.

"Good dog," she whispered. "Good, good dog."

The next morning Jack Summer delivered his draft of the article for the next week's paper. The headline was in huge type. LOCAL FORMER MILLIONAIRE CONFESSES TO DOUBLE MURDER.

Lily read through the text. It was floridly written and every bit as tense and frightening as the actual event had been. It made her stomach lurch and her head hurt to think about it. But it was the truth without more than a hint of embellishment. And it would sell papers like crazy.

She handed the draft to Mr. Prinney and then to Robert. They each read it through and when Robert was finished, they stared at her questioningly.

"I think we should approve it just as it is and print a special edition overnight," Lily said.

"Good!" they said in unison.

"What will become of Mrs. Winslow and Sissy?" Lily asked.

"I'm told that they've moved out of the house and are going to go live with Mrs. Winslow's sister in Cleveland," Mr. Prinney said. "They won't be homeless, but I don't know what their roles will be in the household."

"It's certain nobody will ask them to cook a meal more than once," Robert said.

Lily laughed, but there was an element of sadness in the sound. "We won't have to appear at his trial, will we?"

"I doubt there will be a trial," Mr. Prinney said. "He *has* confessed, after all. He might plead that he was only trying to protect his family's financial wellbeing, but I doubt that will make the least difference to the judge. Major Winslow says he went out for a breath of air during dinner and found Billy lurking at the back of the house. Billy told him what he'd seen on the boat and Winslow said they couldn't talk about it here. That he'd meet him in the woods behind Grace and Favor Cottage. Winslow went inside for a moment, noticed Lily's scarf and took it along so that if there were violence, he could implicate you."

Robert muttered something obscene.

Mr. Prinney went on. "Major Winslow told Chief Henderson that Billy attacked him outside your kitchen door and he went into the house to escape him. But that won't hold up. Winslow has no injuries and Billy had no weapon. He killed him with a butcher knife that was on the counter, tied the scarf around his neck and went back through the woods and calmly finished dinner."

"This has been horrible," Lily said, rising from her chair. "Come, Agatha."

"Where are you going?" Robert asked.

"To take this back to Jack. And to take a very long walk with my wonderful dog."

"Want any other company?" Robert asked.

Lily shook her head. "No, thanks. I need to clear my head of this whole awful experience. I want to forget it ever happened."

Lily and Agatha walked down the path to town and Lily was relieved that Jack wasn't in the office. She didn't feel like talking to anyone. She left the draft on his desk with a note saying, *No changes requested. Publish special edition for tomorrow.*

Then she made her way slowly back up the hill, around the house and to the bench overlooking the river. This was her home and she had helped make it safe. She must keep that in mind. And she wasn't responsible for Mrs. Winslow and Sissy's misfortune. Jonathan Winslow's greed and lack of moral will had ruined them. So why did she still feel so guilty?

She heard the sound of Robert's whistling. He must have been practicing, because his version of "Ain't Misbehavin'" had improved significantly from the day they'd come here.

Lily said to him as he approached, "Why did Billy wait to attempt to blackmail Major Winslow? The boatwreck was months ago."

"Because of us," Robert said, standing and gazing at the river below them.

"What do you mean?"

"Until we actually moved into the house, Billy probably believed that Mimi was going to inherit. She'd told him the truth, that she wasn't Uncle Horatio's child, but he probably didn't believe it. I'd guess he thought that blackmailing Winslow was a little risky. He knew, or suspected, that Winslow had bashed Uncle Horatio with that cane. If I were Billy, I'd figure it was better to just hold onto that information until after I found how much moola my wife was inheriting."

Lily rubbed her eyes. "Good Lord, I think you're right. So it was us moving into Grace and Favor that persuaded him to take the chance of blackmailing Major Winslow."

"Right. Because it was obvious he wouldn't ever get the house or the fortune."

He sat down beside her, saying nothing, not even looking at her. Finally, he spoke again. "This really isn't *such* a bad place to live. I think I'm going to

survive it." He slapped at a mosquito that had
landed on his wrist.

"Me, too," she said, and leaned her head on his
shoulder.

We hope you have enjoyed this Avon Twilight mystery. Mysteries fascinate and intrigue with the worlds they create. And what better way to capture your interest than this glimpse into the world of a select group of Avon Twilight authors.

Jill Churchill branches out with a new series set in the 1930s along the Hudson River even as she continues her very successful suburban Chicago-set Jane Jeffry series. Valerie Wilson Wesley puts Tamara Hayle through her paces in downtown Newark, New Jersey. Carolyn Hart's Annie and Max Darling ward off trouble at their Death on Demand mystery bookstore in South Carolina. Laura Lippman sends Baltimore P.I. Tess Monaghan sleuthing in Texas. And Katherine Hall Page exemplifies small town life with her Aleford, Massachusetts, mystery featuring Faith Fairchild.

So turn the page for a sneak peek into worlds filled with mystery and murder. And if you like what you read, head to your nearest bookstore. It's the only way to figure out whodunnit. . . .

June

Jill Churchill is primarily known for her Jane Jeffrey series, but with ANYTHING GOES she heads off in an exciting new place—and time in history. The Hudson River is dotted with quaint towns that were home to some of the richest people in the United States earlier this century. But in the '30s a lot of these former millionaires were down on their luck—so when Lily and Robert, a brother and sister pair are offered a beautiful mansion with the only stipulation being they must stay there for ten years, it seems like they have finally made it to easy street. But then it seems that their uncle might have had an untimely death. And wait until they meet the neighbors.

ANYTHING GOES
by Jill Churchill

"Who *is* our next-door neighbor?" Robert asked the newspaper reporter.

Jack was surprised. Jonathan Winslow was not only the richest man hereabouts, but he, his wife and his daughter were among the most socially prominent. They'd actually had foreign royalty visit any number of times in the past. He mentioned the name.

"Do they have a daughter they call Sissy?" Lily asked.

"I believe so."

"I went to dancing classes with Sissy Winslow," Lily said, more to herself than to him. "And we were in the Mayflower Girls in grade school."

"Mayflower Girls?" Robert asked.

"We all had names of Mayflower people. Brewster, Bradford, Winslow, Billingslea. It was a joke. I don't think any of us were actually descendants."

Jack was still hoping to get something interesting out of the Brewsters and answering their questions and listening to girlish recollections wasn't accomplishing anything.

"You mentioned Mrs. Prinney having made the lemonade. I understand Mr. and Mrs. Prinney have put their house up for sale. Are they living here?"

"To our enormous pleasure, they are," Robert said.

"Why is that?"

"Because they wished to—and this house is much too big for the two of us," Robert replied cheerfully. He wasn't about to mention that Mr. Prinney controlled the money and served as official watchdog on their movements.

"How could we find out more about our uncle's death?" Lily came back to the subject that most interested her.

"What's to find out?" Jack asked. "The boat sank. He drowned."

"Did anyone else drown in the accident?" Robert asked.

"Nope. But my editor wrote it up pretty thoroughly. You could come to Voorburg someday and take a look at the newspaper morgue."

"I think we'll do that," Robert said.

Jack gave him a long, appraising look. "Why are you so interested?"

"Well, he was our great-uncle," Lily said. "And nobody seems to want to tell us what happened."

"You think there was something suspicious about the accident?" Jack asked, his inquisitive mind making a leap.

"Oh, no. Certainly not," Robert said, too heartily. "We're just curious people."

Jack didn't know whether to believe them or not. Surely Mr. Prinney had explained it all to them. But maybe not. Prinney had a reputation for complete discretion.

Jack waited a minute, debating with himself, then said hesitantly, "I shouldn't be the one to tell you, but I've heard he was murdered."

July

Native New Jersey writer and Essence *editor-at-large Valerie Wilson Wesley tackles the mean streets of Newark in her Tamara Hayle series. Through Tamara's eyes we enter a world that can be hostile and filled with evil, but Tamara's warm heart beneath her tough exterior always makes her the perfect guide.*

EASIER TO KILL
by Valerie Wilson Wesley

What do you know about Lotus Park?" Tamara asked Jake.

"Not a nice place. Unless you're a gay man who doesn't like being gay and who likes dangerous, secretive sex. Don't go there at night."

"Hmm. That kind of place, huh?"

"Yeah."

"There was a killing about a week ago. They said it was a robbery. Did you hear anything about it?"

Jake thought for a moment. "Well, I do know there have been some very violent robberies there recently. Mostly suburban white guys looking for some black or brown action who end up getting more than they can handle. A couple of muggings have turned very ugly—face slashings, beatings, that kind of thing. As a matter of fact, I do remember hearing something about a stabbing last week. He glanced over the top of his glass at me, a touch of amusement in his eyes as he tried to figure out what I was searching for. "So is this your big-time-celeb case?"

"Maybe," I flirted back. "Do you remember anything else about it?" He thought for a moment.

"They said it was a robbery," he leaned back in his chair for a moment and sighed a wistful sigh. "Funny how things stick in your mind. I used to play in Lotus Park when I was a kid. My daddy used to take me and some of the other kids in the block over there and try to teach us how to play like Jackie Robinson. I didn't know exactly who Jackie Robinson was, but I wanted to play ball with pop." He drank some of his water, gulping it as if he were swallowing his memories. "Yeah, the park's definitely changed. Maybe that's why I remembered it when the cop mentioned it.

"This was the first killing, I think, though. Mostly its just been slashings," he continued. "Maybe somebody overheard somebody yelling something about money. I don't know. Maybe it will come back to me."

"The guy who was killed was named Tyrone Mason? He was a hairstylist who worked for Mandy Magic. Does that remind you of anything?" He thought again, narrowing his eyes slightly as he concentrated.

"Mandy Magic? That's the radio lady, right? I don't remember his name, but I do remember hearing somebody say something about her. It could have been the same dude. I can't think of any other reason I'd connect her name with Lotus Park." He shook his head and sighed. "The hustlers who operate out of that place are definitely not nice little boys."

"And you're sure it had something do with a robbery?"

"Yeah. That much I do remember."

August

Carolyn Hart is the multiple Agatha, Anthony, and Macavity Award-winning creator of the most delectable sleuthing couple since Nick met Nora. Annie and Max Darling manage to find quite a bit of murder in their allegedly safe and serene South Carolina island resort. After all, murder is Annie's business—well sort of. She's the proprietor of the popular Death on Demand mystery bookstore and café, and her establishment seems to attract trouble like Annie's pesky felines, Dorothy L. and Agatha, attract furballs. Now, as Annie and Max anticipate a festive summer, the irresistible duo watch their Fourth of July explode not only with fun and fireworks, but with murder as well. . . .

YANKEE DOODLE DEAD
by Carolyn Hart

"Now, Annie." Max shoved a hand through his thick blond hair. "That's absurd."

Annie poured chocolate syrup over the vanilla ice cream. Dear chocolate syrup. Zero grams of fat. She looked at Max. "Zero grams of fat. Do you want some?"

"No, thanks." He shook his head impatiently. "It doesn't mean a thing that Mother was in the rest room."

"Hiding in the rest room." Annie said it pleasantly but firmly.

"Well, I'm sure she'll have a good reason." Max's face was getting its bulldog look.

"Why don't you call and ask her?" Annie plopped on a wicker couch beneath the ceiling fan. Of course their house was air-conditioned, but for the summer in the Low Country one could not have too many methods of cooling. She spooned a smooth dark dollop of chocolate syrup. She'd get to the ice cream in a minute.

Max paced in front of the couch. "Of course she had a good reason."

Annie wondered if he heard the plaintive tone in his voice.

"I'll call her." He strode to the telephone.

Annie edged a smidgeon of ice cream on the tip of the spoon, dipped the whole into the syrup. She closed her eyes and swallowed. And listened.

"Hi, Mother." Max's tone was hearty.

Annie knew he was worried. Otherwise, he would have called her Laurel.

". . . did you realize there was a robbery at the library this evening?"

The spoon moved rhythmically.

"Annie said the general was really angry even though he said nothing was missing." Max held the phone away from his ear.

Annie heard a silver peal of amusement.

"What's so funny, Mother?" he demanded crisply. He nodded quickly. "That's right. Annie heard the general talking to the police." A pause. "Yes, he called the police. What? No, I don't suppose they can do anything about it if the general doesn't say what was taken. But whoever did it could still be arrested for vandalism. Or breaking and entering. Now if you have any idea what—"

Max listened, frowning. Slowly, he hung up the phone. He looked at Annie, his dark blue eyes full of concern. "Do you know what she said?" He rubbed his cheek. "She said, 'If wishes were horses, beggars would ride.' Annie, what in the world does that mean?"

It meant, Annie felt certain, that General Hatch could whistle for his lost property. Whatever it was.

A Speak Your Mind tempted: At the best of times, your mother has the criminal instincts of a cat burglar. Instead, she smiled sweetly. "Laurel is very poetic." She spooned a tiny sliver of ice cream floating in syrup. Be interesting to know what had been taken. But it probably didn't really matter. Be interesting to see how the old geezer behaved at the board meeting in the morning. Annie was sure of one thing only. As soon as the meeting was past, she intended to dismiss Brig. Gen. (ret.) Charlton (Bud) Hatch from her thoughts. Absolutely. Completely.

She concentrated on her last spoonful of chocolate.

September

Laura Lippman has made a name for herself in a few short years. Already an Edgar Award winner for her Tess Monaghan series, she tackles the darker motivations of human nature in her stories. Her sleuth, Tess, being an ex-newspaper woman turned P.I., always is willing to look much deeper to find the "story." But sometimes when the case becomes personal, Tess has to be pushed a bit.

IN BIG TROUBLE
by Laura Lippman

"Just open it."

She ignored Tyner's letter opener and unsealed the flap with her index finger, cutting herself on the cheap envelope. Her finger in her mouth, she upended the envelope. A newspaper clipping that had been glued to an index card slid out onto Tyner's desk, and nothing more. The clipping was a photograph—or a part of one—with a head-and-shoulders shot cut from a larger photograph, the fragment of a headline still attached over the head like a halo.

IN BIG TROUBLE

The hair was different. Shorter, neater. The face was unmistakably Crow's, although it looked a little different, too. Surely she was imagining that—how much could a face change in six months? There was a gauntness she didn't remember, a sharpness to his cheekbones that made him look a little cruel. And his mouth was tight, lips pressed together as if he had never smiled in his life. Yet when she thought of Crow—which was really almost never, well maybe once a month—he was always smiling. Happy-go-lucky, blithe as a puppy. "The perfect post-modern boyfriend," one of her friends had called him. A compliment, yet also a dig.

In the end, it was the gap in temperament, not the six-year age difference so much, that had split them up. Or so her current theory held; she had revised their history several times over the past six months. He had been so endearingly boyish. Tess had been in the market for a man. Now here was a man frowning at her. A man In Big Trouble.

That was his problem.

"There's no sign which newspaper it came from," Tyner said, picking up the card and holding it to the light, trying to read the type on the side that had been glued down. "The back looks like a Midas Muffler ad, and that could be anywhere in the country. Didn't Crow head off to Austin last spring?"

"Uh-huh."

"So what are you going to do about it?"

"Do about what?"

"Crow and this trouble he's in."

"I'm not going to do anything. He's a big boy, too big to be playing cut-and paste. In fact, I bet his mommy lets him use the real scissors now instead of the little ones with the rounded-off blades."

Tyner rolled his wheelchair a few feet and grabbed the wastebasket. "So throw it away," he dared her. "Three-pointer."

Tess tucked the photo and envelope into her note-book-sized daybook, the closest thing she had to a constant companion these days. "My aunt Kitty will want to see his photo, just for old time's sake. See what Crow looks like without his purple dreadlocks. She was his friend, too, you know."

Tyner smiled knowingly.

October

What could be more average than a suburb just outside of Chicago? But though the world of Agatha Award-winning Jill Churchill is overrun by neighborhood parties and soccer moms, next-door neighbors and best friends Jane Jeffrey and Shelly Nowack have developed a talent for uncovering mysteries right in their midst. But how much fun is it going to be to have a dead body turn up outside Jane's house, just as she's meeting her boyfriend's mom for the first time?

THE MERCHANT OF MENACE
by Jill Churchill

"—you volunteered to be hostess?"

Jane leaned back in her chair and sighed heavily. "God help me, I did! Or she volunteered me. I don't remember the gory details. It was sort of like a train wreck. One minute I was chattering along, and the next minute I'd agreed to have the whole neighborhood in for a buffet dinner."

Shelley looked over the cookies cooling on clean pillowcases on Jane's kitchen counter. "Jane, what are these green things supposed to be?"

"Elves," Jane said drearily. "Little nasty Christmas elves. The cutter looked like an elf, but they blobbed out when they cooked."

"They look more like holly leaves—or a fungus growth," Shelley said.

Jane smiled weakly. "But they taste okay. Throw some on a plate and let's make ourselves sick on them. I couldn't possibly let anyone else see them."

"I can't move," Shelley said. "My feet are stuck to your floor."

Jane nodded hopeless acceptance of this criticism. "Corn syrup. I dropped the bottle and the lid came off. I've already washed the floor twice and Willard's licked up as much as he could. Just leave your shoes there."

"Thanks, but I'd rather have my shoes stick than my feet." Shelley tossed some cookies on a plate, her shoes making a sound like Velcro being pulled apart, and sat down across from Jane. She nibbled a cookie cautiously and smiled. "They do taste okay. So, tell me about Mel's mother and why she'll hate you."

"Because he's her only son. He's a successful detective, up and coming, all that. And I'm a widow with three children, one already in college, which is a dead giveaway that I'm older than he is."

"So?" Shelley said.

"So she's going to see me as a predatory old hag, trying to trap her dear boy."

"Jane, you don't know that. She's going to adore you. Well, if you get this disgusting kitchen cleaned up, that is. And do some major repairs to your hair."

Jane shook her head. "Nope, she's not. Mel's already said so."

"He told you this?" Shelley said with amazement.

"Not in so many words. But he keeps mentioning how he's sure she's going to like me and my family. And how he's told her how terrific I am and how he's really, *really* sure we're going to get along great. I can tell he's desperately trying to convince himself of this."

Shelley frowned. "Oh, that doesn't sound good."

November

The creation of Agatha Award-winning author, Katherine Hall Page, Faith Fairchild is a woman who wears many hats. A transplanted New Yorker, she is a minister's wife, mother of two, renowned caterer, and amateur sleuth. Faith has an uncomfortable habit of innocently entangling herself in murder, and a knack not just for puff pastry, but for unraveling a mystery. From Aleford, Massachusetts, to Boston, to Maine, and to New York, Faith grapples with murder, kidnapping, blackmail, and arson, always managing to land on her feet. This time out it's a burglary gone awry which pulls Faith into the world of mystery and mayhem.

THE BODY IN THE BOOKCASE
by Katherine Hall Page

No one in Aleford ever locked their back doors, and they often neglected the front entrances, as well. Faith knocked again at the rear for form's sake. Sarah would certainly have heard the front knocker from her kitchen. A discreet starched white curtain covered the door's window. Faith turned the knob, pushed the door open, and stepped in.

Stepped in and gasped.

The room had been completely ransacked. All the cupboards were open and the floor was strewn with broken crockery, as well as pots and pans. Drawers of utensils had been emptied. The pantry door was ajar and canisters of flour and sugar had been over-turned, a sudden snowstorm on the well-scrubbed old linoleum. A kitchen chair lay on its side. Another stood below a high cabinet, its contents—roasting pans and cookie tins—in a jumble below.

Faith dropped the basket and started shouting, "Sarah! Sarah! It's Faith! Answer me! *Where are you?*" as she moved toward the door to the dining room. She pushed it open; Sarah wasn't there. Nor was she answering. Still frantically calling the woman's name, Faith ran through the living room, then up-stairs, searching for her friend.

The scene in the kitchen was duplicated all over the house. It looked like a newsreel of the aftermath of a tornado. Things were in heaps on the floors, drawers flung on top. But there was no sign of Sarah. "Sarah!" Faith kept calling her name, not sure whether to be relieved or terrified at the woman's absence.

A break-in. Burglars. But surely they wouldn't have entered while someone was home? They must have seen Sarah leave. There had been no signs of life on the street, most of the residents having gone away for the day or already at work. And from the look of things, whoever had been here had worked fast. Sarah couldn't have been in the house. Sarah had to be all right.

In Sarah Winslow's bedroom tucked under the eaves, the bed had been slept in, but the quilt that usually covered it was still hanging on the quilt rack next to the dormer window. The rack stood in its usual place, the spread neatly folded, a note of nor-malcy, but a discordant one in all this chaos. Every-thing else was in total disarray. Shoes and clothes from the closet and lingerie from the bureau drawers had been flung onto the floor. Faith felt sick at the thought of hands touching Sarah's most intimate things, pulling her orderly universe apart. One pillow had been stripped of its case. The other showed the faint indentation where Sarah's head had rested; the sheet was slightly pulled back. Faith's heart sank.

Sarah would never have left her house with an unmade bed.

⫸ JILL CHURCHILL ⫷

GRIME AND PUNISH   CAN

A FAREWELL TO YARNS   76399-0/$5.99 US/$7.99 CAN

A QUICHE BEFORE DYING   76932-8/$5.99 US/$7.99 CAN

THE CLASS MENAGERIE   77380-5/$5.99 US/$7.99 CAN

A KNIFE TO REMEMBER   77381-3/$5.99 US/$7.99 CAN

FROM HERE TO PATERNITY

77715-0/$5.99 US/$7.99 CAN

SILENCE OF THE HAMS   77716-9/$6.50 US/$8.50 CAN

WAR AND PEAS   78706-7/$5.99 US/$7.99 CAN

FEAR OF FRYING   78707-5/$5.99 US/$7.99 CAN

And now in Hardcover

THE MERCHANT OF MENACE

97569-6/$21.00 US/$28.00 CAN